EDGAR TIFFANY

HUES *of* GREEN

A Critical History of
D.M. Thompson's *Colors of War & Peace*

Foreword by
JAMES HUNEYCUTT

FIRST EDITION
Published in 2023

ISBN: 979-8-218-12780-0

Library of Congress Cataloging-in-Publication Data

Library of Congress Registration:
Tiffany, Buster Edgar
Hues of Green, A Critical History of D.M. Thompson's Colors of War & Peace
Registration Number: TXu 2-368-107 | May, 2023

Category: Literary Criticism/Fiction/Vietnam War/Special Forces/MACV-SOG

Written by: Edgar Tiffany

Design & Format by: Eli Blyden | EliTheBookGuy.com

Published & Printed in the United States of America | Tampa, Florida

To Jack de Treville, SFC, USA(RET), U.S. Army Special Forces,
MACV-SOG, Comrade-in-Arms,
Friend and Hero

HUES *of* GREEN

ACKNOWLEDGMENTS

Foremost, appreciations go to D.M. Thompson for his friendship, understanding and lending of *Colors of War & Peace: A Collection of Short Stories* for my scrutiny and admiration; and to Alan Farrell for citation to his "The Green Beret: *Schreckfigur* For the New Age, "*Viet Nam Generation,* 1994", "The Major Won the Croix de Guerre," *Nobody Gets Off the Bus: The Viet Nam Generation Big Book,* Charlottesville: University of Virginia, March 1994 and "Blaming of Parts," *Expended Casings,* Deployed Forward: Lexington, Virginia, 2007; and to Maxine Hong Kingston for citation to her *The Fifth Book of Peace,* New York: Vintage Books, 2003, and *Veterans of War, Veterans of Peace,* Koa Books: Kihei, Hawai'i, 2006, Editor; and to B.K. Marshall (AKA Ken Boyd) for citation to *Dawson's War: A Novel of Friendship Under Fire,* B.K. Marshall: Columbia SC, 2020; and to David Robbins for *War in Pieces,* Four One-Act plays, *The Mighty Pen Project,* 2021; and finally for the yet unprinted treasures of D.M. Thompson, *In Search of My Rune,* Unpublished Journal, *1995, Anamnesis,* Unpublished Memoir, 2007, and *Marble Mountain Redux,* Unpublished Memoir, 2014, and to all the others, famous, infamous, or anonymous cited in the bibliography of *Hues Of Green.* And lest I forget, a remembrance of my guide and nemesis, Edna Wellthorpe, retired.

The *nipa* palm

Casts a sinuous, elegant neck back to peer wistfully up at the sun—languid tropism—laying bare a polished, ebony gorge wayward caress of errant breeze riffling the neighboring gardens…

And this is the Selector Switch which is always released with an easy flick of the thumb and do not you let me fuckin' see you fuckin' filing down that Detent to make a silent safety and be quick drawing you'll blow your fuckin' head clean off it will happen to you and doan worry about that audible click when you flick off that safety. You can do it quite easy if you have any strength in your thumb. The airy summit of the *nipa* with her perpetual nod of insipid assent invites warily, gingerly, coquettishly, never letting anyone see her fuckin' filing down that Detent. And this as you can see is the Bolt.

And the Firing Pin Retainer Clip fifty cent piece of cheap hardware store shit that you will lose in the tall grass and will drop in the mud and will fingerfuck in the dark and then whats you gots is not a Rifle US M-16A1 magazine fed gas operated air cooled selective fire but a fuckin' broomstick on account of without that gizmo it can't not fire nuffin' and won't not nuffin' else fit in that little hole. And the voluptuary *nipa* palm in a silent plié with all the ungainly, chattering, wiry little monkeys skittering backward and forward along her arching back

For today we have blaming of the parts.

—Alan Farrell, excerpt from. "Blaming of Parts,"

CONTENTS

PREFACE

I was 17 when I sat watching *Merrill's Marauders* in a dark, moldy, Swift Creek apartment, while my ratchet-headed brother and oil can friend stripped down a flathead Indian in all its greasy finery and my stomach pitched into my mouth as I watched; I could barely breath but felt exhilaration, then grief, because of the struggle, torture, death and an odd allure, and challenge and, yes, beauty, in the face of such staggering loss, brutish, barbaric, and unmitigated horror from the ravages of a jungle warfare that in 1964, taxed reality, but sparked an imagination, an imagination of what? while mutant Japanese soldiers killed Merrill's malnourished and malarial men, driving them like cows to slaughter. That movie, unbeknownst to me, was depicting the 3507th Composite Group, or the first bona fide military long range reconnaissance group in 1944-45, its roots planted that day so deep and complete in my psyche, reinforced by the childhood documentaries, *Victory at Sea* and *World at War* (narrated by the sepulchral voices of Leonard Graves and Lawrence Olivier), it had struck discordant notes and dreams for this son of a soldier. Two years later, after a year of college, I broke free of my family and civil lashings as sirens with the voices of WW II marauders and oracles beckoned me with the *Ballad of the Green Beret*, as haunting an ear-worm tune as anything Ulysses had ever heard.

Marble Mountain Redux (Unpublished Memoir)
—D.M. Thompson

FOREWORD

> "The process may seem strange and yet it is very true.
> I did not so much gain the knowledge of things by the words,
> as words by the experience I had of things."
>
> —Plutarch, *Parallel Lives*

I've always been an admirer of soldiers. Real soldiers. I am speaking of my cousin, Major General Weldon F. Honeycutt who was commissioned an Infantry Officer upon gradua-tion from Officer Can-didate School, 1951:

WELDON "BLACKJACK" HONEYCUTT

Aide-de-Camp to General William Westmoreland, Battalion Commander of Infantry, most famously of the 3rd Bn, 187 Airborne Infantry, 101st Airborne Infantry Division at Hamburger Hill in May of 1969, and probably one of the most decorated soldiers in any era of the Army, numbering among his multiple awards, the DSC, Silver Stars, Bronze Stars for Valor, Purple Hearts and many more. He has always been the measure of a real soldier for me.

When I was thinking seriously of joining the U.S. Marine Corps in 1978 and being convinced by Marine recruiter Sergeant Skip Krueger in Colonial Heights, Virginia, I was talked out of it by none other than General Honeycutt (he said I had all the advantages he never had and focus instead on business and making money), and my mom (she had three brothers who were Marines in the Pacific during World War II's Island Hopping hell and she saw the cost up close and personal). My parents seemed successful and smart people and General Honeycutt was certainly an authority on all things martial. I listened to them and did not join the Marine Corps. Sometimes, like Pete Starr in Thompson's "Yellow Horse," which is about one man's regret that he did not serve in the hell of Vietnam, I have often thought, "I missed my chance. I'll never know."

I am writing this Foreword because of the intersections between the lives of two real soldier/writers and my own. The first of these soldiers, Edgar Tiffany, is the author of *Hues of Green,* a Critical History of Thompson's *Colors of War & Peace.* I first encountered him in the Richmond Downtown YMCA weight room. "Hiya buddy, my name's Buzz. I got the fuzz. I make the elevator do what she does." Buzz, the elevator operator, is a character in *The Hudsucker Proxy*, a film which came out in 1994, about the time I met Edgar "Buzz" Tiffany. I was in my thirties, and Tiffany in his fifties. But I wouldn't have known it as, at age 50, he was benching 350 and squatting 450, toiling under an Olympic bar rattling with eight forty-five-pound plates, or

EDGAR TIFFANY

maybe more. I cannot remember how our conversations began, but it might have occurred spotting each other at the incline bench. I recall classical allusions being launched, exploding like artillery rounds fired for effect. Totally strange and unexpected to see a long-haired *quinquagenarian* standing above a bench doing the *signum crucis*, intoning from James Joyce:

> "I go to encounter for the millionth time the reality of experience and to forge in the smithy of my soul the uncreated conscience of my race. Old father, old artificer, stand me now and ever in good stead."

He recited randomly, incessant streaming, always new and evocative. Unbowdlerized e.e. cummings:

> *the boys i mean are not refined*
> *they go with girls who buck and bite*
> *they do not give a fuck for luck*
> *they hump them thirteen times a night*
> *they come with girls who bite and buck*
> *who cannot read and cannot write*
> *who laugh like they would fall apart*
> *and masturbate with dynamite*

Totally strange while sweating the three-hour iron-pounding we had enrolled in at the gym.

And finding out about his military service and Vietnam by reading about it in a periodical, I was amazed by the breadth of his daring, experiences and writing skills. A long essay entitled "War & Remembrance" appeared in Richmond's April 1995 *Style Weekly* to coincide with the Twentieth Anniversary of the fall of South Vietnam. It turned out that Tiffany had taken a first trip back to Vietnam after the U.S. embargo was lifted the previous year. This riveting description of a ride into combat in that article is what was added to my image of the intellectual I already knew:

In November 1966, with the beginning of Operation Attleboro, I flew in low over this same treeline, coming into full view of *Nui Ba-Den* [the Black Virgin Mountain] while flying into a base camp named Dau Tieng. The battle here was a fight waged in classical proportions enlisting elements of the 5th Special Forces Group, 25th Infantry Division, 196th Light Infantry Brigade and the First Infantry Division. At 1000 hours my unit, 2nd Battalion, 16th Infantry Rangers, was beginning its descent into a landing zone some five kilometers south of the 28th Infantry action. I remember watching the orange-plumed clusters of high explosive walking in measured step through the towering jungle canopy; ordnance shot from heavy guns poised around that same church steeple. What I recall most vividly, however, was movement high in the wall of trees as the rumbling helicopters dropped under treetop level making a final mad dash to a region of *forêt-clairière* opening like a mine-shaft below. The movement, large and shackled, had been that of a VC soldier roped to a tree in fatal prospicience.

The second soldier/writer is D.M. Thompson. Between me and Tiffany we refer to him as DMZ Thompson. An apt contradiction to introduce a book and a critical study which has so many, for Thompson is anything but a demilitarized zone (DMZ), yet his interpretation of the most military of all experiences has been filtered through a demilitarization. In the short story, "Color Me Red," halfway between his MACV-SOG experiences and his future Special Forces reserve adventures (Tiffany paints the "ambivalence that even the most vaunted and isolated warriors

CAPT. D.M. THOMPSON

felt in the years after returning from the war zone; proud of the pinnacle of the pyramid of combat, but …. doubts about the war and their actions in it, even enough to make one anti-war."), Thompson tells the SF recruiting officer from OPPERCEN looking for former Super Soldiers to fill slots in the now depleting Army reserves:

> "No! Not now, not fucking ever!" I slammed the phone. My armpits were dark moons. I was anti-war, anti-army, anti-Nixon, anti-Republican and we were just coming out of a recession. I had a family to feed and had no intention of going into the reserve.

I started working on a novel several years ago with the title, *Monk Fowler.* I showed it to Tiffany and because I boxed and it had scenes from the Spring Street Jail in downtown Richmond, he showed it to Thompson knowing that he had written a short story/memory of his own golden glove boxing stint and the story named someone I knew well and had trained under, Billy Crowder. Crowder gathered up some of his Golden Glove fighters, Thompson included, and arranged a fight venue with the Warden of the Spring Street Jail for a goodwill exhibition. That coincidence and the fact that like me, Thompson had pursued a writing muse shortly after graduating from college. Thompson's was written much earlier, but these intersections and more got me an introduction to him, and a stalwart position in his ring of admirers.

And boxing may have contributed, along with each man's peak war experiences—one in WW I France, the other in Vietnam and Laos—to Thompson going in search of his imagined Robert Graves. It is reported that Graves, as a schoolboy boxer, knocked out two opponents in a tournament and broke the thumbs of both hands doing it. Like Graves, Thompson was a broken nosed, broken hand-aesthete (metacarpals), never avoiding a fight with principle, and therein the mutual attraction. Whereas I was an athlete and unwilling fighter, I found no Robert Graves when I went searching for my

Paul Bowles; and Thompson's experience with Buddhism and OMEGA Institute, mine with Buddhism and NAROPA institute ("My monk's better than your monk"); him ending up in classes with Sloan Wilson, Larry Heinemann, Tim O'Brien, David Robbins, me in classes with Allen Ginsberg, William Burroughs, *et al.* The learning curve, the edited writing, the redacted writing, perhaps the insults. Paul Bowles said to me once, "It's hard to get past all the grammatical and spelling errors, and when I do I find content that resembles a teenager's drastic inventions." Allen Ginsberg conveyed, "I hope you are better at *Shotokan* Karate than you are as a writer or you're going to get hurt." Strange but they both encouraged me to keep going. And encouragement can always help, but it can't afford you the advantage both of these writers have had; the accumulation of words from their experiences.

I landed in Morocco after graduating from Randolph Macon College at the end of June, 1983, and showed up at 2117 Tangier Socco, and climbed aboard a tiny, creaking elevator which delivered me to within a few feet of his door. A thin, well-groomed man with silver hair, wearing a smoking jacket and ascot opened the door and greeted me. So began a few weeks of afternoon visits, smoking *kif*, listening to Eric Satie, Maurice Ravel and Moroccan folk music, and experiencing the visitor's: Mohammed Mrabet, a Moroccan writer and painter (influenced by Joan Miró), Buffie Johnson and Francis Bacon, both abstract imagist painters, Bacon by far the more famous.[1]

Returned from this grail quest, I chased another ghost and famous poet and began classes with Allen Ginsberg at a converted elementary school on Arapahoe Avenue in Boulder, Colorado. After a meeting in his house on High Street, and noting I was lugging around a heavy Osborne CPM computer which fascinated him, he took me on as a secretary/typist. The one work I helped him complete that year was entitled *The White Shroud*, a collection of poetry described by a literary critic as a "powerful mixture of Blake,

Whitman, Pound, and Williams, to which he added his own volatile, grotesque, and tender humor, [which] has assured him a memorable place in modern poetry."

And like Thompson's Maxine Hong Kingston, the sphere of Ginsberg brought me into the orbit of Buddhism and a whole other cast of characters. NAROPA University founded in 1974 in Boulder, Colorado, by Tibetan Buddhist teacher, Chogyam Trungpa, was known as a "mindful compassion university"; Thompson's OMEGA in upstate New York as a "mind-body retreat center"; and, Thich Nhat Hanh's Plum Village, in Bordeaux, France, as a retreat center for the "study and practice of mindful living." NAROPA, at the time, had hosted a number of Beat poets under the auspices of its *Jack Kerouac School of Disembodied Poetics* foremost, Allen Ginsberg.

While Thompson's foray into Buddhism is explored in *Colors of War & Peace*, we can guess from the writing in *Colors of War & Peace* that the greater dynamic of Buddhism didn't take. In "Yellow Horse," which takes place post-2001, or ten years after his introduction to Buddhism and eight years after his concluding story, "Hello My Little Fear of War!", Thompson is not a Buddhist, but a Catholic confessor to a drunken, rueful, high school buddy.

The book jacket previews for *Hues of Green, A Critical Study of D.M.Thompson's Colors of War & Peace*, states:

> "The author of *Audie Murphy In Saigon* takes a microscope to D.M. Thompson's *Colors of War & Peace: A Collection of Short Stories*, and you may not think of exegesis in the same light after reading this critical history."

And that is the *crux* of Tiffany's book about his longtime friend, military cohort and gifted writer. In *Colors of War & Peace*, Thompson has written something exceptional about the Vietnam War, America's best fighting men and a country they returned to that felt as much Vietnam to them as the triple canopy of the Ashau Valley and Laos. This is not a military history, nor creative writing about the typical *Rite of Passage*; or combat for combat's sake, patriotism, or a "War is Hell" analysis (although *Prairie Fire* is Hell). Thompson's book is a collection of eight short stories of creative non-fiction as layered and referential as the *Ficciones* of Jorge Borges, or *Welcome to the Monkey House* by Kurt Vonnegut.

The first thing to note is that all the stories of *Colors* are written in the first person and that, with the exception of "Yellow Horse" and "Hello My Little Fear of War!", they are chronological. Indeed, *Colors* can be read as a short-story cycle, for it is the same protagonist, the same history, the same life, held together by the memories and trauma of military experiences in eight different vessels. Tiffany's concern in H*ues of Green* was to reduce these eight vessels into surface and symbol, or from symbol to surface. My reading of them noticed, above all else, the visceral events of the stories and gave me an even better understanding of what is meant by the phrase, "real soldiers."

For example, the first tale, "Blue Tattoo," is set in U.S. Army OCS in the gladiator ring that it was in 1967. In Tiffany's reading he locates all the signposts in Thompson's reconstruction of becoming an officer, a gentlemen and an unknowing participant in that future of America, from *Epidaurus*, to David Maraniss, from Northrop Frye, to David Rabe, from the corpse of John F. Kennedy to Muhammed Ali (*aka* Cassius Clay). But it is the story of the pugil pit and the *mano a mano* confrontation between the young David candidate and the older Goliath instructor, which conveys the elemental confrontation in *Colors* that will proceed throughout the book, and rang my bell. For me, it recalled James Jones *From Here To Eternity* where a boxing team sergeant, "Old Ike" Galovitch, harasses and threatens young Robert E. Lee Pruitt because he won't join the boxing team. When he attacks Pruitt with a knife forcing him to fight, (Pruitt ultimately knocks Galovitch out), Pruitt faces a courts-martial. Thompson's protagonist is luckier, but introduces the bad-ass you will follow for the rest of this collection, or composite novel.

And "Walking Point With Sergeant Rock" manages to translate "War is Hell" into "War is Hellarious." Tiffany's deconstruction of it dredges up all the underlying influences, from a poet teammate's famous parody which is used as the epigraph to *Hues* ("Blaming of Parts" by Alan Farrell) to Joseph Heller, to the Marx Brothers, to "Murphy's Laws of Combat." But, as Thompson illustrates, comedy can lie in wait for us, like a precipice. What Thompson does in "Walking Point" is place between the lines of comedy and erudition, the full, visceral experience of U.S. Army Special Forces MACV-SOG operations in the span of 16 pages. You want to know what it feels like to sit a mile from the border of North Vietnam, two miles from Laos with superman training and native Vietnamese (Mung, Bru and Montagnards) as your bulwark to death and devastation? Here it is for you—rain, shit, triple-canopy jungle, death and survival made more digestible with mortal comedy.

In "Boxcar Orange," Thompson has written a story fit for the stage with a Braniff 707 R&R flight containing a cast of traumatized, starched and spit-shined soldiers, a stripped down chassis flying them from Danang, Vietnam to Sydney, Australia for intercourse & intoxication, as the proscenium arch. A particular anecdote, familiar to any former paratrooper who ever jumped from a C-119 "Flying Boxcar," as Tiffany recounts, not only outlines the theme of "Boxcar Orange," but is instructive of what this short story is about. It is the famous airborne story of flying in a C-119. The 1960's anecdote led from a few crashes of the C-119 in the 1950's. In *Not Quite an Ordinary Life* (2009), J. David Joyce wrote:

> [In 1956] I reported to King Salmon Airport with all of my belongings to board an Air Force C-119 transport aircraft. As a few other passengers and I climbed on board, the Loadmaster handed each of us a parachute harness with a parachute and helped us don the equipment. I asked him why we needed parachutes. With a smile, he told me that the C-119 was such an untrustworthy aircraft, everyone on them had to wear parachutes

all of the time. If that didn't bother me much, the answer to my next question did. I noticed the Loadmaster had a red handkerchief sticking out of his parachute pack and asked why it was there. With an even bigger smile, he told me that he always packed his own chute to be sure it would open if needed and the red handkerchief was there to indicate which chute was his. Soon after that time, the Air Force grounded all C-119 aircraft, derisively called the "flying coffin" by crew members, to perform an extensive study to determine the cause of frequent crashes.

By the time of Thompson's airborne training, the mechicals had been fixed, but in the mid-60's this tale had morphed into the learning lesson taught by all Airborne instructors at Ft. Benning, Georgia. This is the one repeated by Thompson as a truism in "Boxcar Orange" out of the mouth of Sergeant First Class Ramon: "And just prior to takeoff each man will elevate his boots perpendicular to and not less than six inches off the floor!" Why? To help the "Flying Coffin," clear the runway "LIKE SHIT OFF A SHOVEL!" Just part of Thompson's technique of signaling danger amidst the banalities of military adventure.

Probably, one of the two best of the book, is "Color Me Red," nicknamed by an old SF teammate of Thompson, "The Vomit Comet," and taking place again in an airplane and in Thompson's head. And this story brings together the authors of *Hues of Green* and *Colors of War & Peace* in a C-7A Caribou equipment jump over Deerfield, Virginia that turns into hell in the heavens. I laughed so hard that I had to, like the co-pilot in the story, hold my hand over my mouth, my "cheeks stretched like a trumpeter," to prevent breakfast from "streaming from either side of [my] mouth like a Fu Manchu."

> If you had been up front and port you would have seen what I saw as I exited the C-7A ramp. The Sergeant Major standing near the rear of the ramp, holding on with his left hand and gripping a barf bag in his right that was sloshing over the brim

and puke streaming from either side of his mouth like a Fu Manchu, him grinning toothy like an opossum in a tree.

Tiffany says of this story, "Now this is how short-story writing should start . . ."

And this is how Thompson has bookended "Color Me Red"—with two rides in the Army's most famous troop and water buffalo transport, the first flight emblematic for all the amazement, randomness and doom of the MACV-SOG experience in Vietnam, and the second playing the best war game money could buy before the advent of personal computers and WANNABE fantasies lived out at a control board in your living room, or basement. In the interest of full disclosure, you can see why I said about reading "Color Me Red," "Now this is how short-story writing should start." And I will say here, "And how short-story writing should end."

"Challenging Disaster" offers up the milieu most familiar to me, taking place in Petersburg, Virginia, with reference to places and characters I even knew. The Dixie Diner, Thompson's unnamed workplace on Bank Street—Anderson & Strudwick—Jeff Davis Highway, the Siege Museum. And it is probably the most layered of Thompson's eight stories, containing, as Tiffany points out, seven circles corresponding to the title event of the story, "Challenging Disaster." As veiled as the referents may be, they are there for the picking and Tiffany picks them, reveals them and Thompson's technique of meaning (as he did in the previous embedded stories). C.S. Lewis is invoked, Bernie Taupin's "Rocket Man" (and by proxy, Ray Bradbury's "The Rocket Man"), Vergil's *Aeneid* by way of Robert Graves' *The Golden Fleece*, by way of Pall Mall cigarettes, by way of a weed-sucking model on a billboard on Jeff Davis Highway (I remember a cigarette billboard, but they must have replaced the smoking, hot blond); the object of the story, the Challenger Shuttle ("Orbits, Oort Constants, Ellison Onizuka, and frozen O-Rings"), a model Lionel train circling the Dixie Diner emitting small O's of smoke in perfect imitation of the Challenger in its last moments, and the lesser hand on a clock turning from 8 am to 12 noon in four circles, "but it feels like a lifetime."

The irony for me, no doubt intended by Thompson, is that if you took a bird's eye view from the Pall Mall Lady's billboard on Jeff Davis Highway looking northeast to Interstate 95, you would see the Phillip Morris Tobacco Company's Marlboro Statue (a landmark known as the "Big Ciggy on 95"), marking the Manufacturing Center for Phillip Morris cigarettes. This world famous obelisk marks the spot where they are still producing 400 million cigarettes per day, or 140 billion cigarettes per year, making it the largest cigarette producing facility in the whole wide world of smoke rings.

I said "Color Me Red" is probably one of the two best stories of the book. The other is Thompson's fifth story, "Black Hand." In this tale Thompson does a deep dive into war trauma, both physical and psychological, using medical texts, Proustian memory, and the hell of Vietnam memory commingled with the goatfuck of a parachute jump into Fort Pickett, Virginia. Thompson weaves between his protagonist's hallucination of a cross-border patrol into Laos gone "Prairie Fire," to his hallucination of the Fort Pickett jump gone awry. While he describes the physical action of both events with a driving narrative, he also inserts his "Anamnesis," or personal medical history, which is a medical dissertation on the last 20 years or more of medical research done on PTSD, traumatic memory, and the related stuffy terminology by the brightest minds in those fields, that really means "broken," and "alienated." His story takes, as it develops, a history of his own military psychological and physical injuries (primarily the severe injury to his right hand in the present tense of the story, hence the "Black Hand") and turns it into one of the finest metaphors for writing, or the inspiration to write ("But if I remembered the pain, used it sparingly, maybe that gnarly, black hand could pen a story that even I could understand.").

I had a chance to join the U.S. Marine Corps, but didn't and that like Thompson's Pete Starr in "Yellow Horse," I often repeat, "I missed my chance. I'll never know." This story was the most personal for me. Thompson has taken his war, his life, and a friend's peacetime, and made them into "Lessons Learned." Tiffany's critical chapter on "Yellow Horse" has distinguished these lessons with facts we probably did not know, but hence Thompson's purpose in telling the story of a Son-of-America who missed *Ia Drang* Valley, LZ X-Ray, never went to war with the "Yellow Horse," and suffered the consequences. The *Ia Drang* Valley battle in 1965 Vietnam became, probably, the most famous (or notorious), next to General Honeycutt's Hamburger Hill, inspiring books and movies for years after the war. But the unit Thompson's Pete Starr didn't accompany to Vietnam, the sister-unit of the one at *Ia Drang*, the 2nd Bn, 7th Cavalry of the 1st Cavalry Division, suffered a far worst fate a day later than that of the much lauded 1st Bn 7th Cavalry in *We Were Soldiers Once . . . and Young.* From Poe's "Raven," to Donnie Rumplestilskin, to Ricky "The Bruiser" Cheney, to Condoleezza RiceErroneous, and the VFW, Thompson lectures those who want to glorify war, having experienced it, or NOT. While Tiffany ends his hermeneutic on "Yellow Horse" saying "Never in the procedural of [it] has there been a moment of one-upmanship," we know that the story ends in a pissing contest that may have taken place, or NOT.

There is a rule among film-makers that says you do not narrate for the audience what they are already seeing. It is the "Show, don't Tell" rule. But in writing, you will find, and Tiffany's interpretation of Thompson's *Colors* is proof in the pudding, that a book, especially one dealing with exotic subjects, fact, or fiction, as *Colors* does, benefits from interpretation and exploration with as much "Tell," don't "Show," as one can give. Thompson's last story, "Hello My Little Fear of War!" is a prime example of this unspoken axiom. In fact, without Tiffany's excavation of Thompson's search for

Buddha, peace and understanding (in a tale Thompson does not include in "Hello") in his biographical/developmental "Introduction" to *Hues*, and deep dive into the real-time travels and meaning behind "Hello," we would have had to take Thompson at his word about his experience of a *sangha*, *bodhisattvas* and the Buddha in *Colors of War & Peace*.

I went to a Norbu Rinpoche retreat with the woman who introduced me to Buddhism in 1983. It came to pass in an old farm house that was formerly a Rosicrucian Enclave going back to colonial times. I recently found my notes on the retreat where I received the Long Life transmission. It was an hours-long bell ringing, chanting, incense burning affair that could impart long-life if you didn't die first. I also re-read my notes from Norbu on the Dharma Teachings: *The Four Dharmas of Gambopa (The Kargu Lineage)*.

I was introduced to Buddhism through a woman named Margherita Pagni. She was an Italian Psychologist studying under Dr. Edward Podvill at Naropa when I arrived there 23-years old with a paperback copy of *The Dharma Bums* in the inside pocket of my leather jacket. We met in Allen Ginsberg's 7:00 pm class on Poetics. She was ten-years older and spoke fluent Spanish, German, and English as well as her native Milanese Italian. She had been a student of Norbu Rinpoche in Italy, and had been a practicing Buddhist for over a decade when we met. I accompanied her to The Rocky Mountain Dharma Center for a retreat in 1984, and then to another in Conway, Massachusetts three years later.

I did what Thompson describes in "Hello": silent for a month, I meditated, ate bland food, attended lectures on The Five Skandhas, The Eightfold Path, and the Four Noble Truths, but I wasn't really the proper vessel for the Dharma at that point in life, having all of the questions Thompson poses, explicitly, or implicitly, in *Colors*. I had no existential, or moral crisis, that had pointed me to this path, unlike Thompson, whose trajectory seems to have been intimated by Maxine Hong Kingston in her *The Fifth Book of* Peace. There, she says that he will return to Vietnam to seek meaning behind the puzzle of a Buddhist Monk on a magic mountain who was the enemy, or not, who he killed, or not, and would embrace the full meaning of his war, or not. After reading "Hues" and "Hello My Little Fear of War!," I don't think Thompson killed a Monk. I'm not even sure he was a Monk and neither is Thompson. And then there are all the "unanswered questions, undeclared questions" that Buddhism is wont to raise (Sanskrit: avyākṛta, Pali: avyākata - "unfathomable, unexpounded"). Was this Monk on the right path? Why was the man a Monk? Are Monks soldiers? And so on. What "Hello" ensures is that Thompson sought Buddha and went to France for all the right reasons, and that he is a gentle man unless, as *Colors of War & Peace* reveals, he is riled.

Ten years after the Vietnam War was over, Tiffany wrote a book review in *American Book Review*, remarking on the industry of Vietnam writing.[2] That was 37 years ago.

> What has been, and is being, written about Vietnam takes up large space. In this year of decennial commemoration it is reported that twelve new books are published on Vietnam each month. The *Vietnam War Bibliography* (Christopher L. Sugnet and John L. Hickey) has 3003 entries chosen from an initial selection of over 7000 titles, and includes analyses, historical treatments, personal narratives, pamphlets, manuscript documents, archival materials and fiction; these in English, Vietnamese, French and other Western languages and Indonesian. One requires a taxonomy to divide the subjects and interests of the Vietnam War.

No doubt, this number of books has grown exponentially to hundreds of thousands, and what is remarkable about Thompson's book is that it is one of only a handful of "literary" books about Vietnam. And Tiffany's "exegesis," as we have it, presents this fact to the reader in revelatory and exciting ways not given to any other fiction volume on the Vietnam War, and certainly not one that bespeaks the pinnacle experience of combat in Vietnam, and its aftermath.

— James Huneycutt, Richmond, Virginia

---

[1] Where Thompson's reading of Graves WW I autobiography, *Goodbye to All That,* led him in search of the poet, novelist and seer, I was blessed with a professor at Randolph Macon, William Shelton Gray (known as "Woods"), a Harvard man who during his early years had hobnobbed with Ezra Pound, T.S. Eliot, W.H. Auden, Edith Sitwell, Osbert Sitwell, E.M. Forster, Somerset Maugham, Aldous Huxley, Evelyn Waugh, Angus Wilson, Cecil Beaton, Princess Margaret, Prince Napoleon Murat, Jean Cocteau, Bernard Berenson, Frederick Durenmatt, and many others. Over his years of friendship with all of these writers/celebrities he had accumulated one of the largest privately held collections related to American and English literature. While T.S. Eliot was the great eminence in his life, he knew Paul and Jane Bowles and his lit classes were my introduction to Bowles' *The Sheltering Sky.*

[2] Edgar Tiffany, "The Triple-Canopied Jungle," *American Book Review*, Vol. 8, No. 1, November-December 1985, p. 7-8.

HUES *of* GREEN

A Critical History of D.M. Thompson's
Colors *of*
WAR *&* PEACE

by EDGAR TIFFANY

HUES *of* GREEN

INTRODUCTION

"How vain it is to sit down to write
when you have not stood up to live."

—Henry David Thoreau

D.M. Thompson, or Dan Thompson as I have known him,
came to writing like he came to military service; with all
the tools to do it, but with none of the training and know-
how to accomplish it. Speaking of his military service in the same
breath with his writing is ironic for now his writing is on display in
inverse proportion to the whole point and purpose of his
distinguished but covert military service in U.S. Army Special Forces,
MACV-SOG (Studies & Observation Group), a highly classified,
Joint Unconventional Warfare Task Force, top secret, special
operations unit which conducted clandestine operations in Laos,
Cambodia and North Vietnam (notionally) from December 1965
until 1972—and his continuation of that service in the post-Vietnam
Special Forces Reserve.

Writing informed his life's journey long before he knew his path.
In his last summer before graduation from Radford University he
purchased a EuroPass and went in search of Robert Graves, the
English poet, translator, memoirist, novelist, and classicist. Graves,
in his premier attempt at autobiography/memoir in *Goodbye to All
That,* published in 1929, inscribed his alienation after the Great War
and his ambition to write. In reading it for the first time, this passage
captured exactly what Thompson knew of his war from a writer who
had been tested mightily a half-century earlier in the trenches of the
First World War:

At least one in three of my generation at school died; because they all took commissions as soon as they could, most of them in the Infantry and Royal Flying Corps. The average life expectancy of an Infantry subaltern on the Western Front was, at some stages of the War, only about three months; by which time he had been either wounded or killed. Of these four, one got wounded seriously, and the remaining three more or less lightly. The three lightly wounded returned to the front after a few weeks or months of absence, and again faced the same odds.[3]

At the Battle of the Somme, Graves was so badly wounded by a shell-fragment through the lung that he was expected to die and was officially reported as having died of his wounds. He gradually recovered and, apart from a brief spell back in France, spent the remainder of the war in England. A young subaltern (Lieutenant) from another War, from MACV-SOG, knowing these odds, was captivated by the mind of the author of *Goodbye to All That*, *The Golden Fleece* (an historical novel retelling the mythology of Jason and the Argonauts), and *The White Goddess* (a study of the mythological muse). Soon to graduate and struggling to define his own war experiences, Thompson found a golden fleece in Graves and sailed to Mallorca, Spain where he knew Graves had been sequestered for 56 years, except for a forced return and sojourn in England during the Spanish Civil War and WW II. Unannounced, uninitiated and unknown as a writer, for Thompson it was as improbable an adventure as the voyage of the Argo. After so many near-death experiences as a recon team leader (One-Zero) along the Ho Chi Minh Trail he was still addicted to risk. How else explain his 7000 mile reconnaissance to connect with this illusive poet? An early short story has his protagonist, a back-packing former American Vietnam veteran, finally arriving at a cafe in Palma on the island of Mallorca.

He was suddenly ravenous and took a seat. The café was abandoned but for an older gentleman with a Roman nose and the scarred forehead of a boxer. He sat at the far end of the cafe with a young lady sipping Perrier. The boxer raked his thick fingers absently through a shock of white hair as he read poetry to the raven-haired, porcelain princess, a young Sophia Loren packed loosely into a V-neck dress; a pendant draped like a finger-bridge between poignant peaks, *terra firma*. She wore yellow, horn-rim sunglasses and matching yellow scarf and studied Talus as he sat studying her. While he studied a waiter approached asking in English for his order. Talus said, "*Uno San Miguel por favor.*"

This is how Talus Moore first set eyes on Graves, as he recorded it in his Golden Fleece diary, capturing the famous exile with his latest youthful muse.

Talus sat contented in shade, sipped beer and listened to the old man's lyrical voice. His bare toes fiddled in and out of carpet slippers while hands clasped blue denim knees. His rich and vibrant baritone melded with an Edwardian accent, had a pied piper appeal. He repeated verses that had been crafted for the baritone voice. (from the unpublished short story, "Talus Moore")

> *Be beauty yours and honor mine*
> *Yet sword and rose be one*
> *Great emblems that in love combine*
> *Until the deal is done*[4]

Sophia rested her chin in the palm of her hand, arm braced on the table. She slowly pumped her crossed legs, dress hiked invitingly to the edge of panty trim, easily visible from where he sat. The boxer finished reading from his book and sat. But for the lack of *caestus*—leather hand wraps—his athletic frame, thick chest and gnarly hands were posed like the bronze sculpture *Boxer At Rest* on the slopes of the Quirinal Hill. It was late afternoon and the lunch crowd had cleared. The boxer paid his bill and strode towards Talus.

You are young and foolish," said the boxer, "but mostly careless."

That is the young Thompson exercising his Robert Graves chops, but sounding more like a young Hemingway. He had aspired to witness and "touch," if humanly possible, that element of Graves' creativity, his *White Goddess*, as if rubbing a brass lamp would cause a genie to appear. But that infatuation passed as did his giant automaton of a hero, Talus. In seeing the "Man," Thompson soon came to appreciate how long Graves had been on earth and the punches life had thrown at the garrulous poet. Thompson said at that time that he harbored, somewhere in the magical department of his grey matter, the quaint notion that any brush with creative genius would inure to the benefit of his vision and enterprise. Always appreciative of the journey and having witnessed the rogue poet and his feminine ideal in the flesh, he realized what a quixotic adventure it had been.

Here is the formative introduction to Thompson in the words of another writer, a very famous one at the time, one who served as an early mentor and guide to him.

Daniel Moen Thompson, a descendant of someone on the *Arabella* (*sic*), the next ship after the *Mayflower*, spoke in the careful voice of a Southern gentleman [by an act of Congress] and Special Forces Green Beret officer. He reads about a Marine LuRP who captures a wounded VC woman and carries her on his back under fire through jungle and rivers. There's a bounty on all slant-eye weasels. His reward for bringing her in would be extra R&R. Dan then tells about a monk, or monks, shadows, he fired upon. "He or they disappeared behind the big bell. I don't know if I hit him. I ran around to the other side of the bell, but nobody was there. Maybe another monk took him away. I'm going back to Marble Mountain to find out what really happened. I just phoned my daughter and told her I'm going to Vietnam again. I want to visit my old haunts inland, and see Da Nang again, and memorize Marble Mountain for my book, Marble

Mountain. I want to know for certain. They couldn't have had rifles. They were monks."[5]

This is a glimpse of the *in vitro* writer, the Thompson who was ready to transition from Virginian jungle marauder/commando to gentleman scholar. Coincidentally, Thompson met Maxine Hong Kingston through serendipitous events after completing his first writing course at Virginia Commonwealth University in Richmond, Virginia (hence the southern gentleman) under the once-famous writer, Sloan Wilson, a preeminent short story writer in the 40's and 50's, author of *The Man in the Gray Flannel Suit* and *A Summer Place*, who was then a visiting scholar seeking to impart 45 years of writing acumen to a select student audience.[6]

"I attended Sloan Wilson's summer writing class at VCU in 1990. My portable Royal typewriter had a worn, inkless tape that left missing letters. When he read my work he said it was like doing a crossword puzzle. I was oblivious to the conventions of writing and handed in single-spaced, unnumbered pages, with no headers. Sloan was irascible and undiminished in the face of such unrefined work. His once arrogant self had been humbled by a now waning career. 'I wrote to meet women, pure and simple.' His crop of white hair and rugged profile had the magnetic allure of a rock star when he did readings. But readers, he'd found, 'Love you and toss you aside like yesterday's paper. It just is. Nothing you can do about it.' He'd refined his presentation, like an actor, with canny New England anecdotes. His mantra was start typing and keep typing. He told of finishing his first book, *Voyage to Somewhere*. It had been given tepid reviews so he gave up and went to work for *Time Life*. He found the unrelenting grind of business sucked everything out of him. 'The top executives worked twelve to fifteen hours a day, barely went home.' The interminable commutes, late nights, pressurized meeting and infighting, chipped away at him. Life had a zombie quality and he wanted off the merry-go-round. He used his experiences to tap into the collective work ethic of big corporations or the lack thereof. He was first to formulate the corporate culture of the

50's, the pre-Mad Men themes—its excesses and ethical conundrums." (from D.M. Thompson's unpublished memoir, *Marble Mountain Redux*)

Thompson said of this beginning,

"Writing a war story, any story, was more than puking it up on the page. Nevertheless, it was hard to curb my bulimic tendencies. Most of what I regurgitated ended in the trashcan. The clue to Wilson's style was only half in the reading. When his course started I'd only read his most famous books, *Grey Flannel* and *A Summers Place*, and had seen the movies." (from D.M. Thompson's unpublished memoir, *Marble Mountain Redux*)

How did the writer come up with his ideas? How did he execute them and make them into a story? He personally didn't have enough mastery of the literary to dissect Wilson's work or derive his creative formula. Thompson said, "There was, however, something to be said for having the listening skills of a Vietnam veteran, who'd seen action and whose bullshit barometer enabled him to listen between the lines."

"After finishing the course Sloane invited me to visit him and his wife Betty on his sail boat, Pretty Betty. It had been tied up in the Richmond Boat Harbor. I stopped at the nearby 7-11 and picked up a six-pack. We sat dockside as the smooth swales of a passing yacht tipped Betty gently, side to side. His sharp and youthful New England cheekbones had been sanded-down, rounded by years of wind, surf, spray and salt. Dressed for a portrait with wife Betty as they stood at the helm of the '54 cruiser, they could have been characters out of a F. Scott Fitzgerald short story. She'd been a glamorous dancer, seventeen years his junior, hot, but he presented more like a synthesis of Tom Rath, Nathan Bond, and Georgie Winthrop, protagonists in his books. The ravages of bipolarity, alcohol, and infidelity had taken its toll." (from D.M. Thompson's unpublished memoir, *Marble Mountain Redux*)

Wilson gave him an A for the course, but more for the prodigious amount of pages he'd produced than for their quality. He confessed, obligingly, how embarrassing it was to read the "shit" he wrote for Wilson these many years later. Wilson barely remarked on the beginnings of his "novel" other than to give encouragement. He didn't learn how to write from Wilson but he learned the value of stick-to-it-ness and the reward of finishing. And Thompson grasped, or learned instinctively from Wilson—to be later iterated and reinforced by other writers—the following truths you will see in all of the formulations of *Colors of War and Peace*:

> "I learned from his talks, more by allegory and anecdote, how his process worked. It wasn't until I actually read his books and connected the sea stories he'd told me, that I saw the direct connection of his work to his experiences. He called them fiction but so much of him was on the page it didn't feel like fiction. He was of the school, go do something and then write about it. How could you write about shit you hadn't stood up and lived? He described in painful detail, as Captain, how he learned that two of his crewmen were having sex in the hold on his Coast Guard Cutter sailing around Greenland during WWII. He spent hours talking about his work, the people he knew when he vacationed at a resort during the summers when he was growing up. It wasn't until I read *All the Best People*, that I connected the characters in his books to the stories he'd told. His books *A Sense of Values, Georgie Winthrop* and *Away From It All* were painted with the thin veneer of fiction but came from the same complex and sometimes torturous inner conflicts the highs and lows of ambition and abject failure, work ethic, money, family and infidelity. They were lifted and exposed from the raw and unabridged feelings from his life. He wasn't afraid to expose his frailties, triumphs, and struggles." (from D.M. Thompson's unpublished memoir, *Marble Mountain Redux*)

After finishing Wilson's seminar, Thompson invited Sloan and his wife over to dinner at his small Cape Cod on Maple Avenue. Normally, the pizzeria next-door provided all necessary food groups to sustain him; pizza, and beer. But on this occasion he fixed his special bachelor-spaghetti concoction. Sloan and Betty found grand delight in the food and finished two bottles of red. Sloan reminisced. They had planned to move the boat to Colonial Beach to be closer to family. Goodbyes were exchanged. "Just keep writing," said Sloan. "You'll get there."

It was by now after 10 pm when he found a copy of a magazine, *OMEGA*, stacked with mail near the front door. He'd never heard of the place or its holistic studies and programs. The magazine chronicled spring retreats and workshops at the Omega Institute, in Rhinebeck, NY. There, advertised on the first page was a week long "Retreat for Vietnam Veterans sponsored by Thích Nhất Hạnh and the Community of Mindful Living." The Vietnamese monk had invited veterans and their families for peace making; meditation, hugging, dancing, dialogue, all bounded by the Buddhist rubric. Thompson was intrigued and inspired but the retreat started the next day? In a mindless effort he threw clothes into a travel case, gassed up the car and drove north on I-95. After the all-night drive, and 428 miles, coupled with an inadvertent turn across the Verrazano Bridge, he arrived at the forested campsite. The community sat in a large circle in the grand hall for introductions. He fell asleep sitting in the lotus position and was awakened by a gentle nudge in the ribs from a man who had that same New England twang of, and resembled, a younger Sloan Wilson. Cole Morton, a former Marine platoon leader, and Dan became fast friends. He made the acquaintance of Maxine Hong Kingston who sat also in the lotus position within the circle across from him. (from D.M. Thompson's unpublished memoir, *Marble Mountain Redux*)

Maxine, long a famous writer and teacher, had deeply connected with Thich Nhat Hanh's Mindfulness Community and believed Vietnam veterans needed a chance to sit in small, intimate groups, tell their stories, reconnect and learn to thrive in community.

It wasn't until the last morning that Maxine broke a week long "noble silence" at breakfast.

"What do you think about starting a veterans' writing group, instead of writing alone in the attic?" She laughed at the cliché.

"It's a damn good idea. When can we start?" said Dan. Others around the table agreed and so the Veterans Writing Group was born.

> They would write the unspeakable. Writing, they keep track of their thinking; they leave a permanent record. Processing chaos through story and poem, the writer shapes and forms experience, and thereby, I believe, changes the past and remakes the existing world. The writer becomes a new person after every story, every poem; and if the art is very good, perhaps the reader is changed, too. Miraculous transformations! So, I added writing meditation to Thich Nhat Hanh's program for veterans.[7]

Worried that veterans would not take instruction from her, a non-veteran, Kingston invited writers she knew who had war experience to help her teach. Among them Larry Heinemann, George Evans, Wayne Darlin, Ho Anh Thai, Le Minh Khue, Fred Marchant and Grace Paley. The core group of 12 to 15 met for the first time as the Veterans Writing Group (VWG) at Omega the following year. This ever-changing, ever-growing group of writers began its work during the first Gulf War and continues to meet and write to the present day. Kingston edited Thompson's first attempt at a memoir, *In Search of My Rune*, and the first drafts of his novel in progress, *Marble Mountain*. Kingston said that the art of writing was in the rewrite. "I rewrite things as many as ten times." What did Thompson take from Maxine's *Woman Warrior*, *China Men*, *The Woman Warrior*, and *Trip Master Monkey*?

> "Maxine's preeminent works were wrapped in mysticism and Chinese mythology. Woman Warrior is a memoir that offers conflicts that rage between realism and fantasy. Her lurid imagination sequences echo the same skill and content of Gabriel

García Márquez. She makes the magical credible then, step by step, leads the reader into the ghostly. She does the same with *China Men. Trip Master Monkey* is a whole different stew although critics say that some of its stylistic elements are similar to *The Woman Warrior*. What intrigued was her use of James Joyce's *Ulysses* and stream of consciousness obliquely and overtly; a Joycean homage. I saw that her path was littered with bodhisattvas, sincerity, brilliance and veterans all the way to Plum Village, France." (from D.M. Thompson's unpublished memoir, *Marble Mountain Redux*)

You will see in "Color Me Red," a distinct influence of his next writing buoy, the novelist Larry Heinemann (*Paco's Story, Close Quarters*) who Thompson studied under in 1996 at the University of Massachusetts (The William Joiner Center for the Study of War and Social Consequences). Heinemann, whose *Paco's Story* was published in 1986, while Thompson was still playing out his pathological war hang-over with reservist Special Forces, posed a challenge for him:

> "Heinemann published *Paco's Story* in 1986, and won the National Book Award. '86 was about the time my life blew up, family, finances and career. He' d been teaching creative writing for fourteen years at Columbia College by then. It would be four more years before I typed my first miserable sentences." (from D.M. Thompson's unpublished memoir, *Marble Mountain Redux*)

In *Vietnam Shadows: The War, Its Ghosts, and Its Legacy*, Arnold R. Isaacs speaks of the alienation of many Vietnam veterans and Vietnam writers. He cites Larry Heinemann's own testimony, whose writing about Vietnam is about alienation as much as anything else. This message was one Thompson had first heard from Heinemann at OMEGA after his introduction through Maxine Hong Kingston. Thompson, somewhat akin to Heinemann, wants "the World" to be his country, his time, and in "Color Me Red" in revealing this search, he can tell you how it was lost, how it slips from his grasp, literally, metaphorically, and absurdly. Arnold Isaacs relates that men surviving battle in the Civil War spoke of "seeing the elephant," another way of saying they had been somewhere foreign and weird.[8] "Color Me Red" shows how Thompson met the elephant, brought it home to a place that no longer seemed to be his country, and remarks half the lessons Heinemann taught him 20 years earlier, and Vietnam taught him 30 years before that. Thompson shared one story about Heinemann that illustrated the riddle of alienated folks:

> "Along with the assignment to write a short story over the first weekend break he handed out a xeroxed essay, *Steal This Article,* and bolted early to get a head start on some serious drinking. The article, by Christopher Hitchens, told how hard it was to legally determine plagiarism. No one understood why he'd handed it out. Was it a caveat, or an inspiration?. I skipped his next Tuesday class and drove to Natick Labs, thirty miles outside of Boston, to do research for a novel, *Marble Mountain.* I hit the jackpot. I'd taken a chance, got into its archives and found the mother lode, exactly what I'd been looking for. The risk had paid off big time. When I returned to class the next day Larry was livid, even after I explained the importance of the find to my writing. 'You only have ten days here to write and you waste my time doing that?' At the end of the week, he shared his publishing contacts with me and we parted company." (from D.M. Thompson's unpublished memoir, *Marble Mountain Redux*)

Unlike Wilson, whose fiction built slowly and stayed close to the bone, Larry's was hyper, overblown, supercilious, combustible, but with eloquent riffs.

> "So he lies there, nearly motionless because of the pain—ticking like a living thing, until he comes to understand it as a living thing, as if some small animal bristling, matted fur had crawled up to him for warmth—and he stares, marveling, into the black and distant, vaulted heavens, his vision blurred by blood spattered dust."[9]

It's not Chateaubriand but it was good enough for a National Book Award. Sloan Wilson's work was at one end of the scale and

Heinemann's hyperbole was at the other. Thompson meets them somewhere in the middle.

Tim O'Brien, whom Thompson followed study under in the same writing program at the University of Massachusetts (and had read his *oeuvre*), proved an even more influential force in his development as a writer and, as you will understand, a narrator:

> "[O'Brien] never removed his BOSOX Cap. During check-in I told him that I'd gone back to Vietnam in '94 and hadn't killed myself yet. It was an acknowledgement that I'd read his *New York Times* article about his return to Vietnam in '94, with his girl friend, Kate, a doctoral candidate. They visited My Lai, where village people had been slaughtered. He told of his days working as an intern and then as a reporter at the *Washington Post*. After check-in he asked for stories to be handed in as an introduction. There was nothing in my acceptance letter, and no correspondence said anything about turning in a story the first day, but I dug a rough draft out of my slush pile entitled *Prometheus Burned*. He handed it back next day edited. I mean edited. The five pages had been sliced and diced as badly as the loser in a Sicilian knife fight. It had been diagramed with sweeping arrows and circles, "lurid," "misspellings," "punctuation," "POV shifts," "writerly tic," pronouncements of gimmicky, reckless, clumsy, and finally on the next to last page, "this is where the story starts." I felt like a cub reporter. After applying a tourniquet to my ego I told him I was thinking about killing myself. Once again, I really learned about Tim's writing by reading *The Thing"s They Carried*, and *Going After Cacciato*. But now sitting before me with all his idiosyncratic and wounded craziness was the primal source of the mythical Vietnam grunt, balding, lily-white skin in a Red Sox hat. For me his meta-fictional writings jelled in those instructions. (from D.M. Thompson's unpublished memoir, *Marble Mountain Redux*)

So *Colors of War and Peace* is a *Things They Carried* (and said, thought and did) in the Army and Army Special Forces, *circa* 1967-1986. It is creative nonfiction and not memoir or autobiography; the fictional events and experiences presented in the short story can be considered as examples of the psychological functions of a character/narrator's autobiographical memories and, like O'Brien's, pose as many meanings yet reach satisfying conclusions in a cascade of events, tensions and reversals with conflicts with solid endings. Frank Hassebrock and Brenda Boyle use a psychological study by David Pillemer, "Momentous Events and Life Story,"[10] in teaching Tim O'Brien's *The Things They Carried* to describe how autobiographical memories of specific experiences and momentous events contain distinctive details about one's self as well as other people, temporal and spatial information, and emotional reactions, in the remembering of events, whether real, or imagined.[11]

Thompson credited O'Brien with examples of a blend of the historical and imagined in such stories as *Going After Cacciato* and *The Things They Carried* as in his mind, he traversed Marble Mountain; its caves, grottos, and the ever-lurking shadows within.

> "In the end I found that creative non-fiction, which uses all of the elements of fiction, non-fiction and memoir, best serves my writing style. The impetuous, energy or idea of creative non-fiction is derived from an event witnessed or experienced by the author, and crafted by his intellect, imagination and skill. It can take the form of a first person narrative, memoir or incorporate any skill used by fiction or non-fiction writers in order to weave a story and arrive at a satisfying conclusion, of which a primary aim is a profound truth. From *The Things They Carried* I learned the art of telling a story is in essence the manipulation with all things necessary, a cascading event set in motion, tension, reversal conflict, place, time and solid ending." (from D.M. Thompson's unpublished memoir, *Marble Mountain Redux)*

For the last eight years, Thompson found himself under the instruction of David Robbins, historian, novelist, poet, playwright, *New York Times* Best selling author of *War of the Rats*, and most recently *Isaac's Beacon*. *War of the Rats*, published in 1999, climbed to the top of the best-seller charts. The plot focused on a 1942 battle between the Nazi Germans and the Soviets set in Stalingrad, Soviet Union.

> For six months in 1942, Stalingrad is the center of a titanic struggle between the Russian and German armies—the bloodiest campaign in mankind's long history of warfare. The outcome is pivotal. If Hitler's forces are not stopped, Russia will fall. And with it, the world.... German soldiers call the battle Rattenkrieg, War of the Rats. The combat is horrific, as soldiers die in the smoking cellars and trenches of a ruined city. Through this twisted carnage stalk two men—one Russian, one German— each the top sniper in his respective army. These two marksmen are equally matched in both skill and tenacity. Each man has his own mission: to find his counterpart—and kill him.[12]

It is under Robbins that his knowledge and skills have integrated. Robbins began a program for veteran writers sponsored by the Virginia War Memorial's The Mighty Pen Project (MPP) in 2014, after teaching creative writing at Virginia Commonwealth University and leading the James River Writers for the previous decade. His twelve-week courses meet once a week and end with a community reading. Robbins has had Thompson's short stories printed in the Mighty Pen Anthology and has recognized and encouraged his creativity and unique portfolio of experience.

Most recently, Robbins fastened on Thompson's short story, "Boxcar Orange" and I was privileged to see his teaching and friendship with Thompson. I knew David Robbins' writing for some years having once lived in Richmond, Virginia, and read his clarion novel, *War of the Rats*, but I only met him recently when he and Thompson entertained at a drink, eat, smoke, bullshit session at Thompson's house in Midlothian, Virginia. The food, cigars and drink-inspired conversation covered a whole range of introductions and interests and as the evening waned Robbins began to talk earnestly about the intent and success of The Mighty Pen Project and advanced a plan to present four new one-act plays converted from short stories by some of the military members of MMP. This project would conclude at the Firehouse Theater in Richmond and each play would be rolled out for several nights over several months.[13] First amongst the stories, Robbins selected Thompson's "Boxcar Orange" and gave a critical assessment of it's "playability," foremost, that it presented its own proscenium arch—an airplane. Thompson explained his aim in the story.

> "I realized in "Boxcar Orange" how plot—where the protagonist sat amongst many characters on an R&R flight to Sydney, Australia, with differing ranks, experience and dispositions—is tied to story. I recognized that the art of writing, drawing the reader into those physical and emotional scenes, was key. I wanted to show how my protagonist physically and mentally reacted to the tension of sitting in the confines of a Braniff Airways 707 stranded on the tarmac of Da Nang Airfield. I wanted the reader to sit beside him and feel every rut, rock, or pothole as the plane rolled down the rocketed runway. And every rut, rock and pothole of my psychological memory." (from D.M. Thompson's unpublished memoir, *Marble Mountain Redux*)

Secondarily, my assessment of "Boxcar Orange" came from Robbins' own stiletto commentary on Thompson and his invention in "Boxcar Orange." To paraphrase Robbins through the mist of single malt and Davidoff Winston Churchill Toros, he offered, among other opinions:

> "'Boxcar Orange' is one of the finest pieces of writing that has come out of eight years and thirty MPP classes. The amazing part was that Dan wrote it for the very first meeting of my very first class. I called friends and read it to them."

From Robbins' intervening classes, Thompson realized that writing was like a Swiss watch. All of the parts had to work in concert. *He was the watchmaker.* If one component was out of synch it stopped the whole process. He better understood how setting could be a character and reveal the makeup of other characters.

While one can instinctually know these things, I learned from Robbins that there were fundamental, manipulatable and reproducible writing techniques that aided the writer. It wasn't all art. There was also structure and application such as tension, asymmetrical information— when one party knows information that the other doesn't. Disagreement, disparity, and dissonance are irreducible components of a well-told story. To practice staying within the span of the "headlights," not straying from the illumination of the story line. (from D.M. Thompson's unpublished memoir, *Marble Mountain Redux*)

Robbins repeated over and over,

Characters say what the writer can't show, they think what the writer can't say, and remember what the writer can't think. In other words, the character should act before speaking, speak before thinking, and think before remembering in stories." He said that he was actually paraphrasing Leonardo da Vinci's observation that the typical hominid "looks without seeing, listens without hearing, touches without feeling, eats without tasting . . . [and] inhales without awareness of odor or fragrance. We under-appreciate and underestimate our sensory powers." (from D.M. Thompson's unpublished memoir, *Marble Mountain Redux*)

Robbins introduced his new writers each session by telling them, "You didn't come to a therapy class, you came to a writing class," belying the old pap of George Bernard Shaw, "Those who can, do; those who can't, teach." Robbins can write with the best of them and his teaching has made "doers" of so many who thought not. And, perhaps, unbeknownst to him, provided therapy.

Outfitted with these apprenticeships, these drills, and these examples, D.M. Thompson saw himself ready to take on "The World." *Colors of War & Peace*, the book for which we now prepare our reconnaissance, is a perfect illustration of something said by Daniel Mendelsohn, the memoirist and essayist, in describing John Williams's novel (the writer, not the composer), *Augustus* (*Gaius Julius Caesar Thurinus Octavianus Augustus*):

". . . the lives we end up with are the often unexpected products of the friction between us and the world itself—whether that world is nature or culture, the deceptively Edenic expanses of the Colorado Territory or the narrow halls of a state university, the carnage of a buffalo hunt or the proscriptions of the Roman Senate, a dirt farm in Missouri or the opulent courts of Antioch and Alexandria."[14]

Mendelsohn spoke of a scene in *Augustus* when a visitor to Rome asks Octavian's boyhood tutor what the young Augustus is like, and the elderly Greek sage replies, "He is a man like any other. . . . He will become what he will become, out of the force of his person and the accident of his fate." What is D.M. Thompson like? "He is a man like any other . . . ."

This critical history of the writing of *Colors of War & Peace* and "a man like any other" was motivated by the respect I have developed for him, my long history in viewing the experiences of this author and a realization, over the four years since its publication, that *Colors of War & Peace* was a far "deeper" read than I allotted it on the first go-around. Leon Edel, who wrote about James Joyce and Virginia Woolf, but whose grand accomplishment was a five-volume biography of Henry James, in his *Literary Biography, 1959,* said that to read between the lines of the best writing

> . . . can indeed be one of the most absorbing pursuits in the world: to catch the flickering vision behind the metaphor, to touch the very pulse of the hand that holds the pen. The critic reads to expound and expatiate on the words that issued from the pen: the biographer does this always to discover the particular mind and body that drove the pen in the creative act.

And, that in taking on these explorations of the terrain of man's imaginative creations,

> . . . we can detect deeper intentions and meanings, valuable both to the biographer and the critic. We thus become tentative geographers of the mysterious psyche, where fancy is bred. What

an enormously difficult task this can prove! Yet how fascinating, mysterious and challenging.

I have always carried Vietnam around in my head as GREEN. It was place that reverberated with hues of green and I have said as much in my own writing.

> H. was thinking about all that green, everything olive drab; the canteen covers, the dull enameled curves of Hueys, B-3 units, polystyrene claymores, H-harnesses, watch bands, the buttressed mangroves with lime waters swirling through gothic root systems and tangled lianas and the almighty wall of the forest that seemed, for the foot-worn infantry, an enveloping *limbus fatuorum* of exotic and deadly beauty.[15]

It is safe to say that these same hues of green have drawn me to the deeper intentions and meanings of Thompson's *Colors of War & Peace*, to catch the flickering vision behind his metaphors and lead, as you will see, to answers fascinating, mysterious and challenging.

Edgar Tiffany
St. Augustine, 2022

------

[3] Robert Graves, *Goodbye to All That*, New York: Doubleday Anchor Books, 1957, p. 59.

[4] Songs of Robert Graves: No. 2, *The King of Hearts a Broadsword Bears*, Marcus Farnsworth. From the Album: Michael Hurd: Choral Music Vol. 2 & Complete Solo Songs.

[5] Kingston, Maxine Hong, *The Fifth Book of Peace*, New York: Vintage Books, 2003, pp. 304-305. Born Maxine Ting Ting Hong, Hong-Kinston is a second-generation Chinese and American novelist. She is a Professor *Emerita* at the University of California, Berkeley, where she graduated with a BA in English in 1962. Her books include *The Woman Warrior: Memoir of a Girlhood Among Ghosts*, in (1976); *China*

Men (1980); *Trip Master Monkey: His Fake Book* (1989); *To Be The Poet* (2002); *The Fifth Book of Peace* (2003); *Veterans of War, Veterans of Peace*; Ed., (2006); and, *I Love a Broad Margin to My Life* (2011). Her writing often reflects on her cultural heritage and blends fiction with non-fiction. These influences came early to D.M. Thompson, because of Kingston's project with veterans and writing, which she intended as catharses, but also revelation.

[6] Born in Norwalk, Connecticut, Wilson was a grandson of US Navy officer and Arctic explorer John Wilson Danenhower. Wilson graduated from Harvard University in 1942. He then served in World War II as an officer of the U.S. Coast Guard, commanding a naval trawler for the Greenland Patrol and an army supply ship in the Pacific Ocean. Wilson published 15 books, including the bestsellers *The Man in the Gray Flannel Suit* (1955) and *A Summer Place* (1958), both of which were adapted into feature movies. A later novel, *A Sense of Values*, in which protagonist Nathan Bond is a disenchanted cartoonist involved with adultery and alcoholism, was not well received. In *Georgie Winthrop*, a 45-year-old college vice president begins a relationship with the 17-year-old daughter of his childhood love. The novel *The Ice Brothers* is loosely based on Wilson's experiences in Greenland while serving with the U.S. Coast Guard. The memoir *What Shall We Wear to This Party?* recalls his experiences in the Coast Guard during World War II and the changes to his life after the bestseller *Gray Flannel* was published.

[7] Maxine Hong Kingston, ed., *Veterans of War, Veterans of Peace*, Koa Books:Kihei, Hawai'i, 2006, p.2. From her Introduction to this anthology of veterans' fiction, nonfiction, and poetry.

[8] Arnold R. Isaacs, *Vietnam Shadows: The War, Its Ghosts, and Its Legacy*, The Johns Hopkins University Press: Baltimore & London, 1997, p.11.

[9] Larry Heinemann, *Paco's Story*, Vintage Contemporaries: New York, 1986, p. 19

---

[10] David Pillemer, (2001). "Momentous Events and the Life Story," *Review of General Psychology*, 5, 123-134. Pillemer describes how autobiographical memories of specific experiences and momentous events contain distinctive details about one's self as well as other people, temporal and spatial information, and emotional reactions. An autobiographical or personal event memory "represents a specific event that took place at a particular time and place; it contains a detailed account of the person's own personal circumstances at the time; the memory includes sensory imagery (visual, auditory, olfactory, or tactile); and the rememberer believes that the event actually happened" (p. 124).

[11] "Memory and Narrative: Reading *The Things They Carried* For Psyche and Persona," Denison University: April 3, 2009.

[12] David Robbins, Canada Penguin Random House, *War of the Rats*, New Releases, 1999.

[13] Postponed since before the pandemic, "War in Pieces" is a world premiere that brings us the stories of four military veterans through their own one-act plays. Written as part of *The Mighty Pen Project*, founded by Richmond writer David L. Robbins, and in cooperation with the Virginia War Memorial Foundation, the four plays are moving and fascinating snapshots of military life, each dramatic in its own way. Performed by a cast of ten, the one-acts are lovingly produced, each enticingly introduced by its playwright in a brief film clip.

[14] Daniel Mendelsohn, "Hail Augustus! But Who Was He?," *New York Review of Books*, August 14, 2014.

[15] Edgar Tiffany, *Audie Murphy in Saigon*, Tampa: A&A Printing & Publishing, 2020, p. 17.

BLUE TATTOO

recall 4.a *Mil.* A call on the trumpet,
bugle, or drum, which calls soldiers
back to the ranks, camp, etc.

— James Jones[16]

The son of a career Army man who performed a military SUPERFECTA—Sergeant Charles John Thompson was at Schofield Barracks, Hawaii with the 25th Infantry Division (27th Infantry "Wolfhounds") December 7, 1941, then jumped into the Netherlands in *Operation Market Garden*, September 17, 1944 with the 508th Parachute Infantry Regiment ("Red Devils") of the 82nd Airborne Division. He was an airborne advisor to the encircled and doomed French at *Dien Bien Phu*, North Vietnam, in 1954, assisting with parachute support from C-119 "Flying Boxcars" for the embattled Legionnaires until their surrender May 7, 1954, and then concluded his long service in Property Disposal in *Long Binh*, Vietnam during the War.

Thompson writes of seeing the red strobe and beacon lights affixed to the 250-foot jump towers in Ft. Benning, Georgia while he was a student in the Army Infantry Officers Candidate School, and before he follows, successfully, or unsuccessfully, his father's large footsteps, which preceded him there 24 years earlier while eyeing the very same towers:

The blinking strobes mocked me; my choice to volunteer for OCS, forego Jump School and the Special Forces training for which I'd enlisted. If boarded out, there would be no Green Beret, Merrill's Marauder's, OSS jumping behind enemy lines. My rebellious nature craved the ideal of self-sufficient insurgency while teetering precariously on this rigid plank of perfectionism. Airborne icons imbued from youth, at once lifted aspirations and loomed as a harbinger of failure. ("Blue Tattoo," p. 12.)

Not to compare *Colors of War & Peace* to Johann Wolfgang Goethe's *Wilhelm Meister's Apprenticeship*, or Gustave Flaubert's *Sentimental Education* in word or deed, the preparation in the first story, "Blue Tattoo," conjures the term *Bildungsroman*. While the *Bildungsroman* is usually a novel of education, or formation—an autobiographical novel that depicts and explores the manner in which the major character answers the reveille call to life, and develops morally and psychologically (and memoirs and published journals have employed this formula; *The Dharma Bums* by Jack Kerouac, and *The Motorcycle Diaries* by Ernesto "Che" Guevara)—Thompson's collection of short stories follows this pattern. And Anamnesis, a big, but obscure word Thompson introduces in his sixth story, "Black Hand," which is every bit present in this one and all that follow:

> Reveille, 0630. The same peppy tune my great-grandfather, Johann, heard in 1863, a hundred years earlier out on the Great Plains during the last Sioux uprising; and my father, Schofield Barracks, December 7th, 1941. From childhood, bugles had structured life; their cadence informed my circadian rhythms. ("Blue Tattoo," pp. 11-12.)

The young Thompson, knowingly, or unknowingly, was already practicing the writing he would take up by his cumulative observations and his intent to stand up and live. "Blue Tattoo" is an allegory for it is set in several arenas, if only on one stage.

> *Far across the Chattahoochee*
> *To the Upatoi*
> *Stands our loyal Alma Mater*
> *Benning's School for Boys.*

The stage is Army Infantry Officer Candidates "School at Ft. Benning, Georgia, in 1967, a grueling test for young, testosterone fueled, perhaps athletically and even scholastically gifted men. The candidate hopefuls are challenged from day one physically and emotionally and can expect early mornings, late nights and torturous repetition, all in the name of an elusive perfection. As the physical and mental exhaustion sets in, OCS transitions from a school to a contest; a means to assess the candidate's stability, character and ultimately, stamina. And in 1967, it lasted 6 months (24 weeks), but the 18th week was the hump week. Upon completion, "a Senior Status Review and formal dinner party [ball] culminates 18 weeks of training and the attainment of Senior [Blue] status."

"Blue Tattoo" is a tale of the journey to that 18th week, a conflict as grueling as any of the hardest combat one of these newly tested graduates will face, without the threat of a waist-high Bouncing Betty, or a bullet between the eyebrows. In Thompson's Candidate narrator's case, the journey is with his sixth platoon, 82nd Company, 1st Battalion, 66th Infantry, and his redefinition of the above:

> Twenty-two OC's braced for the morning ritual, knights bowing to a construct of mission and efficiency. We'd been systematically fixed by OC doctrine and further emasculated by our TACs [Tactical Officers]. Sometimes "cooperate and graduate" gave way to baser instincts; devour the weak. "I want you to compile a list of all building deficiencies," he said, "for the upcoming IG inspection. Every ding, chip, broken tile, loose door knob, cracked window, from top to bottom." He wasn't subtle about my motivation. "This task will reflect directly on your next evaluation." Meaning that if I failed to provide him with an exquisitely detailed and actionable report, I could bend over and kiss my Blue ass goodbye. ("Blue Tattoo," pp. 13-14.)

Candidate Sisyphus low crawling his anxiety up Raiders Creek.

Here we go again
Same old stuff again
Crawlin' down Raiders Creek
Ain't no Ranger we can't beat. ("Blue Tattoo," p. 30.)

The stage in this tale is the pugil pit where the themes of military indoctrination, domination, submission, and victory are reenacted over and over during the climb to Blue status and should end with a championship fight to cull a gladiator from the once company of 200 candidates. But the story is not based on the *Karate Kid.* It is, instead, a major illustration of how life is going to work for these candidates in the new Vietnam era, as the painting of the first circle of Thompson's "Blue Tattoo" subverts the gladiator/hero theme, just as life destabilizes ambition. The story pivots around the *mano a mano* of the pugil pit on Ranger Field overlooked by "Infantry Hall, six stories, brick and mortar; half-million square feet." This pugil pit is like the ancient Greek theater of *Epidaurus* with its stage and limestone seats— an amphitheater, but in this case, one of tin and wood:

> **We marched into sunlight,** came to a halt in front of a large pole barn and bleachers. A tin roof covered wooden trusses, boxed on three sides. We filled the stands with a *can do* crescendo, a low roar that built like *Bolero*, rose in full throated intensity as one hundred and forty voices roared. ("Blue Tattoo," pp. 19-20.)

And this is where the allegorical enters the fray. "We marched into sunlight" begins Thompson's technique of saying one thing but alluding to another, thereby laying the groundwork for implicit meaning, that later becomes explicit. "We marched into sunlight" refers to a book published in 2004, *They Marched Into Sunlight: War and Peace, Vietnam and America, October 1967*, which explicates three coinciding periods in American history: the death and heroism of 1st Infantry Division soldiers in a battle of great loss, student activism against the Vietnam War at the same time in the U.S., and the incompetence and obfuscation of politicians and military leaders in Washington, D.C related to the Vietnam War. [17] The title of Maraniss' book refers to the "Battle of Ong Thanh" in which an Army battalion was ambushed by a superior NVA force and suffered 64 men killed, over a 100 wounded and 2 missing in action. Despite the losses that had been inflicted on the 2nd Bn, 28th Infantry, 1st Infantry Division that day, the U.S. military told the media that the fight at Ong Thanh had resulted in a major, American victory. And "They marched into sunlight" refers to the ending of this battle in a cordite-misted, triple-canopied jungle of Vietnam, when the 28th Infantry exits from the darkness of battle and death into the sunlight of the living. It is no irony that Thompson refers to these events and the October of 1967, for that is when his OCS candidates are completing their rite of passage. Thompson presages his young candidates' order of battle in a kind of reversal, for upon completion of their training and indoctrination walk into sunlight, many of them will walk into the darkness of Vietnam.

Northrop Frye, whose reputation was made by the publication of *Anatomy of Criticism* in 1957 in which he expounds his theory of literary criticism, says that allegorizing is the most common kind of literary activity, whether for writer or critic, and occurs whenever one says, "*that one means this as well as that.*"[18] David Rabe, author of *The Basic Training of Pavlo Hummel,* believed that war is inevitably a part of what he called the "eternal human pageant," a metaphor to illustrate the coercive power of the institution and he used Army military basic training as the metaphor for the "essential" training by which society reshapes all individuals, or just another way, as Frye says, "*that one means this as well as that.*" It appears Thompson read *Pavlo Hummel* at some point in his sentimental education, for Officers' Candidate Training at Ft. Benning, Georgia is, for our autobiographical narrator, Hummel's basic training.

Our Candidate narrator and his classmates will, for the core of this story act out the coerced drill that, while being military training, reverberates the time, culture and history of America in 1967, and will mean to us "this as well as that." And what is the time, culture and history of America in 1967? As Candidate narrator progresses in OCS, four U.S. astronauts have just been killed when fire breaks out in their Apollo spacecraft during a launch pad test. "Respect" was just released, but Aretha Franklin never got any. The corpse of John F. Kennedy was moved to a permanent burial place at Arlington national Cemetery. Tennessee Governor Earl Buford Ellington repeals the "Monkey Law" (officially the Butler Act; c.f. *Scopes Monkey Trial*). *Loving v. Virginia* declares the prohibition of interracial marriages to be unconstitutional. Thurgood Marshall becomes the first African American Justice of the U.S. Supreme Court. Muhammad Ali was arrested because he said "I ain't got no quarrel with them Viet Cong. No Viet Cong ever called me nigger." And the Vietnam War rages, from *Hanoi* to *Vườn Quốc Gia Mũi Cà Mau*—from Bangor to Chula Vista, and Thompson's future SOG teammates are spilling and shedding blood in Vietnam, Cambodia, Laos and North Vietnam. Those are the props behind which the allegory of the "Blue Tattoo" continuum is enacted, and here, the stage.

> Pugil Training was ostensibly designed to teach technique, imbue the heroic toe-to-toe. We battled in the grit pit; wore protective cups and football helmets. But it had little to do with Olympic ideals. Dominance and aggression were key; survival of the fittest, paramount. Nothing made it easer for a TAC to sort out prejudices than testing an OC's mettle in the pit. The training tapped into the primordial, eat or be eaten core. ("Blue Tattoo," p. 20.)

The company on this day will be tested after a procession of commands with the bayonet—high port, whirl, long and short thrust, parry, horizontal and vertical butt stroke, smash and slash—by a Ranger "with steely resolve" recently returned from Vietnam, a "gaunt sergeant, angry fishhook-scar" (now identified as "Fishhook") on his chin who, grimacing, growling, bending his knees and thrusting his "fixed bayonet towards an invisible enemy," appears to be a deranged soul. After this demo, the TAC offers a 10-minute break to prepare the company for a "combat training exercise to enhance unit skills and motivate soldiers under your command." The exercise features sergeant Fishhook confronting a file of six soldiers in the pugil pit, each separated by ten feet, with the NCOIC admonition, "At *no time* will men in the file counter the movements of the aggressor [Fishhook]!"

Sergeant Fishhook proceeds to dismantle the first five candidates in front of our narrator, violating the directions of the TAC to teach the men a lesson, but without teaching the men a lesson.

> Fishhook parried and slashed but followed with a flurry of blows, pads thrashing. The canvas sacks drubbed Jay's head and shoulders. The final smash caught him flush in the face and knocked him down. An angry chorus of boos burst from the bleachers; merged with shrill whistles and catcalls. Fishhook's unrestrained acts of violence awakened deep-seated feelings of abuse, nurtured during the training cycle; embodied by careless restraint. The sleeping giant awoke, rowdy and aggrieved by ferocity unbound. ("Blue Tattoo," p. 25.)

At the beginning of the confrontations, Fishhook had eyed the candidates with disdain, saying aloud, "None of 'em would last two minutes in a fire fight." Other cadre, embarrassed by his remarks, shook their heads and turned away. With this fuel on the fire, our Candidate narrator is faced by the dervish Fishhook and, outrage churning in his gut as one hundred and thirty-four classmates roared, and the bugle played CHARGE in his head, charged Fishhook in a roadrunner cloud of dust before the sprinting TAC officers could intervene and,

> . . . pivoted and threw a horizontal butt stroke that caught Fishhook flush on the chin. The canvas sack struck his twisted mouth and I followed with a smash to the face. His eyes flashed

disbelief as he tilted back on his heels, toppled like a Georgia Pine. I felt my weight shift and shoulders rock, hands and arms powered by pushups struck with such speed and force the Fishhook could only cover up the thrashing. The bugle played on. ("Blue Tattoo," pp. 27-28.)

82nd Company stood as one with an unrelenting roar as they stomped wooden seats and the TAC charged, screaming into his megaphone, "*Stand down!*" Suffice it to say that our autobiographical candidate was a large man, 20 years of age, a talented high school athlete and a boxer before he decided to carry the colors of his father. His violation of the DO IT, DON'T DO IT! law of the pugil pit provides the fulcrum and the multiple interpretations allotted us over the last pages of "Blue Tattoo." The sixth platoon TAC was First Lieutenant Harold McGrit. McGrit replaced in the fourth week the TAC officer who started sixth platoon's cycle, Lieutenant Gray, who the "Army Times listed six weeks later as KIA, Vietnam; popup target, non-electric." McGrit had begun to eye Candidate narrator as soon as he took his replacement assignment authority of 6th platoon's training cycle. Candidate narrator described McGrit's bulldog features and premature jowls "which disparaged a pencil thin neck" and recorded that the platoon quickly named him Deputy Dawg.

Thompson's first impression of McGrit was this homily: "McGrit always said the average life span for a second lieutenant in Vietnam was as long as a fruit fly. That put us at the end of the larval stage." Kind of like saying, your previous TAC was a fruit fly, but I'm FUCKIN MCGRIT! Now, Candidate narrator's berserk moment in the pugil pit had invited the full attention and acrimony of FUCKIN MCGRIT!

> "What the hell you thinking, candidate?" McGrit asked.
> "Sir, may I speak freely, sir?" I picked up the pugil.
> "This ain't no democracy, candidate," McGrit said. "Haven't you learned anything since you've been here? What I want . . .

what interests me, is what possessed you to incite this riot and beat that Ranger like a stepchild." He paused.

"Sir, I was following your explicit orders, sir," I said.

"To what end, candidate?"

"Sir, OCS requires the will to overcome obstacles."

"What about the Tiger Tactics Award?"

"Sir, I gave it my all."

"Brilliant. Maybe your all was too much! What about discretion is the better part of valor?" I mirrored his intense stare.

"I guess I'm no fruit fly, sir." ("Blue Tattoo," pp. 29-30.)

The first thing Candidate narrator expects is his dismissal, but instead, McGrit has the entire platoon low crawl back to the company area up Raiders Creek in ponchos, thinking that such punishment will quell the roaring, seat stomping rebellion but to his unbelieving (lying?) eyes, they respond with the same wild enthusiasm splashing, crawling and singing a Jody Call led first by Meeks, who was yanked aside, then Candidate narrator, who was ordered out of the creek, then by Ricketts, then by Harrell and so on. This is the stuff that leadership is made of and yet, ironically, the OCS TACs are hell bent to crush that quality.

But Thompson has etched also an act that reveals the soft underbelly of this beast, and one could question if it is not the real intent of his story in the first place. It is no accident that racist America has been evoked in the enumeration of 1967; Aretha Franklin, Tennessee's "Monkey Law," *Loving v. Virginia* (that drama unfolded just up the pike from where Thompson was raised), and Muhammad Ali. Thompson inserts subtly, but jarringly, a case example of 1967 American democracy in that least democratic institution of the times, the military (what better irony to unfold misguided dedication and American patrimony). It involves probably the most talented, capable and supreme example of what an officer candidate should be—should have been—Candidate Jeremiah Meeks. Preacher's son, fine athlete, scholar ("3.8 at Yale.

The last IBM punch card ranked him first academically [in the OCS class; but, BLACK]").

> McGrit stopped in front of Candidate Jeremiah Meeks. He made it his duty to spread misery equally; yet thicker for some than others.
> "Why haven't you turned in your quit notice Preacher Man?" McGrit glowered.
> "Sir, Candidate Meeks is not a quitter, sir," Meeks said.
> "Drop and give me fifty!"
> "Uppity!" McGrit said. "I got plans for you." ("Blue Tattoo," pp. 16-17.)

What does Thompson tell us?

> That Meeks was the last person of color to remain in the platoon proved miraculous. Three other blacks had washed out by week eight, four weeks after McGrit took over. Munoz left the eleventh week; boarded at intermediate status. But Meeks' tenacity matched McGrit's singular resolve, that no nigger or wetback would be commissioned from his platoon. In his official capacity as officer and gentleman he'd never said the "N" word, but his prejudice radiated like the neon sign out front his daddy's general store, Holy Pond, Alabama. We all received special attention, but none so special as Meeks. ("Blue Tattoo," p. 17)

Do the math. 6th platoon is now finishing its 18th week. Six weeks left to graduate. The hump week, Senior Status Review, the formal dinner ball and the attainment of Senior Blue status. Thompson paints the dinner ball and procuring a white princess to attend the Infantry School tradition in the latter pages of "Blue Tattoo." His Candidate narrator reports after the conflagration of the pugil pit that he watched, sequestered in the front leaning rest position on the bank of Raiders Creek with Meeks, Ricketts and Harrell, 82nd Company crawl, heartened and undeterred. Later that night he finally makes a covert phone booth call to arrange to escort a Major's daughter to the Senior Ball at the Officer's Club, and returns, marveling at the starry night.

> My boots were shined and poncho folded when I slipped back into the darkened platoon bay. Meeks' bed had been stripped and rolled, locker emptied, all his gear gone. McGrit had fulfilled his final task, purged the enemy from his ranks. ("Blue Tattoo," p. 33.)

Well. Life must go on, and on it goes.

> An innocent kiss and firm embrace beneath a dim porch light, the faint whiff of Jolie Madame and a soft reassuring touch was more than ample reward. As she closed the door with a coy wink, the treble notes of the bugle call *Tattoo*, inescapably haunting, alerted my ear. By tradition it was the same sound that urged innkeepers to send horse soldiers from town back to garrison— and so it did, my first *Blue Tattoo*. ("Blue Tattoo," p. 36.)

It is well to note that Thompson has framed this story between the bugle call of Reveille and the bugle sounding Recall. You will find that the short stories of this collection all do the same justice to beginning and ending. It is no irony that Recall is sounded in "Blue Tattoo" because it is Recall that is the guiding beacon in this book, and no coincidence that "Black Hand" invokes Anamnesis in the structure of that story, for "Anamnesis" and "Recall" are everything Thompson is about here. You hear in this story, and will in the ones to come, the echoes of Thompson's concerns about understanding the duty, honor, country debt he believes he owes in this bewitching, cruel and contradictory era, and the echoes of General MacArthur's "witching memory of faint bugles" first transported to "the treble notes of the bugle call *Tattoo*, inescapably haunting," and it is a *paean* to service, and of course, recall.

---

[16] James Jones, *Viet Journal,* New York: Delacorte Press, 1973, p. 237.

[17] David Maraniss, *They Marched Into Sunlight: War and Peace, Vietnam and America,* October 1967, New York: Simon & Schuster, 2004.

[18] Northrop Frye, *Anatomy of Criticism,* Princeton, NJ: Princeton University Press, 1971, p. 111.

WALKING POINT
WITH SERGEANT ROCK

"Comedy is everywhere, in each one of us, it goes with us like our shadow, it is even in our misfortune, lying in wait for us like a precipice."

—Milan Kundera[19]

After those halcyon days in Fort Benning and Officers' Candidate School etched in the introduction story "Blue Tattoo" Thompson, in "Walking Point with Sergeant Rock," provides the fabric, a site map, of his standing up to live— a lexicon for the visceral experience of MACV-SOG, Command & Control North, *Mai Loc*, Vietnam, as seen through the eyes of his autobiographical narrator, a non-entity, shave-tail SOG 2nd lieutenant.

- MLT-1, Mobile Launch Team-One, sat next to a rutted airfield ten klicks south of Camp Carroll, a Marine stronghold on Highway 9. It was plopped down between the Vietnamese village of Mai Loc and a Montagnards village.

- August 1968, MLT-1 stood on alert. Intelligence informed that a North Vietnamese Army Regiment was lurking about the countryside, eyeing this tasty morsel. The same NVA Regiment had overrun Special Forces A Camp 101 at Long Vei in February. In the aftermath, remnants of the camp were reconstituted and moved to Mai Loc. Newly built and fortified, A-101 anchored one end of the airstrip while MLT-1 sat loosely tethered at the other.

- MLT-1, Studies & Observation Group (SOG) launch site, was a hodgepodge of rusted connex containers, tin roofed bunkers, and moldy GP tents, sagging like green braziers. A darkened doorway in a red mound led underground to the TOC, Tactical

Operations Center. The nearby 4.2 mortar/Jacuzzi pit was filled with brown bilge, pooling in pouring rain. Barbed and concertina wire, trip flares, toe poppers, claymores and bouncing bettys wrapped the porous perimeter.

- Logistically, MLT-1's small airstrip served to refuel helicopters and launch top-secret Recon teams (RTs) across the border into Laos. Tactically, Bright Light teams or Hatchet platoons were launched to retrieve RT remnants, pinned down or overrun.

- As I sloshed between bunkers, the distant report of big guns, 175 mm Long Toms pulsed… With the first deluge of monsoon I'd abandoned military issue inside the wire. Gone were wet socks that rubbed feet raw and sponge-soaked fatigues. No more underwear that bunched into crack and crevice; chafed the crotch. Gone too, the caked jungle boots that hardened into ortho plaster. No matter what the raingear, you were soaked in seconds. I chose the thin, translucent, indigenous poncho for its ease of movement and elegant fit. The cellophane wrap retained no body heat, but it was lighter, quieter and far more pliant than the bulky U.S. Army rubberized poncho.

- By 1968 many of the experienced team leaders, One Zeros, were missing, wounded, dead or just plain burned out. Slots needed to be filled and TO&E [Table of Organization & Equipment] be damned. I was proud and humbled to have been volunteered as cannon fodder for this prestigious unit but mostly for serving with these savvy warriors. Their bravery was legion, mission impossible. ("Walking Point," pp. 39-43.)

If you want the now not-so-secret histories which enumerate this top-secret unit to assist you in understanding SOG, it appears that the once locked caches of these super soldiers have spawned a thousand of them.[20] But Thompson's writing, rather than the more pedestrian and exact study of history, is belletristic and granular.[21]

Why use words meaning "beautiful," and "fine" to describe a journal of hell in a shithole? Because there is a carefully erected scaffolding used in Thompson's particular construction, or deconstruction, of this shithole, a framework supporting the aesthetic, pathos and comedy; you will find yourself admiring the beauty of an image which is confoundingly ugly, or depressing, and laughing out loud in places you probably should be crying. It is no accident, then, that *Wilhelm Meister's Apprenticeship* and *Sentimentale Education* were invoked in his service.

Is "Sergeant Rock" funny? The proper question is, "Why is 'Sergeant Rock' so funny?" Probably why Joseph Heller's *Catch 22* is *so* funny; the satire, the absurdity, the lunacy. As with Heller's aviators in a WW II Mediterranean, Thompson's enemy is on the same side of the fence, high command of a cynical organization that keeps commandos across the border when they are near-dead with exhaustion, and accusing them of a "morbid aversion to dying" and "deep-seated survival anxieties."[22] Hard to be funny about such stuff, but Thompson is, and he employs several forms of humor to do it; "surprise and incongruity," "self-deprecation" (morphing into slapstick), and the "epigrammatic," to name a few.

His "surprise and incongruity" study introduces us to SOG and into a night-time nightmare combining the shits, hard rain, bare-ass naked, flares, .50 cal machine guns, the fear of sappers and—a dog. In his own words, the naked but saran-wrapped 2nd Lieutenant, flip-flop lost, in his own shit, is trekking the barbed concertina wire, trip flares, toe poppers, claymores and bouncing-betty's of Mai Loc's porous perimeter:

> As I glanced into the last bunker a Bru gunner alerted. He leaned forward squinting, scanning the minefield. His hands wrapped the spade grips of a .50 caliber machine gun. He pointed its sleek tapered barrel at movement in the minefield as thumbs pressed the butterfly trigger. The pop-sizzle of a flare ignited his suspicions and the stocky Bru jacked back the operating lever and

seated a round. White light illumined; shadows shifted on a smoky curtain. Rounds exploded from the machine gun as heavy metal, *In-A-Gadda-Da-Vida, chunk, chunk, chunk*, pulse; droned on. The jackhammer recoil lifted and shook the small Bru. Barefoot, I scaled the sand bags to a makeshift tower, searched for the breach, sappers low crawling with satchel charges. Bunkers down the line opened up in quick succession. Hand flares rushed skyward, popped and drifted eerily above the clouds. I clambered up the sandbags in time to see Mango, a mongrel pup, explode with a deafening roar. Shrapnel whizzed past as the .50 cal led a chorus of automatic rifles, machine guns; punctuated by explosions. "*Cease fire! Cease fire.*" The wide-eyed Bru grinned righteously and slumped back against the sandbags. Rain spit and sizzled on the barrel. ("Walking Point," pp. 43-44.)

In sending another flare aloft, the Lieutenant spooked the Bru once again ("… whose tracers rose, wriggling snakes, swallowed by clouds."), this time to skeet-shoot the flare. This started the thunderous *ponk* of a four-deuce mortar as magnesium light still burned dimly above the conflagration.

I hustled over to the TOC and reported the puppy threat terminated with prejudice. An all-clear sounded. After the inquisition and diatribe by a crapulent West Point captain, the mortar tube was plugged, weapons cleared, and soldiers fell abruptly into monsoonal malaise. ("Walking," pp. 44-45.)

The conclusion of this conflagration? "The Bru gunner sulked, saddened by the loss of a culinary delight." And even when the writing seems perfectly descriptive, it is loaded with innuendo and reference. Take for instance his protagonist's preparation for patrol:

With the second strip of tape I wrapped the sling swivels on my rifle and covered the flash suppressor. I squirted a generous load of lubricant over the bolt, thought I heard the mocking voice of my drill sergeant warning "I'll kick any man's ass I find doing that." ("Walking Point," p. 48)

Why? Thompson is slyly referring to probably one of the greatest (and funniest; but least known) poems written about Vietnam, *Blaming of Parts*. It was written by Alan Farrell, a SOG colleague of Thompson's in Vietnam and later with him on operating detachments in the Army Reserves. Farrell wrote it as a parody of the British WW II poet Henry Reed's *Naming of Parts*, in which a lecture on the assembly and parts of an Enfield rifle is juxtaposed with observations about nature in springtime, but Farrell refitted it to an anything but languid tropism in Vietnam. The *Blaming of Parts*; here is what Thompson refers to:

> Today we have blaming of parts. Yesterday, That piece of shit M-16 we fuckin' tol' you wouldn't work didn't. And Tomorrow morning,
> We'll fuckin' plant Waziscowicz, L J, 042 36 3842, who we found deadern' a mackerel cleaning rod slammed down the barrel of his piece no spent brass nowhere so he like didn't even get off round one before the Dinks popped him fuckin' tol' him you slather that goddam Lubricant comma Semiautomatic all over the fuckin' Bolt it'll fuckin' lock up on you tol' him that shit was no good would he lissen, fuck, no… But today, We have blaming of the parts. The *nipa* palm Casts a sinuous, elegant neck back to peer wistfully up at the sun—languid tropism—laying bare A polished, ebony gorge wayward caress of errant breeze riffling the neighboring gardens…[23]

Like Joseph Heller, Farrell also is such an appropriating parodist of a lunatic war. And no better place to introduce Ken Boyd, a.k.a. B.K. Marshall, the third member of an influential SOG quartet to be introduced, along with, Thompson and Farrell. In his novel, *Dawson's War*, Boyd's autobiographical protagonist is Alan Dawson, like D.M. Thompson, a young 1st Lieutenant whose rite of passage Boyd etches in MACV-SOG, 1968-1969. Boyd introduces a Staff Sergeant "with his arm in a sling, for a detailed briefing."

"My name is Fallon. I got dinged up on a hatchet force operation out of Kontum last month," he said motioning to his arm. "So, I haven't been here long. But, I've been here long enough to know that you're probably not going to get into this target," Fallon said bluntly.[24]

This briefing takes place at the TOC of FOB 1 (at the time) in Phu Bai, and Sergeant Fallon will provide intelligence information to Alan Dawson and his Recon Teams throughout the rest of the novel. This Sergeant Fallon character is none other than a fictional portrait of Alan Farrell, and the Mai Loc Dawson arrives at, preparatory to Thompson and his crew, is the same Mai Loc described identically from two different precipices (unlike Akira Kurosawa's *Rashomon*). Boyd's is a portrait painted a month before Thompson arrives in Mai Loc, but there is no mistaking it as the place described in Thompson's opening of "Walking Point With Sergeant Rock."

A helicopter landed on a partially completed runway. Dirt, stirred by the whirling blades, blew through the cabin as the chopper shut down. After two weeks of work, the Mai Loc launch site was nothing more than a few tents, not even protected by sandbags, surrounded by a couple of strands of concertina wire. Dawson stepped out, carting a duffle bag. Looking around, he saw hills to the south and mountains to the west. The rest was a flat plain. He followed the helicopter crew through a rudimentary gate, guarded by a grinning, dark-skinned Asian.[25]

In an aside to Lieutenant Dawson, who hears of his reassignment to Mai Loc, one of his enlisted team mates, Sergeant Rogers, apprises Dawson of the shithole Mai Loc is. Dawson asks him if he is going with him. Rogers answers, "Not me LT. I'm smart enough to stay away from places where they don't have running water and toilets." Dawson, as Thompson's LT will find, learned that when there is no running water and toilets, you shit down your leg and let the Monsoon take care of it. It turns out that Thompson, surreptitiously, stuck Boyd/Dawson in "Walking Point With Sergeant Rock." After the perimeter conflagration with the Bru machine-gunner and Mango, the exploding dog, Sergeant Short gives the Lieutenant an after-action report: "One casualty," Short Round said. "El-Tee Boykin fell in the mortar pit and broke his leg!" When Thompson and Boyd exchanged books these many years later, El-Tee Boykin/Boyd/Marshall corrected Thompson. "I didn't break my leg. I just twisted some strings." Thompson said of Boyd's book:

Reading *Dawson's War* is like strapping on a ruck and jumping aboard a H-34 chopper with a recon team just before it lifts off. You are shoulder to shoulder with Dawson as he's inserted into high risk missions in Laos, or afterwards donning a 9mm w/shoulder holster and catching a Blackbird to Saigon for three day R&R, twilight delight. Dawson, a ground operator assigned to SOG, through hard nosed persistence, raw intelligence and sardonic wit, learned to overcome daunting challenges. His task: learn quickly or go home in a body bag. In order to live, he had to outsmart a crafty adversary while on target and an absurd, ambitious and out of touch Headquarters. This book is historically accurate down to the smallest detail. I was proud to serve with warriors like Dawson. Strap in and enjoy the ride, I did.

Thompson's real, but ludicrous situations, are secretly informed with snatches of Marx Brothers-like dialogue reminiscent of *Duck Soup*, *A Night at the Opera*, *Horse Feathers*, and *Monkey Business*, among others. But Thompson's humor, and slapstick as it appears, is far more self-deprecating than the Marx Brothers, or Farrell's (and as it unravels, self-defecating). In this theme, our anonymous 2nd Lieutenant narrator's vacation sojourn in Mai Loc has given him the shits.

Splashing forward my sphincter spasmed and a warm discharge spilled down my legs. Brown sluice slid down the back of my exposed legs. By the end of my first month I'd purged twenty pounds from a raw and ravaged blowhole. Nothing plugged the rush, which at times like now breached amid step. Hard rain flushed the skunk-works. "What's that smell?' Short's muscular legs hung from his cot. "Smells like shit!" Short studied my see-through duds. My stomach cramped; a sphincter twitched. I pulled a bottle off paregoric from my rucksack and took a healthy swig. A finger in the dike. [Gathered in the dank, underground tuberous TOC with the commander, Major Clyde Sincere and the patrol] My ass spasmed and I let loose silent but deadly gas. Sincere scowled. "Who shit?" I shrugged. Short Round coughed, Matson gagged. The crapulent XO pinched his nose. ("Walking Point," pp. 42, 43, 45, 50.)

- (*Monkey Business*) Groucho Marx: You call this a barn? This looks like a stable. Chico Marx: Well, if you look at it, it's a barn. If you smell it, it's a stable.

- (*Horse Feathers*) Reginald Barlow: Professor Wagstaff, now that you have stepped into my shoes… Groucho Marx: Oh, is that what I stepped in? I wondered what it was. If these are your shoes, the least you can do is have them cleaned.

- (*Duck* Soup) Zeppo Marx: General Smith reports a gas attack. He wants to know what to do. Groucho Marx: Tell him to take a teaspoonful of bicarbonate baking soda and a half a glass of water.

And "Sergeant Rock" has its "Catch," albeit an apparently life-saving one, at least for those in their right mind:

Second lieutenants, goats [of which our narrator is one] on the Special Forces totem pole, had to earn their *stripes*, much as a snot-nosed PFC——but there was a catch. There were no slots in Special Forces Table of Organization & Equipment (TO&E) for either. ("Walking Point," pp. 42-43.)

- (*A Night at the Opera*) Chico Marx: Hey, wait, wait. What does this say here, this thing here? Groucho Marx: Oh, that? Oh, that's the usual clause that's in every contract. That just says, it says, "if any of the parties participating in this contract are shown not to be in their right mind, the entire agreement is automatically nullified." Chico Marx: Well, I don't know… Groucho Marx: "It's all right, that's in every contract. That's, that's what they call a sanity clause. Chico Marx: Ha-ha-ha-ha-ha! You can't fool me. There *ain't* no Sanity Clause!

"One casualty," Short Round said. "El-Tee Boykin fell in the mortar pit and broke his leg!" Short Round unbuttoned the tent flap. "Be careful out there today, El-Tee." "Break a leg?"

- (*Duck Soup*) Groucho Marx: I have here an accident policy that will absolutely protect you no matter what happens. If you lose a leg, we'll help you look for it.

Gathered in the dank underground around Sincere; Sergeant Rock, Short Round, Matson, demolition specialist, the radio operator, pudgy XO and me. "I've coordinated with the Ruff-Puff, A-101, and marines, about patrolling this area," Sincere said. He circled a spot on the map five kilometers east of the camp. "Enemy activity reported here." "I patrolled that area two weeks ago," Rock said. "Nothing but rice paddies, hedge rows, and buffalo." Sincere cast a withering gaze. Rock braced but never blinked. ("Walking Point," p. 49.)

- (*Duck Soup*) Louis Calhern: I am willing to do anything to prevent this war. Groucho Marx: It's too late. I've already paid a month's rent on the battlefield.

The surly major stared at me. 'You'll be going out with Sergeant Garland." Sincere spread misery evenly like peanut butter on B-2 crackers. SFC Garland had served three tours. His chiseled cheekbones, three-day beard and square jaw resembled *Sergeant Rock,* whose iron fist could knock out a T-54 tank. ("Walking Point," p. p. 48.)

- (*Duck Soup*) Chico: I wouldn't go out there unless I had one of those big iron things that go up and down. What do you call those things? Groucho: Tanks. Chico: You're welcome.

The XO looked at me. "So you've got nothing to show for a busted mortar, two wounded and one dead?" he asked. "Sergeant Garland executed the patrol order, found bunkers and suffered casualties from a booby trap," I said. The debrief was drifting towards the army tradition of *pin the fuck-up on the donkey*, and I was the nearest ass. "The 4.2 mortar was in support, but remained under MLT command and control." "Who asked you?" "I believe you did, sir," Rock said. ("Walking Point," pp. 60-61.)

- (*A Night at the* Opera) Robert Emmett O'Connor: Am I crazy or are there only two beds in here? Groucho Marx: Now which question do you want me to answer first, Henderson?
- (*Horse Feathers*) Zeppo Marx: You're talking to the wrong team. Groucho Marx: I know I am, but our team wouldn't listen to me!

Self-deprecation, is also another one of Thompson's ironies. A self-deprecating Special Forces bush-master, redundant mutilator, eye-shooter, widow-maker, name-taker, *isolato*, and outrider, whom, "when walking among them made you feel like you were being watched from hundreds of hidden caves,"[26] seems oxymoronic, but Thompson gives the Marx Brothers as good as Lenin, Trotsky and Stalin gave Karl Heinrich Marx and his four sisters. But the epigrammatic is especially poignant because the counter-intuitive nature of it makes war funny, if it don't kill you.

1. When in doubt, empty your magazine;
2. If the enemy is in range, so are you;
3. Don't look conspicuous, it draws fire;
4. The easy way is always mined;
5. Try to look unimportant, they may be low on ammo;
6. If you can't remember, the claymore is pointed at you;
7. A "sucking chest wound" is natures way of telling you to slow down;
8. Never draw fire, it irritates everyone around you;
9. If your attack is going well, it's an ambush;
10. Anything you do can get you shot, including nothing;

11. If you are short of everything but the enemy, you are in a combat zone;

12. Never forget that your weapon is made by the lowest bidder;

13. If you are forward of your position, the artillery will fall short;

14. Incoming fire has the right of way;

15. Friendly fire—isn't;

16. Radios will fail as soon as you need fire support desperately;

17. The only thing more accurate than incoming enemy fire is incoming friendly fire;

18. Make it tough for the enemy to get in and you can't get out;

19. When you have secured an area, don't forget to tell the enemy; and (DRUM ROLL)

20. Professional soldiers are predictable, but the world is full of amateurs.

It started with Murphy's Law, a timeless epigram that states, "Anything that can go wrong, will go wrong." [27] Every soldier, marine and sailor knew, or heard of, Murphy's Laws of Combat. While there are many, those listed above seem to be the most prescient about the risks of war. These "Laws" are epigrams and follow the "Anything that can go wrong, will go wrong" paradigm and Thompson has interposed them literally, or figuratively, throughout "Sergeant Rock." Thompson's Bru machine-gunner applies the first of these with verve and gusto:

- Number 1: When in doubt, empty your magazine (or ammo belt).

His hands wrapped the spade grips of a .50 caliber machine gun. He pointed its sleek tapered barrel at movement in the minefield as thumbs pressed the butterfly trigger. The pop-sizzle of a flare ignited his suspicions and the stocky Bru jacked back the operating lever and seated a round. White light illumined; shadows shifted on a smoky curtain. Rounds exploded from the machine gun …. ("Walking Point," p. 43.)

- Number 10: Anything you do can get you shot, including nothing.

  Gotta go," I slid the case beneath the cot.
  "Maybe you should secure that in the TOC."
  "No time."
  "Things disappear around here."
  More people than things, I thought. ("Walking Point," p. 47.)

- Number 15: Friendly fire—isn't.

  "What about marine patrols?" Rock asked.
  "The walking dead?"
  "Fucking jarheads see Bru, they'll fire us up."
  Sincere nodded. "But that would be friendly fire." ("Walking Point With Sergeant Rock," p. 49.)

- Number 13: If you are forward of your position, artillery will fall short.

  "First of all, *sir,*" Rock said, "the propellant ain't all that stable in rain." He challenged the major with a mixture of sarcasm and respect. "Second. Four-deuce rounds at maximum distance can deviate wildly and third ..." ("Walking Point," p.p. 49-50.)

- Number 2: If the enemy is in range, so are you.

  Firecrackers, AK-47 rounds, sputtered and cracked overhead. Meng pointed across an open field at bunkers, dirt mounds with firing ports, connected by trenches. Rock's face went slack. "That ain't good." ("Walking Point," p. 54.)

- Number 14: Incoming fire has the right of way.

  Rock radioed. "Jack Black this is Chicken Little ... one round, Willy Pete." Rock gave coordinates for the fire mission." I listened. "I know you're at *max range,*" he yelled. "That's *your* fucking problem!" But that wasn't exactly true. Once Short dropped that eighteen-pound mortar round down the tube, it was our fucking problem. ("Walking Point," p. 54.)

- Number 17: The only thing more accurate than incoming enemy fire is incoming friendly fire.

"I've got the call sign and frequencies for Camp Carroll, FDC." "Are you fucking crazy," Rock said. "Who do you think the camp is named after? [Captain Jack] Carroll was killed by friendly fire." "Worse than enemy fire?" I asked. "Dead is dead." ("Walking Point," p. 56.)

- Number 7: A 'sucking chest wound' is nature's way of telling you to slow down.

Vegetation spread concentrically from a large crater. Nip had triggered the booby trap. The broad leaf foliage was blown sideways and folded back, its red speckled underside exposed. An arm wedged high in a stand of bamboo, finger pointing like a washroom sign towards the crater. ("Walking Point," p. 59.)

These laws, prescient and concise, seem casual, but to experience any of them in Vietnam combat drew the same observation. "It don't mean nothin," we said. That response was both human and oracular and was the coping mechanism in Vietnam used to dismiss witnessing or experiencing the *horrida bella*, or express relief that we had avoided being killed, even if we were ugly-injured, or secretly maimed. Thompson knows that the mechanisms of irony, self deprecation and the epigrammatic, while easing you into the center of the conflagration, also provide an existential distancing from the conflagration. And, as Thompson's humor establishes, it also allows covert reconnoiter, at least one more time.

But ignore the humor, if you can, "Sergeant Rock" is a serious portrait of the limits of man's fortitude in combat. John F. Kennedy wrote in an April 11, 1962 memorandum to the U.S. Army after his inauguration of Army Special Forces and the Green Berets, that they were "A symbol of excellence, a badge of courage, a mark of distinction in the fight for freedom." Thompson's former teammate, Alan Farrell who blamed the parts, explains it best. Farrell is as canny and brilliant a contradiction as exists to that old slaggard, "intellectual writer" Umberto Eco, who said in *Foucault's Pendulum*:

> "'And the boasting was empty?' Diotallevi asked. 'Often. Here again, what's amazing is the gulf between their [speaking of the *Templars*] political and administrative skill on the one hand and their **Green Beret style on the other: all guts and no brains.**'"[28]

Farrell, an Army Reservist Team Sergeant, former SOG warrior, classical language professor, essayist, and poet who rose to the rank of Brigadier General at Virginia Military Institute in the early 2000's, probably defined best the fighting force John F. Kennedy imagined in the Green Berets. In "The Green Beret: *Schreckfigur* For the New Age," Farrell turns to a former WW II French commando *qua* war journalist and novelist, Jean Lartéguy, and his *The Centurions*:

> Have you noticed that throughout military history no regular army has ever beaten a well-led guerrilla army? If we use the regular army in Algeria, we will lose. I'd like France to have two armies: one for parades with handsome fieldpieces, polished tanks, little tin soldiers, bands, general staffs, and lovable old curmudgeons to command it... the other would be for real, composed of nothing but young men super-trained, all volunteers, wearing camouflaged fatigues, whom you'd never see in town but from whom the impossible would be asked and to whom we would teach all the tricks. That's the army I'd like to fight in.[29]

Who? Those French fuck-ups? But Farrell knows of what he speaks and D.M. Thompson knows Farrell:

> The Green Beret, you should know, traces his heritage variously from a number of sources, but it was the French who, so far as I know, from my experience inside Special Forces, really colored the grander American notions of strategy in Vietnam. But the French intellectualized their war, as the paradigmatic writings of Colonel Roger Trinquier indicate. And so it was with

the first of the Green Berets, who read Mao, and Trinquier, and Jean Lartéguy, in whose *Centurions*, with its literate captains and thoughtful, athletic colonel they found their models.[30]

And to the real legacy of SOG and U.S. Army Green Berets, Farrell quotes from a little known Lartéguy essay explaining the dedication devoted toward the indigenous natives of Vietnam both French and U.S. Special Forces turned to and employed who lived where they lived, went were they went, fought who they fought and died where they died. The Special Forces and Vietnamese mountain peoples, each tough, versatile and accustomed to living in wild conditions, formed an affinity for each other and bonds that have not been broken by time and the tide.

> The Montagnards were encouraged. For them the enemy was the Vietnamese interloper, communist or anticommunist. But the American took the place for them of the French GCMA [*Groupes de Commandos Mixtes Aéroportés*], who had protected them up till now. Many American officers and agents spoke French well, and some even passed themselves off as French.[31]

ALL GUTS AND NO BRAINS? My ASS! And to do the French one better, the U.S. government created the *Groupes de Commandos Mixtes* Aéroportés on STEROIDS. And Thompson, Farrell, and Boyd were all deluxe models in this new *Groupes de Commandos,* and they even packed their muscle around with them. Our SOG Lieutenant has hauled a mysterious suitcase, "cheap laminate sides swollen and separated," halfway round the world. He tells us that his father had lugged *the very same* home from Europe, as he planned to do from Vietnam. It was wrapped heavily in duct tape, the latches were sprung; "It was more totem than tote-able." Early in "Walking Point," the Lieutenant needs some tape to wrap his sliced foot and cuts some of the duct tape from the battered suitcase. What's in the suitcase? He divulges this at the end of "Walking Point," after the killing patrol, after the debrief, and after the *pin the fuck-up on the donkey*. He cut the tape on the worn portmanteau and exposed its contents.

> Two twenty-five pound plates fit perfectly squared in the suitcase. On top were two ten-pound plates and dumbbell bars. The side pockets were stuffed with rolled newspaper. It may as well have been a chest of pirates gold. ("Walking Point," p. 61.)

SFC Short (Round), lying in his cot and unseen by the Lieutenant, exclaimed upon spying the contents of the mystery case, "Dumbbells? Jesus, sir, you hauled weights all the way from the states? That's what you been hiding under your bed?" Surprised by Short and not having words to express why he'd carried Dad's suitcase stuffed with steel hallway around the world, he loaded a single curl bar with the two twenty-fiver pounders and, sitting, attempted a preacher curl and miserably failed. Sergeant Short, thick forearms and barrel chest, moved over to him and asked, "This is going to save your ass El-Tee?" And he bent and removed the two twenty-five pounders and replaced them with the ten-pounders. "Try that." The Lieutenant, his arm twitching and straining, burned hot, and failed again. Short took off the tens and handed him the empty bar. "Sometimes it's good to find our limitations, sir." and stepped into the rain. ("Walking Point," pp. 61-62.)

The Lieutenant beat the dysentery, finished his two tours and followed Sergeant Short's advice. Years later, as his life unraveled, "wife, house, kids ... the full catastrophe," the Lieutenant found himself fixing a leaky pipe in a stank-ass basement, smelling oddly reminiscent of a TOC.

> I moved a box and there, sealed with tape, the suitcase I'd carried home, just like my father. I cut the thick duct tape and lifted the lid. The scent of gun oil, rust, and moldy earth wafted up, unloosed a flood of memories; Mai Loc; monsoon, dysentery, Nip and Nok—always smiling, Meng—pointing at the sun. I slid two plates on the rusted bar and curled it until my muscles screamed 'Stop!' But muscle memory, my savior—kept pumping. ("Walkiing Point," p. 62.)

In *Dawson's War*, Ken Boyd probably gives the best encapsulating remark about SOG and its legacy. He places it in the mouth of Fallon/Farrell. After a particularly existential trip into the woods with his Recon Team, and the subsequent intel briefing at Phu Bai, Lieutenant Dawson asks Sergeant Fallon, "Then what's the point in going out and getting our asses shot off?" Fallon answers:

> "That's a good question, maybe it's why SOG is classified for twenty years. By the time your kids are grown up and you can tell them what you did, I'm sure they'll have come up with something."[32]

Boyd/Marshall/Dawson tops off the ultimate translation of Fallon's remarks near the end of the book and after the culminating battle in Laos pitting Dawson's RT and his Bru counterparts against North Vietnamese Army regulars and VC, as the Bru refer to them. The battle has encompassed everything SOG did in making these small unit forays into Laos, Cambodia and North Vietnam. The Special Operations helicopter pilot who had flown Dawson and his team under fire from their Hell in Laos to Quang Tri, for further transportation to Da Nang, asks him to wait while he refuels so that he may have the privilege of flying them, himself, to Da Nang.

> "Give us a chance to refuel and we'll take you," the pilot offered.
> "That would be great, Thanks a lot."
> "Don't thank me. This is a story I'm going to tell my grandchildren. How I flew into Laos and rescued, I don't know, whoever you people are."
> "SOG," Dawson said. "You'll be able to tell them about it in about twenty years, when it gets declassified."[33]

Speaking of declassified, a mechanical explanation is called to mind when thinking of Thompson's technique in "Sergeant Rock." The first OV-1 Mohawk arrived in Vietnam in 1962 with the 23d Special Warfare Aviation Detachment, about the same time as the

Army Green Berets. By the end of the war, highly classified, photographic, side-looking airborne radar (SLAR), and infrared radar Mohawk models were under direct operational control of field commanders. The SLAR capability provided long-range surveillance of moving targets, especially at night and in poor weather conditions, and the advanced infrared system mounted on the OV-1C could detect heat traces from small cooking fires, a recoilless rifle flash, or from truck engines that had been parked for as long as 16 hours, allowing surveillance through darkness, camouflage or jungle cover. The addition of these new types of classified imagery from the systems on board the Mohawks led to the name change from photographic intelligence (PHOTINT) used since World War I to imagery intelligence (IMINT) still used today. Thompson's writing here is IMINT. It may invoke in some ways the sense of a camera, but its long-range surveillance is imagery, imagery, imagery.

---

[19] Milan Kundera, "Comedy Is Everywhere," *Quadrant, 1978, Vol. 22, No. 5, p. 44.*

[20] Start with John Plaster's *SOG: The Secret War of America's Commandos in Vietnam*, John Meyer's *Across the Fence*, Thom Nicholson's *15 Months in SOG: A Warriors Tour*, Robert Gillespie's *Black Ops Vietnam*, Lynne Black's *Whiskey Tango Foxtrot*, Jim Morris' *Above and Beyond*, Kenneth Boyd's (aka B.K Marshall) *Dawson's War*, and Richard Schultz Jr.'s *The Secret War Against Hanoi*.

[21] Chisholm, Hugh, ed. (1911). "Belles-Lettres." *Encyclopedia Britannica*, (11th ed.). Cambridge University Press. p. 699. Literally, *belles-lettres* is a French phrase meaning "beautiful" or "fine" writing. In this sense it includes all literary works—especially valued for their aesthetic qualities and originality of style and tone." The term thus can be used to refer to literature generally. The *Encyclopedia Britannica Eleventh Edition* describes it as "the more artistic and imaginative

forms of literature, as poetry or romance, as opposed to more pedestrian and exact studies."

[22] Joseph Heller, *Catch 22*: Simon & Schuster, 1961. p. 297. "You have a morbid aversion to dying. You probably resent the fact that you're at war and might get your head blown off any second." "I more than resent it, sir. I'm absolutely incensed." "You have deep-seated survival anxieties. And you don't like bigots, bullies, snobs, or hypocrites. Subconsciously there are many people you hate." "Consciously, sir, consciously," Yossarian corrected in an effort to help. "I hate them consciously."

[23] Alan Farrell, "Blaming of Parts," This poem appears in *Expended Casings*, Lexington, Virginia, 2007, a collection of 12 poems which a poet, playwright critic said "Evoke rondeaus, with their song-like structures and Kipling ballads, with their skillful use of demotic GI language." The same critic said, "[He] stands out as one of the few unique voices among Vietnam War veterans."

[24] B.K. Marshall, *Dawson's War: A Novel of Friendship Under Fire*, B.K. Marshall: Columbia SC, 2020, p. 95.

[25] Marshall, *Ibid.*, p. 136.

[26] Michael Herr, *Dispatches*, New York: Vintage Books, 1968, p. 25. In "Boxcar Orange," Thompson will describe his now battle hardened and promoted 1st Lieutenant looking at himself in the toilet mirror of his Braniff Airways R&R flight: "Eyes peered from moon craters." p. 77.

[27] The claim, however, is that Murphy's Law originated at Edwards Air Force Base in southern California, the same place where Chuck Yeager broke the sound barrier in 1947. Around that time, a team of Edwards engineers was working on Project MX981, a mission to determine the amount of force a human body could sustain in a crash. In the late 1940s, the team received a visit from an Air Force captain and reliability engineer named Edward A. Murphy. A documentarian, Nick T. Spark, who interviewed the surviving witnesses more than 50 years after the fact, said that it was generally agreed that Murphy was there to deliver some new gauges for the apparatus. The gauges malfunctioned. An irritated Murphy allegedly blamed the problem on underlings, grousing, "*If there's any way they can do it wrong, they will.*" The person who transformed Murphy's complaint into Murphy's Law was Colonel John Paul Stapp, the flight surgeon who put his life on the line in the sonic sled to test the team's theories. When a reporter asked about the project's inherent danger, Stapp allegedly replied that the team was guided by a principle he called "Murphy's Law." It's supposed to be, 'If it can happen, it will,'" "Not 'Whatever can go wrong, will go wrong.'" The disaster-minded approach worked. MX981's experiments resulted not in high-speed tragedy but in research that revolutionized air and road safety.

[28] Umberto Eco, *Foucault's Pendulum*, translated from the Italian by William Weaver, London: A Harvest Book, 1988, p. 82.

[29] Jean Lartéguy, *Les Centurions*. Paris: *Presses de la Cité*, 1961, p. 296.

[30] Alan Farrell, "The Green Beret: *Schreckfigur* [Scary Figure] for the New Age," "*Viet Nam Generation* 5:1-4 (March 1994). Essay.

[31] Jean Lartéguy, *Un million de dollars le Viet*. Paris: *Raoul Solar,* 1965, p. 156.

[32] Marshall, *Ibid.*, pp. 236-237.

[33] Marshall, *Ibid.*, p. 343.

BOXCAR ORANGE

"Be the pilot of your own flight. Not the passenger."

— Giovannie de Sadeleer.

Boxcar Orange" starts with a reference to the rainbow airplanes of Braniff International, which took over the pursestrings of Braniff International Airways in 1965. It was the "can't miss" airline in the 1960's and any of us who served during that time took a ride on these Disney "wet dreams" at least once. And rainbow is a useful arc under which to fit the layered themes of "Boxcar Orange" for the story is, like a rainbow, multi-tiered.

Suffice it to say, our SOG narrator in "Boxcar Orange" gets his first ride via a R&R (Rest and Relaxation)—or as Vietnam veterans would thereafter ever refer to it, I&I (Intercourse and Intoxication)—given to him courtesy of a SOG recon teammate who had been hit, turned up missing, or was killed in action. Our now war-grizzled SOG 1st Lieutenant has been presented a seven-day R&R to Sydney, Australia. He has, with a command lottery device, filled the seat of one of his SOG teammates, another young 1st Lieutenant Pete (or Mac) McMurry, who unbeknownst to our Lieutenant, was killed on one of those "Mission Impossible" targets that he will speculate on, dream of, or hallucinate for the rest of his life. Speaking of lotteries, in the seat behind him sits the infantry cousin (nick-named Raspy McMurry by Thompson) of McMurry, a soldier of the 1st Bn, 14th Infantry Bn, Fourth Infantry Division, who had been advised of his cousin's death before boarding the plane and is not taking it well (and will not be meeting Pete in Sydney as planned). What are the chances of that, or to use another idiom, "Who da thunk it?" While this puts our Lieutenant at the center of his universe, this degree of connectivity is anachronistically expounded on some 20 years later with regard to that sometimes "War Hero," actor Kevin Bacon.[34] Their lives and coincidences intercept on this ride in the orange boxcar and that is the story in a nutshell, for the *mise en scène* is the arch of a Braniff 707 fuselage with a few other poor players strutting and fretting their hour upon that chassis. Connectivity, coincidence, or irony, or all? We think Thompson intends all.

> I squeezed into the small seat of a Braniff Airlines 707 Freedom Bird, painted cool, popsicle orange, on Da Nang airfield. . . . I thumbed through the in-flight magazine, *BI Pages*. Braniff International wanted to make a splash, so it hired Alexander Girard, graphic designer, to draw from a wild palette of colors for its planes——lemon yellow, metallic purple and bright orange——spruce up its go-go image. *Pages* showed how Emilio Pucci had modernized and accessorized the sleek, Star Trek uniforms of their stewardesses. ("Boxcar Orange," p. 65.)

The Military Air Command (MAC) flight our now battle-worn 1st Lieutenant narrator rode in to Sydney hadn't been given the commercial treatment, for instance, of those Braniff 707's flying the Dallas to LA tour. As Thompson mentions, these military servicing planes (contracted with for Braniff by a good buddy of the President of these United States of America at the time), while retaining a veneer of the pomp and coloratura of the celebrity Braniff, had been field-stripped.

> My narrow seat was unlike the spacious digs touted in the ads; eccentrics, Andy Warhol and Salvador Dali. Inside the boxcar they'd removed all first and business seats and crammed in forty smaller ones. Inside, no ice-cool air pumped through overhead jets. I cinched my seat belt to stay tethered. Time melted like a Dali watch. A hostess, blond beehive, smiled and checked seat belts. She strolled gracefully in a plum dress, cut fashionably above her knees. Her yellow print scarf draped loosely around a thin white neck. Four hundred eyes tracked pink Pucci pumps with green heels down the aisle. ("Boxcar Orange," pp. 66-67.)

We know that Braniff stuffed that plane with 200 American servicemen, cut-rate. So Gucci used a series of nautical themes for crew uniforms; so Pucci used "space age" themes, including plastic Space Helmets and Bolas (as dubbed by Pucci);[35] so Beth Levine created plastic boots and designed two-tone calfskin boots and shoes; so later uniforms and accessories were composed of interchangeable parts, which could be removed and added as needed. Do you think Thompson's military passengers gave a shit about Pucci, Gucci, Girard, Levine, Warhol, and Dali while waiting to be mortared on an airstrip near the *Troung Son* mountains? However, the lucky boys did get glimpses, as he says, of plum dresses above the knees, yellow print scarfs around thin white necks and pink Pucci pumps with green heels served with an occasional Texas twang; a little Pucci clad-ass for 200 khaki-clad asses who wanted to get levitated.

It is not enough that 200 sweating service-men in Class-A uniforms are sitting in a phosphorescent-orange air bus, but so much else is on our Lieutenant's mind under this psychedelic arc. It is not that he is mired among movie idol-handsome Quartermaster captains, dumpy pay clerks, tanned beach-going privates and other assorted logistical personnel, or that he is fraternizing with the white Christian brotherhood and patriotic knights of Rear-Echelon-Mother-Fuckers (REMFs), but that the powers and brains that be have left all 200 of em sitting on a mortar azimuth. This is the first thing that abides his mind:

> Outside the window, the hulk of a C-130 lay smoldering on the tarmac, mute testimony to the luck of NVA rocketeers. An oval frame, charred whale ribs lay crumpled on cement beach. Who in their right mind would sit in a bright orange bull's-eye on this tarmac? The garish plane taunted enemy spotters to vector 122 mm rockets from the rocket zone, two klicks north. Sitting exposed like this was counter-point to everything I'd ever learned about survival in Vietnam—camouflage, cover and concealment, never walk a trail, never sit in an orange plane in broad daylight.

A muffled scream inside yelled, "*Get the fuck out!*" I stuffed a pillow in its mouth. ("Boxcar Orange," p. 66.)

While he can't avoid existing in his own consciousness, he has a Greek chorus surrounding him; the loud sergeant in a seat near him, or a pair of F-4 Phantoms rushing skyward with their afterburners blazing like the blue tips of welder's torches.

> [As a hostess bent over the loud sergeant near him to check his seatbelt] "Just keep it tight," the hostess said. "Tight is right." His eyes flickered. "Like this little piece of fabric would save my ass if this here plane went up like a roman candle." He laughed and elbowed the sergeant next to him. ("Boxcar Orange," p. 68.)

But we can depend on his deep inner-feelings, mostly free of any intellectual concerns, because they are visceral communications with the place that is Vietnam, its encumbrances and its symbolisms.

> Brakes squealed as the plane came to a grinding halt. The bright orange bull's-eye sat idly at the end of the runway. I checked my watch, counted, figured we had a minute, two at most. The brakes released and the wheels began to roll. The pucker factor climbed as I checked my watch, 67 seconds. The clueless captain relaxed. As the plane accelerated every bowl and bump registered in the pit of my stomach. I awaited that flash of light that would rip off the tail or wing. I gauged the ground speed and at the perfectly timed moment, lifted my feet perpendicular to and not less than six inches off the floor. Tradition, or superstition—it had gotten me this far. ("Boxcar Orange," pp. 73-74.)

And his Greek chorus again confirms our lieutenant's stream of consciousness; the entire manifest of the flight, or a Specialist sitting in his commentator seat.

> No one spoke or moved a muscle as the plane's nose tilted skyward and I felt that smooth carpet ride sensation and the cabin exploded with, "*Yeeaaasssss! Get sum! Sin loi motherfucker!*" The wheels retracted with a high-pitched squeal. As the plane banked sideways and headed out to the China Sea I looked down at a

white plume of smoke rising from the runway. "Holy cow!" the Specialist said. "That rocket could have blown us to kingdom come!" ("Boxcar Orange," p. 74.)

And he, busy in his stream mind-mapping the things that are concerned with multiple military propositions, some traditional (as foreshadowed in his pre-takeoff foot lifting preparation) or, others the grist of those adventures in MACV-SOG, or their interpretations, like the simple parody of *Big Rock Candy Mountain* sung by McMurry's seat mate, who our grizzled Lieutenant has named "Sidekick."

"Operation Green Thunder, NVA blunder, we put a thousand gooks asunder!" Sidekick said. [He] sang to the tune of *Big Rock Candy Mountain, "We was buggered sore, like Charlie's whore, on Chu Pac misty mountain!"* (Boxcar Orange," p. 69.)

The word "asunder" triggered our Lieutenant's classical reading, albeit military, to cross his map again as the plane cabin calmed in the last minutes before take-off.

The plane grew quiet. Captain snooze to the left of me, specialist to the right, Raspy behind, shattered and sundered, as we sat, all sweaty two hundred. ("Boxcar Orange," p. 73.)

Do you recognize that *metre*? If "Sidekick" could parody Bob Seeger doing Harry McClintock in *Big Rock Candy Mountain*, then our Lieutenant could parody Alfred, Lord Tennyson, writing anonymously as A.T., in *The Charge of the Light Brigade*:

> *Plunged in the battery-smoke*
> *Right through the line they broke;*
> *Cannon to right of them,*
> *Cannon to left of them,*
> *Cannon behind them*
> *Volleyed and thundered;*
> *All the world wondered.*

Cossack and Russian
Reeled from the sabre stroke
Shattered and sundered.
Then they rode back, but not,
Not the six hundred.

Something as simple as a sort-of-rhyming echo of Sidekick's riff on Bob Seeger, dredges for our Lieutenant, always, a more serious military overtone to the story. The sweaty 200 are, in so many ways, no different than the 600, the Light Brigade of the British cavalry (the 4th and 13th Light Dragoons, the 17th Lancers, and the 8th and 11th Hussars), an historical example of a glorious, military goat-fuck, where young men in their prime are delivered in a suicidal assault on some objective that will live forever in nothingness and anonymity (unless Alfred, Lord Tennyson, 1st Baron and Poet-Laureate of Great Britain under Queen Victoria, commits it to posterity); an experience some of the youthful, testosterone fed passengers of Flight Boxcar Orange had already been privy to themselves, foremost the SOG 1st Lieutenant.

And this back and forth in military memory proceeds. For any young soldier (and perhaps the occasional airman, sailor and marine) who attended Airborne school at Ft. Benning, Georgia during the 60's, and jumped out of a C-119 "Flying Boxcar" in at least one training jump will recognize Thompson's two-page anecdote about Sergeant First Class Ramon, Senior TAC NCO of 45th Company, Airborne! The Army son comes full circle and jumps from the self-same craft his father launched out of in his on-the-job training in 1944 over Holland, and commandeered over *Dien Bien Phu* in 1954. But the anecdote introduces an elemental theme in airborne training a half a century ago.

[Sergeant Ramon] Scanning the formation, his eyes fixed me with a steely gaze. "And just prior to takeoff each man will *elevate* his boots *perpendicular to* and *not less than* six inches off the floor. This maneuver will enable your plane to rise *expeditiously* from this runway! Is that *clear!*" "We roared in unison '*Clear* sergeant! *Airborne!*'" ("Boxcar Orange," p. 71.)

From this Thompson exposits that first jump from the C-119 Boxcar, bucket of bolts rattling, tail-boom swinging, *Hail Mary full of grace*, Pratt & Whitney engines screaming, gooney bird bouncing, until, WHOOOOOSH, the son blew out the door at 1200 feet like an automatic grenade launched. AIRBORNE! All the sticks of virgin airborne troopers squeezed into the confines of that flying boxcar had assisted all 14 tons of that fuselage and cargo off the runway with 50 pairs of spit-shined Corcorans "elevated *perpendicular to* and *not less than* six inches off the floor," and the "flying coffin" cleared the runway like shit off a shovel.

The inspiration for this *intermezzo?* The Lieutenant's seat next to the Hollywood captain:

> The engines throttled up, bucked, as the pilot tested brakes. My stomach tightened. I bent forward and lifted my boots off the floor. The suave captain opened one eye and looked down. "Tradition," I explained. "Superstition." His patrician nose wrinkled as though he'd smelled a fart. "Superstition?" I squinted at the leg captain. I set my boots down. Tell that to the burning bush, Sergeant First Class Ramon, Senior TAC NCO of 45th Company . . . ! ("Boxcar Orange," p. 70.)

Classical readings are necessary to paint the central reference in "Boxcar Orange," and it starts with the "Boxcar Orange" epigraph, which at first seems to have no context, but in the interweaving of his story, has every relevance: "In battle, since shields were worn on the left arm, the right flank, right of the line, had to be the strongest." The reference is to the overheard conversation of Raspy McMurry and Sidekick behind him who both wore golden dragon patches of the 1st Bn, 14th Infantry of the 4th Infantry Division; "*Right of the Line,* curled beneath a slue-footed dragon."[36] Peter McMurry's cousin, Raspy, is acting out over the news of Peter's death and is looking for a fight. Seeing Raspy's name tag, the Lieutenant realizes he must be talking about the "McMurry assigned with me."

"Me and Pete was going to Sydney," Raspy said. "Kick it hard. What the hell they tell you first day of basic training?" he said. "Don't volunteer! What'd he do? Signed up for Airborne Special Forces." ("Boxcar Orange," p. 69.)

After Raspy punches the back of the seat in his frustration the Lieutenant sits up and turns to glance back at the gaunt, red-faced soldier who. . . stares at his fist "then at me with a 'What the fuck you lookin' at?' expression. I cocked an eyebrow."

"Cool it!" Sidekick said. "They'll throw your ass off the plane!"

"He's cool," Sidekick said. His forearm pinned the struggling pug. My fingers touched the green beret folded crisply and tucked securely beneath my belt. ("Boxcar Orange," p. 73.)

Finally in flight, the Lieutenant aimed a cool stream of air from the overhead jet at his face. He looked back and checked Raspy's name tag again. McMurry. He questioned if Raspy was talking about the McMurry in his unit?

Pete, we called him Mac; more shadow than silhouette. His thin frame bent like a Bedouin as he crossed the sandy confines of our camp. His quick wit balanced an irregular stride. An infectious grin belied his penchant for mischief. I recalled the *Top Secret* shithouse rumor weeks before. Mac and his hatchet platoon were part of a strike force tasked for a *Guns of Navarone* mission. Argosy hacks couldn't dream up this cockamamie scenario, a mix of pulp fiction and Greek tragedy. ("Boxcar Orange," p. 75.)

The Lieutenant allows his heated memory to redraw Pete McMurry's last arena. Thompson uses a command planner's vision drawn up by a real-life character from his past. That character was Major "Speedy" Gaspard, who was a longtime and legendary Special Forces operator, not the average run of the mill SF savant. He had a certain *Je ne sais qua*, that attracted both the famous and infamous. Donning civilian attire in Saigon during a CORD-like tour, he projected a sophisticated air and specific knowledge about spies, double agents, saboteurs and unconventional warfare that his press corps peeps devoured. With his murky past, graduation from the first Special Forces Q course, and journalism background he proved to be intriguing, erudite and brazen enough to hang with media heavyweights like Peter Arnett, Neil Sheehan and David Halberstam.[37] Gaspard's Napoleon vision in 1968, like most best laid plans of men and mice, however, ended in a goat-fuck as Thompson divulges in this fictional aside in "Boxcar Orange":[38]

> Major "Speedy" Gaspard, S-3, ordered a task force of Special Commandos, to set down on top of the infamous Co Roc Mountain, located just across the Laotian border. The Japs had hollowed out a huge network of caves during occupation, WW II. NVA took ownership. Cannons rolled out from its caves on rails, fired and disappeared inside. During the siege of Khe Sanh, NVA spotters directed 122mm rockets and heavy artillery at the camp. The continuous pummeling of the impregnable fortress by B-52 bombers proved futile. Inside the honeycombed massif, worker bees buzzed safe and sound. I pictured Mac, last time I saw him, standing in the door of a bubble-nosed H-34 helicopter lifting off the helipad. The chopper resembled a bullfrog, eyes recessed high above its round nose. Mac, cammied up, tiger-striped uniform and green cravat, sat in the door. He stared west toward Co Roc Mountain, Sepon River coiling at its base. (Boxcar Orange, p. 75-76.)

Alan Farrell, who also knew "Speedy" Gaspard," had a more jaundiced view of leadership from the rear as this epigraph to his short story, "The Major Won the Croix de Guerre," illustrates.

> *The Major won the Croix de Guerre... Paaaaaaaaaarlez-vous?*
> *The Major won the Croix de Guerre... Paaaaaaaaaaarlez-vous?*
> *The Major won the Croix de Guerre,*

> *But the sonuvabitch was never there...*
> *Hinky dinky parlez-vous?* (from a WW I trench song)

He distinguished this view by differentiation; those who lead from the front, and those who serve that only sit in S-2, S-3, S-4 *et al*, at least those who served in "The Major Won the Croix de Guerre."

It is the curious duty of an officer in war to impress the stamp of human will on the random array of nature and event and not infrequently to disregard or even disdain the driving surge of fact and certainty which could forestall action. But to impose will is not to impose order. You can beat the odds, but you can't change them. Sheer dogged, dumb, blind, human obstinacy--*grit* we might call it--can often countervail the insistency of a real and physical world, of the genuine and relentless momentum of destiny. To do so, of course, an officer must galvanize the inevitable inertia of those he would lead... often by taking that *first* step first out beyond safety's embrace. Follow me![39]

There are echos of Jean Lartéguy in that, *certainement*. Our *Schrekfigur* Lieutenant looks back at Raspy thinking the McMurray he knew was either back at FOB-4 celebrating the mission or playing King of Co Roc Mountain. As you will see, the specter of McMurry will chase him, first to Australia and then for the rest of his life:

There was no way he was dead. *No fucking way* was I sitting in *his* seat on the way to Sydney in this orange boxcar with blond showgirls prancing in pinks and plums. But then Special Forces are practiced in the art of self-deception and plausible denial. Our trademark was twisting truth into a slipknot. We denied the obvious to attain the impossible. ("Boxcar Orange," p. 76.)

The plane had leveled off at cruising altitude, the drink cart came and went, dinner served and removed, lines formed at the lavatory and dwindled, lotus eaters slept and the muffled roar of jet engines faded to a smooth vibration. The Lieutenant stood, stretched and looked down at Raspy and Sidekick. They were engaged in a heated exchange but Raspy looked up and sees the Lieutenant's green beret tucked in his belt.

"SOG," Raspy said, nudged Sidekick; looking more like a mate off the Sloop John B.

> *Did he say, SOG?* I pressed toward the back of the plane.SOG—Studies and Observation Group, was cover for a clandestine unit whose specialty was sneak and peak, cross-border spy operation. Minimal Studies and little Observations; since it was virtually impossible to land a helicopter undetected anywhere near the Ho Chi Minh Road. By 1969 much of it had been paved. The mission was mostly a goddamn waste of brave warriors. I caught myself. McMurry was *not dead.* Missing, wounded perhaps—*not dead.* ("Boxcar Orange," pp. 76-77.)

He made his way to the cramped lavatory, drained a lily, scratched, stared at an alien image in the mirror with bristled, blond hair, tapered cheekbones, rounded chin and eyes that peered back at him from moon craters. Stepping again under the proscenium arch, he rested his head on the galley wall to listen to the muffled roar of engines, but was rudely interrupted.

> "Two words," Raspy said. "Pete McMurry." I lifted my head and took measure. His sturdy frame had been rendered of all fat in the jungle cauldron. His eyes flickered nervously; temple pulsed with each heave of the chest. Straightening, I pressed forward into the isle, flexed knees, shifting weight to the balls of my feet. I found the smooth handle of my stiletto with two fingers. *Mind zap. Whoa, slow down.* ("Boxcar Orange," pp. 78-79.)

Raspy pulled a worn telegram from his pocket and said, "They think I'm stupid." Raspy is blocking other piss-weary soldiers from the lavatory and the Lieutenant asks him what makes him think they think he's stupid.

> "Lieutenant Pete McMurry died, deep in enemy territory," he read.

"Right of the Line!" I read the motto on his patch. "What the hell does that mean?"

"Civil war? he said. "I don't rightly know." ("Boxcar Orange," p. 78)

When Raspy moves into him, the Lieutenant pivots smoothly on a heel and in one movement parried his arm, spun him sideways and pinned him in the cramped passageway, freeing up the piss line, and wedging his own arm (in a cast) under his chin and pressed hard. "I know you," Raspy seemed to mock him.

"You don't know shit, sergeant."
"I seen you at Marble Mountain," Raspy said, "At the club."
His breath smelled vinegary.
"Never been there."

Raspy had been there and his SOG cousin, trained in all manner of deception and misdirection and knowing the risk if Raspy had been caught, had broken the rules to bring him into the Top Secret encampment.

"I seen the skull with Green Beret, refrigerators, showers and that cement blockhouse with all them antennas," Raspy said, "All you prima donnas." ("Boxcar Orange," p. 78.)

Raspy is still struggling to free himself from our Lieutenant but the grip tightens, and the body leverages with a knee to the groin. When a specialist exits the lavatory and pushes by, he says excuse me "Sir" to our Lieutenant. Clueless Raspy had failed to notice the Green Beret was an officer, and clueless to think that he should fuck with a Green Beret in the first place in that passive-aggressive drama going on in his wee, small head. Released, Raspy explaining that all he saw was the green beret, still expresses an urge to go after every other mutha fucka on the boxcar. Raising the telegram, he asks the Lieutenant, "Why?" "*Why?*" The Lieutenant answers, "Maybe it was just his nature," and proceeds to tell Raspy a quick story of the the scorpion and the frog. Scorpion asks a frog for a ride across the river on his back. Frog accedes and half way across the river the scorpion stings him. Like Raspy, the frog asks, "Why?" for now they would both surely die. The scorpion answers, "It's just my nature."

> "What the fuck that got to do with anything?"
> I lifted my cast from under his chin and pointed to the motto on his patch, *Right of the Line.*
> "Well, maybe Pete worked *Left of the Line.*" ("Boxcar Orange," p. 78.)

Just his nature. Hmmmm. A light bulb goes on for Raspy. "I never thought of it that way." Lieutenant says, "You have your traditions and we have ours." The Lieutenant, seeing Raspy staring at the crumpled magazine he held showing an advertisement for a frosted Margarita staring back at him said, "I'm hoping she does the trick when we get to Sydney." Raspy licked his cracked lips and tucked in his rumpled shirt and said, "Yes sir. Me too. But what if it doesn't?" The Lieutenant provides the only answer suitable for this brick-headed, American infantryman: "Then it won't."

A sleeping boxcar orange slips into a contagious comfort until the beautiful stewardess, who earlier narrative has revealed to us is from Love Field, Dallas, having augured a Margarita from clues given in the earlier conflict on stage, wakes our Lieutenant and offers him a Margarita, advising him that it's not the real thing, but when questioned as to where to find the real thing, she replies, "Where else? the Texas Tavern, Kings Cross." With this summation, boxcar orange is descending on Sydney while our Lieutenant provides a final soliloquy on the genetics of a warrior, how repetitive acts trigger memories and the repetitive acts, unnamed, are of course, the military, the military, the military:

> It doesn't matter whether they are born of fact or fiction, truth or superstition—it's all the same. Raising my feet perpendicular to and not less than six inches off the floor allowed me to concentrate on the things I could control and forget about

things I couldn't. A lifer should understand traditions are born of feelings imprinted deep in our bones; conscious deeds bonded to memory, past and future fused into one present wordless moment of clarity. Traditions allow us to look out the door of a Flying Boxcar into chaos and know we can survive the jump. ("Boxcar Orange," p. 83.)

"Conscious deeds bonded to memory, past and future fused into one present wordless moment of clarity." You could say that "Boxcar Orange," now a moment of the past, is a foreshadowing that will allow our Lieutenant to see his future in "Color Me Red," in wordless, but recorded moments of clarity. "I & I" in Sydney past, an anonymous flight back to Rocket runway Da Nang, and land transport to FOB-4 at Marble Mountain, the Lieutenant is told of the circumstances and death of Lieutenant Pete McMurry on Co Roc.

> The Air Force bombed it around the clock before the assault. The 500 pounders did little more than stir the nest. It was a kind of twisted irony that he was killed by the frog he'd ridden across the Sepon River. A Vietnamese pilot misjudged final approach and careened into the LZ; hit so hard that it pitched sideways toward McMurry who stood nearby. A rotor clipped his head, killed him instantly. The task force was extracted with seven wounded and three dead. ("Boxcar Orange," p. 83.)

What "Boxcar Orange" has revealed is that the forces that have led the planeload, our Lieutenant and Lieutenant Pete McMurry to their service and fates in their military service, Special Forces and SOG, are in their "natures." Nature, as a metaphor, is the inflection point which leads to glory, or to doom, and while, as the Lieutenant thinks, his devices of survival will "[allow] me to concentrate on the things I could control and forget about things I couldn't," there is a far more overriding philosophy of war at work all of the time here, and in *Colors of War & Peace;* one enunciated out of the mouth of a hardened soldier of the Guadalcanal campaign in James Jones The *Thin Red Line*. Sergeant Maynard Storm says,

"No matter how much training you got, how careful you are... it's a matter of luck whether or not you get killed. Makes no difference who you are or how tough a guy you might be. If you're in the wrong spot at the wrong time, you're gonna get it."

But, to be fair, Thompson has also made a nod to Rudyard Kipling:

> *If you can keep your head when all about you*
> *Are losing theirs and blaming it on you,*
> *If you can trust yourself when all men doubt you,*
> *But make allowance for their doubting too;*
> *If you can wait and not be tired by waiting,*
> *Or being lied about, don't deal in lies,*
> *Or being hated, don't give way to hating,*
> *And yet don't look too good, nor talk too wise:*
>
> *If you can talk with crowds and keep your virtue,*
> *Or walk with Kings—nor lose the common touch,*
> *If neither foes nor loving friends can hurt you,*
> *If all men count with you, but none too much;*
> *If you can fill the unforgiving minute*
> *With sixty seconds' worth of distance run,*
> *Yours is the Earth and everything that's in it,*
> *And—which is more—you'll be a Man, my son!*[40]

The real Peter McMurray (aka McMurry) was indeed killed on Co Roc and awarded the Silver Star for his bravery on that eminence. The Silver Star General Orders read:

> For gallantry in action while engaged in military operations involving conflict with an armed hostile force in the Republic of Vietnam: First Lieutenant McMurray distinguished himself by exceptionally valorous actions on 27 August 1969 while commanding a reconnaissance operation deep in enemy controlled territory. His objective was to infiltrate an area held by a large

enemy force, establish a tactically defensible position, and hold that position. Shortly after helicopter insertion, Lieutenant McMurray and his men arrived at the desired area. Their presence, however, had been observed by the enemy force, and being followed by hostile elements they were probed by automatic weapons fire before defensive positions could be set up. Realizing the need for immediate defensive tactics Lieutenant McMurray made his way to where the enemy fire was heaviest in order to encourage his men and direct their return fire. When the adversary's suppressive fire gained in intensity, pinning down many of his men, he took control of a mortar tube and began placing devastating fire on the attackers. Holding fast under barrages of automatic weapons fire directed at his position, he delivered round after mortar round on the enemy until they broke contact and pulled back. Having gained a foothold in the adversary's midst, Lieutenant McMurray then radioed for reinforcements and resupplies of ammunition in preparation for artillery and airstrikes which he could coordinate against the enemy. When supply helicopters arrived, he exposed himself to sniper fire to guide the aircraft into a clearing.

McMurray did die from the injuries inflicted by the "frog" he rode into Co Roc. Returning to evacuate his patrol's dead and wounded, the same helicopter he ferried in on took his life.

Two helicopters had safely landed, but as a third ship made its advance, it suddenly went out of control. While attempting to warn a fellow soldier to move from the area, Lieutenant McMurray was killed instantly when the disabled helicopter crashed and struck him. First Lieutenant McMurray's gallantry in action, at the cost of his life, was in keeping with the highest traditions of the military service and reflect great credit upon himself, his unit, and United States Army.

Only 22 years old, the Lieutenant's truncated lifetime of experience already fills his recall constantly, and the memories and mutters of his battlefields reverberate like the meanings of General Douglas MacArthur's memorable farewell speech at West Point in 1962, after his 60 year military career came to a close:

"I listen then, but with thirsty ear, for the witching melody of faint bugles blowing reveille, of far drums beating the long roll. In my dreams I hear again the crash of guns, the rattle of musketry, the strange, mournful mutter of the battlefield. But in the evening of my memory, always I come back to West Point. Always there echoes and re-echoes: Duty, Honor, Country. Today marks my final roll call with you, but I want you to know that when I cross the river my last conscious thoughts will be of The Corps, and The Corps, and The Corps. I bid you farewell."[41]

To young men who saw the pinnacle of combat, upon return to "The World" the experience of a year, or two years, made them feel that they had lived 60 years, mistaking, perhaps, that that experience meant wisdom. And, perforce, why this young Lieutenant was now ever merged in duty, honor, country, and, like MacArthur, will hear the echoes and re-echoes of it, but in ways so much different from the *fin de siècle* doctrine and patriotism of his father, and General MacArthur.

In "Boxcar Orange," Thompson has managed to invoke history, literature, music, philosophy, religion and finally, art, in support of his major goal—to show the indelible imprint war has on the mind and memory of the young who go to war, even when those young are the most dedicated and capable of all. He concludes "Boxcar Orange" with this haunting memorial to Peter McMurray.

Years later as I wandered through an exhibition of Rodin, I happened upon the statue of *Walking Man*. I was struck by the sculpture's exquisite detail and physicality of its muscular legs and torso. Something struck me about how he'd captured motion. The headless form only served to accentuate his powerful stride. Marveling the craftsmanship, the form sparked a vague memory. The forward tilt of Walking Man reminded me of Lieutenant Pete McMurray. Its unique form conveyed the very essence of Pete; his drive and sense of perpetual motion. To this day, I see him pitched forward—braced against the swirl, taking his last, long, eternal stride. ("Boxcar Orange," p. 84.)

---

[34] Ruthven Alexander, "Kevin Bacon is the Center of the Universe," April 7, 1994. "I know a guy who knows a guy who knows a guy who knows a guy . . . ."

[35] These clear plastic bubbles, which resembled Captain Video helmets and which Braniff termed "RainDomes", were to be worn between the terminal and the plane to prevent hairstyles from being disturbed by outside elements. "RainDomes" were dropped after about a month because the helmets cracked easily, there was no place to store them on the aircraft, and jetways at many airports made them unnecessary. Besides the 1965 and 1971 Collections, Pucci designed new Braniff uniform Collections in 1966, 1968, 1972, and 1974. As one would imagine, all of the vintage Pucci attire designed for Braniff are now quite valuable.

[36] In recognition of the 14th regiment's heroic performance of duty during twelve of the bloodiest campaigns of the American Civil War, General George Meade, awarded the Infantry Regiment the place of honor at the "Right of the Line" in the Grand Review of the Armies in Washington DC at the end of the war. This is where the regiment takes its motto "The Right of the Line". But the origins of course, are much earlier, let's say about 2,600 years earlier. The first usage of the term *phalanx* comes from Homer's "φάλαγξ", used in the *Iliad* to describe hoplites fighting in an organized battle line.

[37] Thompson reconnected with Gaspard after Vietnam and maintained a long friendship with him until his death in 2018. He wrote: 'As a 1st Lieutenant, I worked for Major Gaspard as an Assistant-S-3 in July 1969 after finishing my stint with Recon Team (RT) Rhode Island. At the conclusion of my time working for him he wrote one of the best OER's (Officer Evaluation Reports) in my file. He was fair, level headed, professional, and a superb writer, having no doubt took lessons from Arnett, Sheehan and Halberstam."' (from D.M. Thompson's unpublished memoir, *Marble Mountain Redux*)

[38] Robert Burns, *To a Mouse*, 1786. It tells of how he, while ploughing a field, upturned a mouse's nest. The poem is an apology to the mouse. "But Mousie, thou art no thy-lane,/In proving foresight may be vain:/The best laid schemes o' Mice an' Men/Gang aft agley./Aj'lea'e us nougat but grief an' pain,/For promis'd joy!" *Translation from the Scottish*: But mouse-friend, you are not alone in proving foresight may be vain: the best-laid plans of Mice and Men go oft awry, and leave us only grief and pain, for promised joy!

[39] Alan Farrell, "The Major Won the Croix de Guerre," *Nobody Gets Off the Bus: The Viet Nam Generation Big Book,* Charlottesville: University of Virginia, Vol. 5, No. 1-4, March 1994, p. 1.

[40] Rudyard Kipling, "If," written 1895, appearing in *Rewards and Fairies*, Doubleday, Page & Co., 1910.

[41] General Douglas MacArthur's Farewell Speech Given to the Corps of Cadets at the West Point Military Academy on the Hudson, NY, May 12, 1962.

COLOR ME RED

"They've promised that dreams can come true—
but forgot to mention that nightmares are dreams, too."

— Oscar Wilde

"Color Me Red," starts like a snippet from Christopher Robbins' 1978 non-fiction book, *Air America: The Story of The CIA's Secret Airlines*,[42] or a little *Operation Dumbo Drop* (though nothing so sappy as that trivialized piece of history where the film lands like the elephant—with a thud). And we are in another plane, this time one built for popping off and dropping onto runways targeted by 122 mm rockets, and mortars. It is the all-purpose C-7A Caribou, a delight to fly in if you prefer heavy gliders and 50 foot stops, but not so much if you fear vomiting pilots and side-ways landings (which always make it easier to stop in 50 feet), and this glider has a water buffalo, probably a large, angry water buffalo. Now this is how short-story writing should start.

I sat buckled in the hold of a C-7A Caribou flying to *Mai Loc*, near the Laotian border, 1968. I'm wedged against boxes of LuRP and C-rations, ammo cans, and a tightly tethered water buffalo with brass nose ring. The camouflaged bush plane smelled of dung and ammonia, chicken feathers floated. The Caribou, designed for short take off and landings, drifted, dropped and rose again in the Asian thermals, as the powerful flanks of the buffalo edged ever close. ("Color Me Red," p. 87.)

So this CIA-like plane ride into the secret SOG Command & Control base *Mai Loc* with that large brass nose-ringed, rice-paddy beast lurching ever closer to our Lieutenant, who sees a "vast checkerboard of emerald paddies, rolling hills and jungle" unfold from the just dropped tailgate of the plane, is a mesmerizing glimpse of man and machinery. The Lieutenant, "intrigued and allured by the vivid splash of colors," stepped to the precipice of that dropped tailgate and slipped his hand through a nylon handhold and peered down:

> My tethered hand felt a vicious tug, feet lifted and torso stretched into the slipstream, bull rider hung on an eight second ride [but the bull is still in the plane]. My arm shook violently, hand tore loose and I tumble through space until I arched my back and spread my arms into a stable free fall position. Amazed to be alive, every nerve in my body fired as I plunged toward a bright red strip of clay surrounded by jungle. I felt for my ripcord handle and realized I had no chute, . . . everything went red. ("Color Me Red," p. 88.)

OOOOOPS! No static line, no drogue, NO RIPCORD! What the fuck?

It's okay. Nothing but a dream, the wife's soothing hand rubbing his back. "It's alright," she hushed. "Yeah. Just a dream, nobody gets hurt." And a good thing because the stable body position will only slow you to 120 miles an hour without a chute and SPLAT! And, suddenly, we are back in "the World"—back in the U.S. of A. with a job, a wife, a mortgage, and progeny.[43] But are we? The answer is yes and maybe.

Our dreamer is now a discharged Captain from the Army and back in "the World" working for a realty company after a "brief but unspectacular career with Merrill Lynch, Pierce, Fenner and Dildo." Seems he went from strap-hanging in MACV-SOG to strap-ons with Merrill Lynch ("We'll make you a small fortune, if you have a large fortune!"). He receives a phone call, now in the late 1970's, from a Major Evans, identified as an OPPERCEN official Head-Hunter for former Special Forces officers to fill Army Reserve slots. The OPPERCEN major conducts his track on the Captain as covertly as the Captain used to stalk North Vietnamese minions down the Ho Chi Minh Trail. Get them in your sights and pull the trigger.

"What about those hard won memories?" he asked. "Here's one, I read in the *Journal* [*Wall* Street] where Uncle Sam thinned the ranks, RIF'd officers with combat experience for the 'convenience of the army' and now you need weekend warriors to take up the slack?" "Needs change in every business," he said. "But there are benefits." "No! Not now, not fucking ever!" I slammed the phone. My armpits were dark moons. I was anti-war, anti-army, anti-Nixon, anti-Republican and we were just coming out of a recession. I had a family to feed and had no intention of going into the reserve. ("Color Me Red," pp. 91-92.)

Perhaps the thought never entered his head after leaving *Mai Loc*, Vietnam, hospitals, the dying, the dead, for "the World," certainly not seven years later with family, the job, the obligations, but …?

But the major's phone call had sparked some latent thirst, ignored or denied; tantamount to a dry alcoholic watching a beer commercial. Two words, Special Forces, threatened to pierce a carefully constructed facade of normalcy. I'd worked hard to rebuild my identity in the intervening years, but mostly; remembered to forget. Too much remembering can kill you. ("Color Me Red," p. 93.)

Like the *Mai Loc* nightmare that has pierced his sleep for a decade, the Special Forces Reserve does pierce his carefully constructed facade of normalcy. But unlike the tender and consoling touch from his wife after his dream and his rejoinder, "Just a dream, nobody gets hurt," when he pulls closeted, mildewed boxes in search of his old jungle boots and camouflage fatigues, she stands behind him and asks, "Going hunting?" There is no consoling touch from her this time. His explanations of deciding to add Special Forces Reserve service to his full menu of life are met with stunned anger. "What about work—the kids?" Her eyes flashed.

"It's the reserves, for God's sake," I said. "I'm just checking it out!" "What does that mean?" "It's just one weekend a month." "So you've already made up your mind?" "Maybe I can train some men to ..." "Survive?" she asked. "Really? When were you going to tell me?" "I can't explain," I said. "They called; offered me a slot." "You've got a slot," she said. "Family slot. Right here!" She shrugged and retreated in silence. ("Color Me Red," p. 97.)

To convince her, and himself, the Captain yelled after her, "I'm just checking it out. Nobody gets hurt."

But it is no dream this time, and our newly minted Reserve Captain (but old hand) shows up for his introduction to his new Operating Detachment A team (ODA), in canvas and camouflage per schedule. But here's what is not in his book, or "Color Me Red." Let me read from Department of The Army Warning Order dated for a Special Forces training operation scheduled April 6-8, 1979:

> *2. As planned in isolation phase, this drill will involve a night parachute infiltration at EDWARD DZ, Deerfield, Virginia, utilizing three C-7A aircraft. 3. Company communications section will establish CP at Deerfield, VA, vicinity EDWARD DZ. 4. Rations will be C-rations and LRRPs. Uniform will be camouflage fatigues, bush hat and as follows: LBE, Rucksack, Rifle, Blank adapter, 4 magazines of blank ammunition, survival knife, Compass, Flashlight, H-harness, Lowering line, Jump helmet. 8. CPT Daniel M. Thompson, USAR, has joined the company as Commander, ODA-212. CPT Thompson is from Petersburg, VA, and is a veteran of the 5th SFGA. He has commanded a long-range reconnaissance company in combat. CPT Thompson will be a definite asset to the unit and to ODA-212.[44]*

I retained this old Warning Order for 40-odd years because this is the day I met Thompson, and then jumped with him from his "daymare" Caribou C-7A, albeit sitting with another Operating Detachment across from him in this railed, vomit-roiled cattle-car; Thompson, the new Commander of Operating Detachment A-212, me with Operating Detachment A-211. And this is how Thompson has bookended "Color Me Red"—with two rides in the Army's most famous troop and water buffalo transport, the first flight emblematic for all the amazement, randomness and doom of the MACV-SOG experience in Vietnam, and the second playing the best war game money could buy before the advent of personal computers and WANNABE fantasies lived out at a control board in your living room, or basement. In the interest of full disclosure, you can see why I said about reading "Color Me Red," "Now this is how short-story writing should start." And I will say here, "And how short-story writing should end."

It is because the story delivers us the anatomy of war and its pathology in a *précis* that seems to be about misunderstanding, but is all about understanding, from Alpha to Omega. How is the *vomitorium* (the ancient Roman *vomitorium* was actually a quick exit from the crowded confines of entertainment, not a room to vomit in; something, however, Thompson's C-7A fulfills in perfect duality) ride and the ill-fated Reservist "daymare" jump that brittle April day a bookend to the *Mai Loc* nightmare and its Omega in the understanding of the arc of Captain Thompson's war? As in "Blue Tattoo," "Walking Point with Sergeant Rock," and "Boxcar Orange," the themes of duty, honor, country reverberate, but always in the same obscure—NO—the same covert, ways.

The Captain's trek is one of constant misunderstanding but, in the language of war and its pathology, provides us with an "oracular and existential" understanding for our own reading of it. And we hear the echo of another theme, "Into the valley of Deerfield rode the 600; in this case, jumped the half-hundred," because the landing zone for our jump looked like the Crimean valley between the *Fedyukhin* Hills and the Causeway Heights at the Battle of *Balaclava*. But it existed, instead, between the Allegheny mountains of West Virginia and the Shenandoah mountains of Virginia, consisting of farms, hunting areas, old plantation houses and all the scenic views of mountains you don't want to see just before you make an exit out of a slop-sloshed aisle of coughing, regurgitating, redundant mutilators, not to mention a gulp-gulp-gulping copilot and crew. It is one of those scenes that, if played on the big-screen for a popcorn-eating audience, would have had them hooting and rolling in the aisles, but in actuality was an apocalyptic, interminable hour of suffering and broken promises (for the half-hundred). It was climaxed by Captain Thompson (and his avatar; in the digital technology sense of the word) having his arm left hanging by a string because the flat nylon edge of the static-line had wrapped, then sawed through his biceps like a bandsaw. As gravity generated exit speed toward the terminal velocity of his dream jump over Mai Loc, reality was replaced by Occam's Razor.[45] He was unable this time to assume a stable-body position, but he still had a parachute.

Here is what Thompson has done in "Color Me Red." He has illustrated two axioms that arise in combat, recurrent as they seem. "Don't tempt the Gods," and "Don't repeat the things that almost got you killed the first time." But, ironically, he has placed them in an arena that should insulate the former SOG captain from duplicating them. He is a married, productive civilian living in "the peacetime World" which would appear to eliminate the challenges of these contests.

It is understandable that the Captain has brought home the neural imprint of Vietnam and war, and his opening nightmare in the Caribou C-7A offers this illustration and reinforcement for "Don't tempt the Gods," but "Color Me Red" paints that rehabilitation period in a few conversations that give an accurate synopsis of his return to "the World." The ambivalence that even the most vaunted and isolated warriors felt in the years after returning from the war zone; proud of the pinnacle of the pyramid of combat, but …. doubts about the war and their actions in it, even enough to make one anti-war. This in spite of building successful lives, finishing educations, establishing good careers and raising families. Thompson testified:

> "No! Not now, not fucking ever!" I slammed the phone. My armpits were dark moons. I was anti-war, anti-army, anti-Nixon,

anti-Republican and we were just coming out of a recession. I had a family to feed and had no intention of going into the reserve. ("Color Me Red," p. 92.)

You see in this story a distinct influence of one of his writing teachers, the novelist Larry Heinemann (*Paco's Story, Close Quarters*) whose *Paco's Story* was published in 1986. As mentioned in the Introduction, Arnold R. Issacs speaks of the alienation of many Vietnam veterans and Vietnam writers. He cites Larry Heinemann's own testimony, whose writing about Vietnam is about alienation as much as anything else.

> When he came home, the writer Larry Heinemann recalled years afterward, "I had the distinct feeling (common among returning veterans, I think) that this was not my country, not my time."[46]

Thompson wants "the World" to be his country, his time, in "Color Me Red," but he is now allergic to his own history, as separated as Gregor Samsa, that poor alienated cockroach in Franz Kafka's *Metamorphosis*, but he is not quite vermin yet.

This Reservist night jump, postponed because of weather from the night before, becomes a day jump, and here are 24 cockroaches making a full-equipment, imitation combat-jump from a twin-engine Caribou into the Valley of Deerfield. How do I remember it was full equipment? Because the Warning Order said, "Individual equipment will be as follows: Rucksack, Rifle, LBE, H-harness and lowering line"; that means you are squatting, walking, sitting, jumping with a one-hundred pound back pack between your legs that you've got to adjust, then grasp quick release straps to lower the bundle after you exit a perfectly good aircraft so you won't break your legs on landing, if you haven't already severed your arm on launch. Thompson's Captain confirms this fact:

Buckled in the hold of a C-7A Caribou I stared across the floor at another A-Team rigged for a combat jump; rucksacks and rifles. Ashen faces and drool betrayed steely constitutions.

And no better place to introduce Jack de Treville, Thompson's A-team Sergeant, and the fourth member of my SOG quartet. Jack was a MACV-SOG trainer of reconnaissance teams with Special Operations Detachment 5891 at the Long Thanh Special Forces training camp during the War. He, I would learn later, was a crazily, fearless, or was it a fearlessly, crazy crusader attempting to get to know the new company commander on this short, but seemingly endless, "vomit comet" introduction to him.[47]

I was looking forward to jumping from 1250 feet into total darkness, carrying my M16 rifle, 95 pounds of equipment, and wearing a 42 pound parachute. But, to my disappointment, the jump was postponed until the next morning. I was the ranking enlisted man on our A team as the C-7A Caribou left Byrd Airport headed for the Deerfield DZ. I was anxious to get to know our newly assigned detachment commanding officer, Captain Dan Thompson. We were seated next to each other. Later, when it came time to jump, Captain Thompson would be the first off the plane's tailgate then I, and the rest of the team, would quickly follow.[48]

Captain Thompson, the new man in ODA 212, is preparing to lead his men out of this bouncing betty; the sooner, the better. The Caribou was acting like a championship bucking bronco that had never been ridden the full eight seconds and I sat at the rear of that bronco, on the left side of the fuselage facing the tailgate, near the step-down from the cockpit where a vomiting co-pilot would soon exit. It is not that Thompson was anonymous, for all of us who had a little background in Vietnam, airborne infantry, or special operation forces, knew exactly what a former leader of a SOG Reconnaissance Team meant.

The formula for service in a war arena went something like this. Less than ten out of every one-hundred soldiers (one-hundred thousand out of a million) were assigned a combat arms MOS (Military Occupational Specialty), which still didn't mean they actually saw combat, and then there was a pecking order existing among combat arms roles; cross-border operands in Studies and Observation Group (Marine Force Recon, Navy Seals, Army Special Forces) sat on the tip of this pyramid of bad-ass and carried out, by far, the most dangerous combat missions in the war venturing into and among superior enemy strongholds in Cambodia, Laos and North Vietnam; next were the LRRPs (Long Range Reconnaissance Patrols) and Rangers who carried out all in-country reconnaissance (LRRPs evolved into Ranger units in Vietnam in an organizational table change in 1969); then the straight-leg and airborne infantry (Army and Marine) carrying out large unit search and destroy missions seeking massed-force confrontations with the enemy. The wing of Navy, Air Force, Army and Marine pilots shot down over enemy territory defined an entirely separate category of service and sacrifice. Everybody else in that ten percent should crowd in under these warriors as the foundation blocks of this combat pecking order. And then there was the other 90 percent.

When I say "tip of the pyramid of of BAD-ASS, I mean Mount Everest. It's true that in 1979, the general population didn't know SOG from Strokes Of Genius, Shots On Goal, and Son-Of-a-Gun and wouldn't for another two decades, but they knew about the "Green Berets," and John Wayne, but the important thing was what I knew about SOG. To illustrate, Michael Herr writes about what he calls "Lurps" in his book *Dispatches*, first published in 1968 and expanded and republished several times over the next 20 years, a book that became the first huge best-seller about the Vietnam War.

In his portrait of these Lurps, (LRRP for Long Range Reconnaissance Patrol; Thompson uses Herr's term for LRRP throughout *Colors of War*, a backronym created from the sound of the acronym) Herr strap-hung with the Lurp team assigned to the 4th Infantry Division (the same Division of Raspy and Sidekick of "Boxcar Orange" infamy) and he tells one of those journalist-Hemingway stories, to impress us about tough men in the war, but also to impress us about the tough journalist. Anyway, he paints a portrait of these 4th Infantry Division Lurps:

> His face was all painted up for night walking now like a bad hallucination, not like the painted faces I'd seen in San Francisco only a few weeks before, the other extreme of the same theater. In the coming hours he'd stand as faceless and quiet in the jungle as a fallen tree, and God help his opposite numbers unless they had a least half a squad along, he was a good killer, one of our best. The rest of his team were gathered outside the tent, set a little apart from the other division units, with its own Lurp-designated latrine and its own exclusive freeze-dry rations, three-star war food, the same chop they sold at Abercrombie & Fitch. The regular division troops would almost shy off the path when they passed the area on their way to and from the mess tent. No matter how toughened up they became in the war, they still looked innocent compared to the Lurps.[49]

What's the point of this illustration? Well, when SOG got done eating their chop-chop, Abercrombie & Fitch, freeze-dry *foie gras* and Wagyu, and playing five-finger fillet with their K-Bars, the Lurps would shy off the path as SOG passed their area on their way to and fro. Now that's the real story. Sure those straight-leg infantry might have been a little nervous around the Lurps, but not as fucking nervous as those Lurps would have been around SOG. Am I making this shit up? I served with a qualified LRRP unit in the First Infantry Division a year before Thompson got there and I know that of which I speak. And Thompson didn't just strap hang with a Recon Team in SOG, he pointed it as One-Zero in an almost two-year career of valorous leadership that only SO's, GO's, awards and decorations can now reveal. Knowing that, Thompson's new coterie, including me, would have followed him into the Valley of the 600. Instead, I followed him out of his daymare C-7A.[50]

> An hour into the flight the plane dropped precipitously into a roller coaster plunge and my stomach floated in zero gravity. I looked down the line of the newly assigned A-Team as the plane reversed its plunge, lifted violently. My stomach compressed into a ball and pressed hard to exit my ass. I gripped the seat webbing over my shoulder with one hand and the aluminum bar with the other. Each vicious sheer and upward reversal torqued the aluminum frame as wing grommets groaned and stomachs sloshed. ("Color Me Red," pp. 97-98.)

Even SKYDIVE! from Gonzo Games & Electronic Arts, the latest and best in simulated parachute jumping, can't give you the inside of a jolting C-7A ride with roiling stomachs—and sloshing gangways.

> A gaunt, green sergeant across the aisle looked up, Adam's apple bobbing. He swiped drool from his mouth. His pallid face and wondering eyes conveyed a desperate need to exit. Jumpers covered mouths with both hands, struggling not to breach. One man blows, we all go. ("Color Me Red," p. 98.)

All of this is unravelling as I feel, see the co-pilot climb down the stairs to the hold and crawl/scurry past me holding his lunch between his fingers.

> The gangly co-pilot in baggy flight suit gripped the ladder, climbed slowly from the cockpit. He sat and scooted along the floor, hand over mouth; cheeks stretched like a trumpeter. He gripped the anchor line cable stretching from bulkhead to floor at the rear of the plane. He floated momentarily then slammed violently. A brown stream shot from his mouth. ("Color Me Red," p. 98)

Thompson doesn't describe our Sergeant Major Jump Master, but here's how that looked. During this roller coaster ride the Sergeant Major stood with a barf bag in his right hand and held onto the bulk head at the rear of the plane puking his guts out. He filled one bag and after the tail door opened up he walked to the edge and threw the bag out. The bag disappeared below the cargo ramp then, to everyone's chagrin, as if an illusion, levitated and shot (boomeranged) back into the cabin. So after he threw out the first bag, no lessons learned, he began immediately filling another one. I asked Thompson later to describe those images to me. He said:

If you had been up front and port you would have seen what I saw as I exited the C-7A ramp. The Sergeant Major standing near the rear of the ramp, holding on with his left hand and gripping a barf bag in his right that was sloshing over the brim and puke streaming from either side of his mouth like a Fu Manchu, him grinning toothy like an opossum in a tree.

Jack de Treville offered this description, adding some additional bedaubed, yet revealing details, that only he remembered so well because he was sitting/standing on top of it.

Then, approaching the mountains, the thermals aloft began tossing the Caribou around like a leaf in a wind storm. As it got worse, a few of us including myself and Thompson kept our cool. Many, including the copilot, the crew chief, a lot of the other team across the aisle, and our Jumpmaster, a Sergeant Major, RALPHED up breakfast, some more than once. A young Sergeant (Sergeant Northrup) next to me vomited all over his reserve and equipment bag, stood up trying to wipe the mucous, stringers and chunks off himself, and slid and fell. When he hit the deck, his ruck came apart and TO&E spilled out. I swear I saw a pair of pink undies in the mess. This was at about the six minute stand-up and a couple of his peer group helped him pack all of his *ejecta* just in time for him to slide out the rear end. At jump time it was a relief to get out of what I would later call, "The Vomit Comet." I toggled away from the barbed wire fence to a safe landing thinking to myself what a nasty job the C-7A ground crew would have cleaning up that fucking mess.

I felt like some watcher in the skies when a new smell comes round the bend ("rotten eggs and Limburger"), or like brave Thompson when with eagle eyes he stared out the tailgate at the Shenandoah—and all his men gazed at each other with wondering eyes.[51] Would our fate be like the mythological wax-winger's who flamed in as the sun rose over Samos? Did he also feel his stomach preparing to exit his ass? Only there was no sea here. When all was said and done, this C-7A would be a stack of kindling somewhere below in a Blue Ridge ditch.

> *In Breughel's Icarus, for instance: how everything turns away*
> *Quite leisurely from the disaster; the ploughman may*
> *Have heard the splash, the forsaken cry,*
> *But for him it was not an important failure; the sun shone*
> *As it had to on the white legs disappearing into the green*
> *Water, and the expensive delicate ship that must have seen*
> *Something amazing, a boy falling out of the sky,*
> *Had somewhere to get to and sailed calmly on.*[52]

Like Icarus' anonymous death when everyone turned away, fixing the fence line, plowing the corn, or erecting another silo and no one gave witness. As Thompson writes it, we survived, but you can't be quite sure from the last words of "Color Me Red." In the opening lines of "Blue Tattoo," Thompson invokes the 255 foot-tall jump towers of Ft. Benning, Georgia, topped by "incessant, winking, red-eyed Cyclops."

The blinking strobes mocked me; my choice to volunteer for OCS, forego Jump School and the Special Forces training for which I'd enlisted. If boarded out, there would be no Green Beret, Merrill's Marauders. OSS jumping behind enemy lines. Airborne icons imbued from youth, at once lifted aspirations and loomed as a harbinger of failure. ("Blue Tattoo," p. 13.)

There are all of the key words in this consideration to foreshadow exactly what is going on there, in the now, in Deerfield. Not known to Thompson yet, electrical lines strung between giant, lattice, steel, transmission towers await below (if the night jump had come off, he'd have been able to see the red-eyed Cyclops winking at him, incessantly). His nightmare C7-A Caribou has predicted things mostly correctly, except for the slouching beast:

> The Pratt & Whitney engines strained as the plane lifted and fell. It rattled and rolled as I glanced upstairs into the cockpit. The co-pilot knitted his brow and studied his landing checklist. I strained to see out the port window as the din and discord of hydraulics squealed, flaps lowered, engines slowed and wheels dropped. The tailgate folded down, exposing a vast checkerboard of emerald paddies, rolling hills and jungle. ("Color Me Red," p. 87.)

And this *leitmotif:* "The tailgate folded down, exposing a vast checkerboard of emerald paddies," in his nightmare, has been adumbrated at the end of "Color Me Red," with "The tailgate folded down, exposing a checkerboard of black and gray. Barren trees brushed the gunmetal sky," in his daymare. Careening against the bulkhead, slipping on mucoid vomit as the plane rose and dropped, Thompson's Captain gripped the nylon seat netting with his right hand and his static line in his left while another jumper slipped and crashed to the floor.

> The plane bucked and shimmied on the final approach. Green light lit to a dissonant chorus of gratitude and groans. I reached the edge of the ramp and bunny hopped; awaited the tug of a smooth opening. Instead I felt a savage jerk on my arm and my body unfurled like a banner. My head snapped back and something ripped. I reached for the toggles of the MC-1-1 but one arm hung limp along my side. I pulled the other toggle and my chute spun like a top. I drifted toward electrical lines strung between lattice steel transmission towers. I blinked hard and tried to wake. As my chute spun and I dropped ever close to the power

lines the stark realization came that I was drifting, completely out of control. I listened for her soft voice, 'Same dream?' and the soothing rub of her hand on my back. Everything went red. ("Color Me Red," p. 99.)[53]

In the real world, I came stumbling, sliding and tripping out of the Caribou, probably 25 seconds after Captain Thompson, breathing deeply like a man freed from a prison cell, going through my parachute checklist and finally looking earthward, transmission towerward, mountainward, and wayward. In the warp of memory I thought the fences that surrounded the property in that valley were of the old wood-railed, Manassas type, and that the fields and corn rows and ridges were yellow, brown and sere, winter just done, and spring yet to break its bloom, but Thompson, without regard to a spinning chute, a dangling left arm, and transmission towers, described a different DZ, one which unraveled for him like a gauntlet and ended when he found himself gazing at sharpened wood stakes, beckoning, to add to the insult of everything that had already happened to him, "How bout a six-foot stake up your ass?" Here is how he described it:

From the air the drop zone (DZ) looked like a long par five stretching east to west between two steep ridge lines, carpeted by giant oak, maple, spruce and pine. At the east end of the DZ drooped thick electrical wires that carried power through the valley. The wires, strung between massive towers rose with open arms to greet the chutists. The wind rushed headlong from the west was squeezed between and amplified by the narrow valley walls. The blustery wind swept the shaken, but not stirred captain towards the onerous power lines. A slight humming sound was first detected as if the synchronized warmup of a Greek chorus. It grew in intensity as I slipstreamed towards the lines; now the buzz of an active bee hive. Closer still, the sound was similar to the whine of a dental drill, in overdrive. The DZ was bisected by a barbed wire fence, stretched between and anchored by many large wooden posts which, when seen from the air, looked like the freshly sharpened pikes Centurions once decorated with severed heads. (from D.M. Thompson's unpublished memoir, *Marble Mountain Redux*)

Taking in gulps of crisp mountain air, and thanking the Gutter Gods that I'd survived this slime ride, I prepared for landing, landed and packed equipment. Once freed, I noticed a gathering movement of camouflage a long distance up the sloping field toward the fence line. The thronged camouflage was men of Captain Thompson's Detachment 212 doing what we'd all been taught to do in combat, rendering medical aid and assistance. We know that Captain Thompson did not buy the Deerfield farm. Even though everything went red, he survived his daymare, much as he awakened from his nightmare, and we know from reading, that in another short six years he would be challenging disaster once again. The Captain eschewed any medical help that day, though upon examination, team medic SFC Courtney Griffin said, "His humerus was stripped like a chicken bone. A clotted sack of torn muscle congealed like blood pudding at the crotch of his arm." It ballooned darkly and reminded him of Popeye. Ironically, it was the same force that threw the Sergeant Major's vomit back in his face that instantaneously caused Thompson's static line to wrap his arm as he exited the plane, and before he could get hands on his reserve. Unknown to any of us in A Company at the time, it turned out that this was not an uncommon occurrence when jumping the C-7A.

"He stuck the limp arm into his field jacket pocket, grabbed his gear and moved out with his team." The Captain had drilled and rehearsed his A-Team for a successful night attack on an enemy target and rode home on a bus. Luckily, Colonel Lithgow, on active reserve duty at Fort Lee, an orthopedic surgeon from a prestigious Chicago hospital, had seen all to many of these injuries but was skilled at repairing Thompson's biceps at oh-dark-thirty of the next Monday morning.

"Two words, Special Forces . . . ." If there is a major theme in the story here, and the ones ahead, the Captain was the equivalent of a "dry drunk" or, more seriously, a dope addict who thought he'd beaten the "habit" but when finally confronted by his old pusher (the ARPERCEN Major), after having gone cold-turkey for several years, couldn't resist just a wee taste, line or shot of the opiate he been fed in his SOG days ("Color me Red"). He'd run the gamut—RT missions, flew Covey, been inserted into the Heart of Darkness, fire fights, dangled 10000 feet above a verdant jungle on strings, and lived the thrill and agony of tracking the enemy and being tracked.

Maybe those dreams that came from the dark depths of his unconscious foretold of another life. But more likely the prophetic words of Brutus proved all the map he needed:

> *There is a tide in the affairs of men,*
> *Which taken at the flood, leads on to fortune.*
> *Omitted, all the voyage of their life*
> *Is bound in shallows and in miseries.*
> *On such a full sea are we now afloat.*
> *And we must take the current when it serves,*
> *Or lose our ventures.*[54]

It is the Frog and the Scorpion, just better said by Will Shakespeare in 1599. Maybe Thompson's Captain hoped the view from the ramp of that C-7A would be a "vast checkerboard of emerald" (as in his dream) and symbolize new life, a rebirth of the high he'd been on all those years ago. Or maybe his feeling that he'd failed civilian life, convinced him that he'd been called back to his destiny. Or maybe this was a do-over, a way to physically and mentally rearrange the ignominious end to his war. But the irony of chasing this field of dreams was that this disjunction, one foot in each world even while in a tactical airplane, signaled something to come that was winter blasted and sere, "a checkerboard of black and gray." That Thompson, since his return from Vietnam, had built a carefully constructed façade of normalcy," would even consider being lured back into the Army had him now teetering on the extreme edge of absurdity. That he wasn't jerked back from the abyss by the vicious tug on his extended arm, his body flapping like a flag in the 110 mph slip stream of the Caribou, speaks to his latent, "I have a need, a need for speed" addiction and his inability, like the scorpion of "Boxcar Orange," to be anything except what he was. This theme foreshadows "Challenging Disaster," "Black Hand," and "Yellow Horse," as we will see.

---

[42] "Air America's pilots flew dangerous missions, those no one else would fly, frequently under enemy fire. Many missions were in fact aid-oriented missions to provide logistical support and food to allies who were fighting the war along with the South Vietnamese and the US. Most of the time, pilots did not know what they were delivering, just when and where, no matter what the weather was like, or whether it was day or night." Wikipedia, *Air America* (book).

[43] Arnold R. Isaacs, *Vietnam Shadows: The War, Its Ghosts, and Its Legacy*, by Arnold R. Issacs, The Johns Hopkins University Press: Baltimore & London, 1997, p. xi. "In the soldiers' slang of the Vietnam War, home was commonly called 'the World.' It's a telling phrase, expressing their sense that they had been sent to someplace so distant and strange it felt like another planet. They were not the only soldiers to feel that way (in the Civil War, I have read, men who had experienced battle spoke of 'seeing the elephant,' another way of saying they had been somewhere foreign and weird). But for many reasons, those who fought in Vietnam were left feeling particularly shut off from the country whose uniform they wore."

[44] Enclosure as *Annex 1*, DOA, Company A, 2nd Special Forces Bn, 11th Special Forces GP (ABN), Michelli USAR Center, 1305 Sherwood Avenue, Richmond, Virginia 23220: Subject: LOI for

MUTA-5 on 6-8 Apr 79, Quentin Crommelin, Jr., MAJ, Armor, USAR, Commanding, 20 Mar 79.

[45] This philosophical razor advocates that when presented with competing hypotheses about the same prediction, one should select the solution with the fewest assumptions, and that this is not meant to be a way of choosing between hypotheses that make different predictions. That Thompson's static line acted like a razor after he left the plane is the solution with the fewest assumptions and the correct prediction.

[46] Arnold Isaacs, *Ibid.*, p. 11.

[47] Jack enlisted in 1955, and after his first Airborne service with 456th Division Arty of the 82nd Airborne, did one of those little known tours in Army history in the early 1960's. He was assigned to the 557th Airborne Quartermaster Co, in *Evreux*, France, SHAPE, where he became good friends with another young NCO, Robert L. Howard. Both Jack and Howard ("Bob") were destined to become Green Berets and serve in MACV-SOG, at different times, different places. Howard went on to a 35 year career and retired as the most decorated soldier in Vietnam service, and probably, in modern military history. Not only did he receive the MOH, but was nominated two other times for it, and like Audie Murphy, one of his childhood heroes, received every decoration for valor in the military pyramid.

[48] Jack had played football for John Marshall High School in Richmond, Virginia in the early 1950's and that became a point of conversation with Thompson on the ride out to Deerfield. Jack said, "The first part of the flight was smooth and easy, and as we engaged in small talk, I found him to be friendly and approachable. He told me he was from Petersburg, and when I said I was a Richmonder and mentioned while in high school playing against Petersburg High and never winning, but coming home with Petersburg's cleated boots up our asses, his ears perked even more alertly into friendship."

[49] Michael Herr, *Dispatches*, New York: Alfred A. Knopf, Inc.. 1977. pp. 6-7.

[50] All of the above was true of Jack de Treville.

[51] With a nod to John Keats' sonnet, "On First Looking into Chapman's Homer," 1816. "Then felt I like some watcher of the skies/ When a new planet swims into his ken;/ Or like stout Cortez when with eagle eyes/ He star'd at the Pacific—and all his men/ Look'd at each other with a wild surmise—/ Silent, upon a peak in Darien."

[52] W.H. Auden, "Musee des Beaux Arts," first published as "Palais des beaux arts," *New Writing, Spring,* 1939.

[53] J.D. Heckman and M.I. Levine, "Traumatic Closed Transection of the Biceps Brachia in the Military Parachutist," *Abstract,* "Static line Injury to the military paratrooper's arm occasionally produces an unusual muscle injury: closed transection of the belly of the biceps brachii. A review of twenty-eight untreated paratroopers so injured demonstrated significant residual weakness and deformity. Attempts at late repair resulted in only minimum improvement. The results of twenty fresh injuries treated by either surgical repair or aspiration followed by closed reduction and splinting are presented."

[54] William Shakespeare, *Julius Caesar,* Act 4, Scene 3, 218-224.

CHALLENGING DISASTER

Up, up the long, delirious, burning blue
I've topped the wind-swept heights with easy grace
Where never lark nor ever eagle flew—

— John Gillespie Mage Jr., "High Flight"

W hat do Elton John, astronauts, U.S. Army Special Forces Reserves and the reverberations of MACV-SOG, a model Lionel train on a circular track in the Dixie Diner, the Henderson & Fenwick Brokerage Firm leveraged buy out, Pall Mall cigarettes, the 1986 Challenger space launch disaster, and time itself have to do with each other? The simple answer is D.M. Thompson. The more complex one, "Challenging Disaster," is a circle representing Thompson's observations of risk and calamities in life—his own and some of the actors in his own history and ours.

Circular narratives begin and end in the same location. They place emphasis on knowledge gained through the events and, perhaps angst, in between. Often the characters will behave differently when they return to the original location because they have learned something during the story, or not. Consider *The Lion, The Witch and The Wardrobe*, which both begins and ends with children at a train station—three children evacuated by their parents from World War II London in the 1940 German *Blitzkreig* on England. That is not to say that C.S. Lewis, was read by, or informed our author, but you can say that "Challenging Disaster," like *The Lion, The Witch and the Wardrobe*, begins safely at a train station and ends safely at a train station.[55] This is one of the circles of seven delineated by Thompson in "Challenging Disaster," but nothing to do with the circles of the Hell of Dante's *Inferno* in his 14th-century epic poem, *Divine Comedy*.

Thompson's concentricity in "Challenging Disaster," while perhaps broaching, on one hand, some of the seven deadly sins, has more to do with painting a moment in time that is circular, and, indeed, his circles are composed of circles. It begins with the epigraph of John Elton's lyrics to "Rocket Man," the use of a Diner table for Army Reservist administrative paperwork and a model Lionel train that circumnavigates the Dixie Diner on a lone track placed above its customer's heads.

Elton John's rock hit "Rocket Man," introduces the first circle(s) in "Challenging Disaster," the theme of orbit and the fascination of the space age and astronauts and, of course, the events of the story's setting, January 28, 1986, which loom large over this eponymous tale. The full lyrics of Thompson's epigraphic contraction say:

> *And I think it's gonna be a long, long time*
> *'Til touchdown brings me 'round again to find*
> *I'm not the man they think I am at home*
> *Oh, no, no, no*
> *I'm a rocket man*
> *Rocket man, burning out his fuse up here alone.*

While the pioneer spirit of exploration was not a new concept in the 1980s, space exploration was. "Rocket Man" debuted right around the time that the Apollo 16 mission sent astronauts to the moon for the fifth time, Neil Armstrong and Buzz "Lightyear" Aldrin having made the first journey in 1969. Elton John's lyricist, Bernie Taupin, took the inspiration for "Rocket Man" from Ray Bradbury's science-fiction short story, "The Rocket Man." Bradbury's story, written 10 years before men would go into space, and almost 20 years before they ventured to the moon, surmised at that very, early date that being an astronaut in the future would become a sort of everyday job. If you can believe it, space travel now so mundane, Bradbury's rocket man brings back the stuff of that space travel for his curious son to assay:

> And from the opened case spilled his black uniform, like a black nebula, stars glittering here or there, distantly, in the material. I kneaded the dark stuff in my warm hands, I smelled the planet Mars, an iron smell, and the planet Venus, a green ivy smell, and the planet Mercury, a scent of sulphur and fire, and I could smell the milky moon and the hardness of the stars. I pushed the uniform into a centrifuge machine I'd built in my ninth grade shop that year, set it whirling. Soon a fine powder precipitated into a retort. This I slid under a microscope. And while my parents slept unaware, and while our house was asleep, all the automatic bakers and servers and robot cleaners in an electric slumber, I stared down upon brilliant motes of meteor dust, comet-tail, and loam from far Jupiter glistening like worlds themselves which drew me down the tube a billion miles into space, at terrific accelerations.[56]

The story embraces the same sensual and tactile images of the labyrinths of space as Thompson's does the *limbus fatuorum* of the SOG warrior's Vietnam. So the song is purposive, a beacon for his story, for the main theme is the struggles between adventure and peace, danger and comfort. The rocket man is torn between his love of space travel and a sense of responsibility to his family. As he relates in the story, being in one place always makes him long for the other place. Where, I ask you, have you heard that theme before? And of course, a related theme is the acceptance of death and its cost to survivors. In "Rocket Man," his wife admits to coping with her husband's absence by considering him dead; however, his actual death is even worse, as he perishes on a final apogee to the sun (where were Oort's Constants in that orbit?)—pretty prophetic of some of the events to come in Thompson's challenging day.

Rocket men (and two rocket women) headlines greet him in the local newspaper as he finishes his breakfast on the fateful morning: *Challenger Attempts Launch Again Today - Local School Set to Watch*

Christa McAuliffe - First Teacher in Space. Brea, the waitress serving our Captain *qua* Branch Manager/stockbroker and reading over his shoulder the headlines from the local rag, crooned in his ear:

> *"She packed my bags last night preflight. Zero hour, nine a.m."* Glittery nails slid the ticket across the table.
> "Don't you just luvvvv Elton John?"
> *"Til touchdown brings me round again to find."* She hoisted a Heinz ketchup bottle and sang into the mic, *"I'm not the man they think I am at home."*
> ("Challenging Disaster," pp. 105-106.)

Breakfast finished by 8 a.m. The seven astronauts are boarding the derrick elevator to their slingshot ride. Brea amped her vocals as he headed out the Diner door. *"And I think it's going to be a long, long time.*

Returning to his office on Bank Street, he removes a portable TV and hauls it up to his second floor office to watch the launch of the Challenger. Thompson's description of the office makes it sound more like a speakeasy after closing time:

> I lifted a pillow and afghan blanket from the King Edward couch where I'd slept the night before. I surveyed the office, stepped into the bullpen. Two rows of desks were littered with holding books and buy/sell tickets. Cigarettes floated in coffee cups, ashtrays brimmed. Cursors winked mindlessly, blank screens of quote machines. ("Challenging Disaster," p. 108.)

Turning on the TV, the Captain adjusted tin foil flags on the rabbit ears and muted the sound. "Watching television during work felt strange, but the anticipation of flight produced a kind of euphoric recall." Television and stock-brokering didn't mix unless it was viewing an exchange ticker tape low-crawling across the wall, but Thompson is recalling an age that many of us still remember. From the time Alan Shepard made the first sub-orbital flight in 1961 in the Mercury-Redstone spacecraft he named Freedom, and John Glenn the first orbital flight, through every launch afterward, any day a launch event took place was a TV holiday whether you were a first grader, or royalty. Tuesday, January 28, 1986 was the kind of day you remember, like Friday, November 22, 1963; you remember exactly where you were, what the sun looked like, if you could see it, and exactly what you were doing. I was 40 miles north of Thompson's office, in Richmond, Virginia, walking up Main Street to find lunch at one of the cafes near my office and noticed a large crowd standing outside a store display window with TVs blazing. The hum of the unbelieving crowd had already started and the images of Challenger began to repeat and repeat and repeat. Yes, January 28, 1986 was a stockbroker holiday, or so our Captain *qua* broker thought.

The second circle(s) presents itself in the cloak of the Captain's Reserve obligation and the constant reverberations of Vietnam and his SOG experience. Like the Rocket Man, the Captain is torn between his love of the next adrenalin rush and a sense of responsibility to his family. Being in the one place makes him long for the other just as the mathematics of this exploratory ambivalence was formulated in "Color Me Red." And so it continues:

> I penned evaluation reports, EERs for my A-Team, reviewed next month's training schedule, lesson plans, IG inspection prep, requisitions for parachutes and Q-school for the newly assigned. The army doesn't march on its stomach, it low crawls on paperwork. ("Challenging Disaster," p. 103.)

Thinking ahead to the central crisis of the story, a highly speculative, and maximum monetary risk project, a leveraged buy out (LBO) of the brokerage company he now worked for, our Captain searches the interiority of his risk identity, or the Army, Special Forces Reserve and MACV-SOG:

> Vietnam had expanded my tolerance for risk far beyond the normal range. Just how far? I hadn't a clue. Absolute risk or as close as I could get to it in civilian life was deferred to weekend drills in the Special Forces Reserve. I was an adrenaline junkie and got my fix with fly-aways; night drops in Panama, leaping

from Mark-IV SOC boats into the shark-infested Caribbean. ("Challenging Disaster," p. 104)

Speaking of the pending action awaiting him in the planned LBO, the Captain says:

Other than trading puts and calls on the CBOE [Chicago Board Options Exchange] this was the first investment that provided the kick he need to feel alive; though far less intoxicating than flying nap of the earth in a C-130 Blackbird out of Hurlburt Field; rigged and ready for a night jump. This private placement had financial elements of chance that far exceeded its risk ratio. But it was still a two-dollar fix for a hundred-dollar habit. ("Challenging Disaster," p. 104.)

As he watched the pre-launch news briefs, he completed the EERs for his A-Team and greeted his late arriving secretary, Elsa, tall, broad-shouldered Slav, who dropped an armload of mail on his desk in prelude to the stockbroker business that will break out in the fourth circle, she asks him if he is on the Executive Committee meeting over the weekend with the "titular head."

"Weekend Drill." I said.
"Another jump from a perfectly good plane?" she shook her head
"Airborne." ("Challenging Disaster," p. 110.)

In addition to trying to make a waitress out of Elsa (bring the titular head a cup of coffee when he comes in), he charges her with updating portfolios, and has trained her to do the Reservist's monthly training schedules, requisitions and evaluation transcriptions.

"Yes, drill sergeant." She saluted awkwardly.
"Any chance of that raise?"
"About the same as that shuttle lifting off," I said,
"And yes, sir will do just fine." ("Challenging Disaster," p. 111.)

The Captain has surrounded himself with the artifacts of his mercenary soul on display after a walk through a long hallway "dark and drafty as a French prison," and a climb up pitted stairs with mahogany balusters to his second floor mezzanine.

An alabaster bust of Odysseus sporting a green beret stared vacantly from the fireplace mantel. A drawing of me bandaged like a mummy and strapped on a cargo pallet, leaned against the mirror. A row of army plaques, statues, awards and decorations filled the mantel. At the far end, Green Berets rigged for a water jump, squint into the lens. The framed article: *President Reagan Attends 200th Anniversary of Yorktown Special Forces Provide Airborne Excursion.* ("Challenging Disaster," p. 108.)

When, on the TV, the shuttle begins to vent steady streams on the launch pad, the Captain remembers high school, John Glenn's first orbit and playing hooky from school as he did whenever a NASA launch was scheduled. And then that reverie slips into the Valley of the Shadow:

I missed the moon landing when in Vietnam. The only lift off I was worried about that day was the UH-1D chopper and snatching us up on a hot LZ. All systems were a go as me and my team ran for our lives in the Ashau Valley. Neil Armstrong must have had the same exhilarating feeling about the time he stepped on the moon. While he took one small step for man, I took one giant leap for my kind, into a hovering chopper. The pilot pulled collective and plucked us, *deus ex machina*, in a hail of gunfire. It was funny how indiscriminate memories, events, men, dead and alive, popped into my brain like that. One minute I could be sitting in my chair the next whizzed off to a jungle firefight. Seemed like it happened more and more often. ("Challenging Disaster," p. 109.)

F.W. Henderson, the principal stockholder in Henderson & Fenwick ("second-generation silver spoon, had been born on third based, but believed he'd hit a triple"), was viewed through the Captain's second-floor window disenthroning his 1967 pale green, Pallas Citroen parked on Bank Street in front of the office. This car transports him backward again:

It reminded me of another Citroen, blown upside down on Highway 1 outside Da Nang, wheels spinning lazily. I blinked and shook my head, annoyed by the intrusion. ("Challenging Disaster," p. 111.)

The Captain sees a tall, gaunt man with a thin black comb-over, slumping posture, rounded shoulders exacerbated by head tilt, and a dead eye (glass). These features send our Captain whizzing once again:

His dead eye reminded me of a Nung striker who stepped on a mine, exploded in front of me. Truth was I couldn't remember what he looked like, just laying on my back, trying to breathe, head ringing and bleeding from the ears. It felt like a heart punch. Sergeant Dixon screaming soundlessly, "You all right? You all right?" His lips moved. No words sounded. ("Challenging Disaster," pp. 111-112.)

The dead-eyed F.W. is revealed in a military aside. Once in the Captain's office, he stared at a picture on the mantel of the Captain standing at attention in front of a company formation.

"Officer and gentleman," he said.
"Award ceremony."
"Green Beret? I was 4F, didn't believe in that war."
"War's an article of faith. Intelligence nets, dark arts, double agents and plausible denial. The key word is plausible."
"I read *The Green Beret.*"
"You know that's fiction."
"It's like this business; lies fly and truth arrives on a stretcher," he said. "How'd that song go . . . *fearless men who jump and die?*" ("Challenging Disaster," p. 112-113.)

To presage the repetition of circles in "Challenging Disaster," the Dixie Diner employs a toy Lionel train that circumnavigates the Diner on a track built round the interior, and overhead. It is the third circle(s).

The high-pitched whistle of the Lionel train circled the room and passed overhead. Small Os puffed from the engine's smoke stack. A gust of cold air swept the isle as the front door opened. ("Challenging Disaster," p. 103.)

The Lionel serves as a Greek Chorus to sound the central theme of the play, the voice a high-pitched whistle, the actor's props, small Os puffed from the engine's smoke stack. And this chorus closes the play drawing our Captains eyes inevitably toward it:

My eyes were drawn toward the high-pitched whistle of the Lionel train as it circled the room and passed overhead. Small Os puffed from the engine's smoke stack. It gave a subtle reminder with familiar reprise. The truth was simple—everyone lies.

But the crux of "Challenging Disaster," and the fourth circle(s), is the Captain's adrenalin enterprise in the stock market world and the attempted leveraged buy out of the Company from the degenerate son of old, southern money. This story, centripetal and encircling, contracts toward center stage of "Challenging Disaster," while the rest of the action seems to be searching for ways to break orbit. How so? Thompson's meaning for January 28, 1986, was intended to unravel in the insulation of small-town America at the same time that a larger event was disclosing on the world stage, and neither the twain should meet; or so we thought.

In the second circle of business, penning evaluations reports, EERs, *et al*, the Captain reviewed his, and a few of his associates', Private Placement Memorandum (PPM), a Stock Offering for Henderson & Fenwick. The Captain and eight younger associates in the Company, spread from Washington D.C., to Virginia, to Florida, as Thompson relayed to me later, were "all young meat-eaters" who were described by old-timer bond traders as the "Young Turks." Using the PPM ("highly speculative, high risk shares in the Company"), the "Young Turks" will buy enough shares, 51%, to gain a majority ownership and unseat the *status quo ante*, of Henderson & Fenwick. They had subscribed to the PPM a week earlier, or so the Captain believed.

As Thompson explained it, this take-over offered the same kind of high-risk adrenalin rush that Special Forces offered—but not quite. Unexplained, but implicit in the events and dialogue of parsing the LBO, not all of the "Young Turks" were meat-eaters after all. It turns out that some were vegetarians and this changed the complexion of dinner and the dinner table. F.W., via vegetarianism, had discovered the take-over scheme and scheduled a weekend, surprise "Committee Meeting" in the Richmond office. The original Board Meeting was scheduled after the close of the stock offering (the "Put-up, or Shut-up gesture" of the "Young Turks") the week before, but F.W., forewarned of his ouster, scheduled a Saturday night massacre, surprise board meeting. In the aftermath, because the Captain hadn't attended due to a Special Forces Reserve weekend drill, F.W. called him at home. Under the ruse that he'd never visited the Southern office, he called the night before the disastrous launch to let the Captain know that he would be making an "office visit." This is dimly revealed to us in his conversations with his secretary, his own thoughts and ultimately in a challenging disaster in his office, for the plot below did not unfold as planned.

> As one of the Young Turks, a loose confederation of branch managers and hotshot brokers, we conspired to take the high ground; dislodge Henderson as president and grow the company. Subscription completed, the die had been cast. Henderson would soon be voted out as president. Today's meeting, I guessed, was a lame attempt at prolonging the inevitable. ("Challenging Disaster," pp. 104-105.)

Having found out about the "coup," F.W. arrives at our Captain's office to cut its head off and successively end the Captain's career as a licensed trafficker and stock monger. Once revealed as having invested his money and signing the subscription, he was now going to swing in the wind. The conversations evoking the Captain's military service with F.W. were prelude to the massacre on Bank Street.

I stepped from the heart of Dixie into a frigid blast of arctic air. The wind chafed. I looked down Bank Street toward the Siege Museum. The morning sunlit the imposing Greek revival architecture, four white column and Doric edifice. ("Challenging Disaster," p. 106.)

F.W. dispenses with the weather conversation ("First time I've seen the operation . . ." "Now remind me . . . how long we been here?" "Remarkable space."). The Captain searches F.W.'s good eye for any hint of enlightenment. But, as he says, "If the good eye was a lantern into his soul, than F.W.'s was coated with lampblack. Or, the lights were off and nobody was home." Leaning back with lit cigarette, F.W., blew a steady stream of Pall Mall smoke at the Captain, brought up the demise of Big Tobacco in southern Virginia. "They're made in Petersburg," the Captain reminded him. "Not for long," said F.W., reminding him of the factory closing. "Four thousand jobs. All that money, poof, up in smoke!" and with a laugh, "Big tobacco is dead."

A man who hears a Pall Mall sucking, third-base born, one-eye Nung laughing at the prospect of 4000 people losing jobs, and their livelihoods signals the Captain he is dealing with a fucking barracuda and things are about to get bloody. In getting out his shiv, F.W. even makes a side-swipe at the Vietnam show.

Referring to the Challenger delay scrolling on the office TV, F.W. says, "It's a tricky business. Like any business." Thinking that F.W. is referring to Astronauts in general, the Captain says, "It doesn't look good."

"All that planning, preparation and money." One eye stared out the window. "Timing and execution. Unintended consequences, like Vietnam. The waste of blood and treasure, idiots running the show. Sometimes you just have to wave the white flag and say, 'Well we tried,' and walk away." "Didn't we do that?" ("Challenging Disaster," p. 116.)

Still in synchrony with the delayed astronauts, the Captain answers F.W., "They know the risk when they volunteer. Six days they've been strapped on their backs."

But F.W. is talking about Brown & Williamson now, and his Captain, his Captain.

> "B &W pours millions of dollars into this community. Now they're leaving and there's nothing to replace it. We needed capital," he said, rubbing his hands together. "Like you said, everybody knows the risk"
>
> "What are we talking about?"
>
> "You" he said, "Taking the risk."
>
> "What risk?"
>
> "We're closing this office," F.W. said. He dropped the cigarette into his cup. It doused with a sputter.
>
> "The most profitable office in the company?"
>
> "It's a greedy business," he said. "But I've weathered coups before." ("Challenging Disaster," p. 117.)

Old F.W. then reveals something our Captain knew, but apparently had forgotten; that there are few humans more cut throat than brokers and bankers.

> "Nothing more cut throat than brokers and bankers," he said. "Talk about nets, informants and double agents. Talking is their business and they can't stop. Never met a broker who could keep a secret." ("Challenging Disaster," p. 117.)

The conclusion? F.W. delivers the punchline advising the Captain that some of his partners, the vegetarian ones, had decided not to invest leaving the LBO gambit a little short. "I'm still majority stock holder." With that, F.W. stood and announced that all of the Captain's brokers were being transferred to the Richmond office, as would his client portfolios, and said "Never too late for a new career. I'm hungry," and headed to that central degustation outlet recommended to him by the Captain, the Dixie Diner, no doubt lighting a new Pall Mall on the way.

The vindictive F.W., having visited upon the Captain his own disaster, introduces the fifth circle(s) of "Challenging Disaster." They are those fine cigarettes made in Winston-Salem, North Carolina, and not at the B&W of Virginia as I had earlier suspicioned. How fine? So fine that the individual packs address us in Latin.

> F.W. slid his hand inside his coat and removed a pack of Pall Mall. "You mind?" he said, without looking up.
> "My mother smoked Pall Mall, I said. F.W. searched the pack for the last cigarette.
> "Ashtray?" He fingered the pack, waved it like a red flag.
> "Died of emphysema," I said. There was no urge to accommodate.
> "Sorry, must have missed that," he said, coughing. The secondary smoke was less an affront than the logo on the red pack. The inscription: *Per aspera ad astra*, "through hardships to the stars." F.W. lit the cigarette, crumpled the empty pack, tilted his head back and exhaled a perfect O like the mysterious woman that once graced the billboard on Jeff Davis Highway. ("Challenging Disaster," p. 114.)

The perfect circle has taken the Captain back three decades in memory to that billboard on Jeff Davis and his great excitement and anticipation, as a child, to see a glimpse of Miss *Misteriosa*.

> I had only seconds to study her face as we passed the Jeff Davis billboard on the way to Richmond; just seconds to study her rounded red-lips, blond hair and expressive eyes. I pressed hard against the window to see her inscrutable smile and perfect Os of smoke, big as a bike wheel, pumping effortlessly through white teeth. Whatever the hour, day or night, she puffed unerringly. The wonder of the smoke rings and sheer satisfaction delighted me. ("Challenging Disaster," p. 114.)

Pall Malls and Latin. What do you make of that? Even the name Pall Mall is from the Latin *palla* and *malleus* meaning ball and hammer (Thompson has F.W. dissertate the word for him: "Pall Mall," he said, posing like Edward R. Murrow. "Taken from a 17th Century English game with a ball, *palla* and hammer, *malleus*.").

The Latin signifiers on Pall Malls seem to be friendly for the pending Challenger launch, but, as we will discover, are *ignis fatuus*:

> On the same pack: *In hoc signs vinces*, "In this sign you will conquer." I looked up the meaning during Miss Doan's Latin class. On my way to lunch, I spied her sitting in the teachers' lounge, smoke purling from a cancer stick. She fell asleep in bed and burned up. I figured she'd taken "to the stars" literally. Then, too, her morning breath smelled of bourbon. ("Challenging Disaster," p. 115.)

Even his mother. When he sins against the light, like stealing a carton of her cigarettes, or staying home from school to watch John Glenn in his Mercury spacecraft circle the earth three times, she gives him kudos for honesty for he had learned that she always knew when he was lying, but she quotes him biblical text then whips the backs of his hands with a thin belt:

> "If the eye offends you pluck it out, if the hand causes you to sin, cut it off," she said sternly, hands trembling from withdrawal as she lit a cigarette and took a deep pulls. The thing was, I wanted to save her the pain. I was willing to endure hardships so she wouldn't go to the stars. But nicotine, it turns out, was as addictive as heroin, and she never broke its grip. ("Challenging Disaster," p. 115.)

The Captain knew of what he spoke when he defined addiction (*cf.* "Color me Red"; " . . . tantamount to a dry alcoholic watching a beer commercial. Two words, Special Forces, threatened to pierce a carefully constructed facade of normalcy . . ." p. 93). One day the child Captain passes the billboard where the smoking, hot blond had always been. She was gone—the sign torn down and hauled away.

> "Where is she?" I asked.

I searched my mother's face for an explanation as she fished for the last cigarette in her pack and lit up. She tilted her head back and blew an O, for the first time. But her head wasn't poised at that perfect angle. Her lips were neither round nor red, hair wasn't quaffed but eyes were wide with desperation. As she exhaled that O I recognized the gaiety of my billboard blond had been replaced by nothing more than a tawdry habit. The physical contentment on my mother's face bore sad resemblance to despair. The mysterious Os were nothing more than empty lies, fueled by addiction. But then again we all have addictions, at once masking and exposing our tolerance for pain. ("Challenging Disaster," p. 121.)

We should all heed Kurt Vonnegut when it comes to this tubular circle maker. He once said that "smoking was a classy way to commit suicide." In the Preface to his book, *Welcome to the Monkey House*, he embroidered it:

And one time a pretty girl came up to me at a cocktail party, and she asked me, "What are you doing these days?" "I am committing suicide by cigarette," I replied. She thought that was reasonably funny. I didn't. I thought it was hideous that I should scorn life that much, sucking away on cancer sticks. My brand is Pall Mall. The authentic suicides ask for Pall Malls. The dilettantes ask for Pell Mells.[57]

Kurt Vonnegut calls them Pall Malls. H.W. called them Pall Malls. Miss Doan called them Pall Malls. Mother called them Pall Malls. Pall Malls and the perfect Os generated from these Latinate cigarettes lead us inevitably to the tragic O.

The sixth circle(s): Orbiters, Oort Constants, Ellison Onizuka and O-Rings. From Rocket Man, who would have been better served with Oort's Constants on his last journey to the sun, to astronauts from Alan Shepard, to Ellison Onizuka, to the orbiter Challenger and its frozen O-rings. Trains and boats and planes. For some reason the melody of that 1960's hit sounded for me when I read this story, even though the reference is so muted, and immaterial, but there is mention of a Lionel train, Mark-IV SOC boats, C-130 Blackbirds, UH-1D helicopters, and the beautiful, but doomed, Challenger.

In the course of the morning events, the Challenger had three delays, the first when during the night a stiff north wind blew across the external tanks and an eye wash fountain, left on, covered the solid rocket boosters with a sheet of ice. A notice scrolled across the Captain's screen, FLIGHT DELAYED. The second occurred just before F.W. unAssed his pale-green Pallas Citroen in front of Farmer's Bank and the third as F.W. begins his farewell monologue:

> SHUTTLE DELAY scrolled across the TV. Smoke venter from the tanks. F.W. leaned forward and squinted at the small screen.
> "Always wanted to do that," he said. "I'm a pilot, you know."
> "Never too late for a new career."
> "It's a tricky business," F.W. said, "Like any business."
> "It doesn't look good." I drummed my fingers. ("Challenging Disaster," p. 116.)

If the Captain had only known. He could have said to F.W., "Hey, Sky Pilot! I wish you were sitting in that cockpit right now."

Between F.W. 's exit from his office and the launch of the Challenger there is a brief interlude (a dish best served cold). The Captain, in a moment of fitful anger, and weakness, takes a small revenge.[58] Seeing F.W.'s car parked below in a NO PARKING/BUSES ONLY/TOW ZONE, he dialed the Captain of the Police Department ("one of the perks of living in a small town; breakfast with the police chief at Kiwanis was one of them.").

> "Morning captain," I said. "Hell of a blow last night." We bantered
> "Someone left their car out front last night. Looks like it's been damaged. Could you send a wrecker and have it towed? Thanks." ("Challenging Disaster," p. 119.)

A half-hour later a tow truck showed, hydraulics hissed, a bar lifted the pale-green Pallas Citroen. Old Cyclops, slippin and slidin from the Dixie, is screaming, "That's my car!"

"Well it's a tow zone," said the driver. "Besides, you can't drive it with a block through the window."
"What the hell?"
"Can't you read? NO PARKING/TOW ZONE?"
"This is my office," he said. "MINE!" My brokers, my rugs, my furniture, MINE!" ("Challenging Disaster," p. 119.)

F.W. cried out with West End credulity as the tow driver told him he could ride to the city impound and pay the charge. "Then I'll haul it wherever you want." F.W. looks up to see the Captain gazing down at him from his second floor window and screams "I don't know how, but I know you had something to do with this." The Captain opens the window and gives him a middle-finger salute, *digitus impudicus*, as the tow truck turned the corner and was gone. As he is closing the window, the TV programming cuts away to the launch pad at Cape Canaveral.

I turned up the sound, " . . . three, two, one zero." Engines ignited, a torrent of smoke and flame washed over the pad, boosters firing, hold down bolts exploded. "We have *lift off!*" The Challenger's silver wings lifted majestically like a home sick angel. I cranked the sound all the way up to hear that special crackling STS-1 engine; 418,000 pounds of thrust. It sent a bolt up my spine, same as when I was a kid. "You are a go at throttle up," a TV voice said. "Roger, go at throttle up," shuttle commander, Dick Scobee said. ("Challenging Disaster," p. 120.)

About 72 seconds into the flight a voice from the shuttle said, "Uh Oh." The kind of "Uh Oh"'a doctor says in the middle of heart surgery. The kind of "Uh Oh" a paratrooper says when no parachute appears. The kind of "Uh Oh" nobody ever wants to hear when it is followed by a massive ball of detonation, fire, smoke and rocket parts corkscrewing across the sky.

The solid boosters collapsed, tore loose from the shuttle and painted a double helix across the blue sky. The shuttle wings sheered off as the crew cabin reached 65,000 feet, lost momentum and fell fluttering like Icarus into the sea. All that was left were Os hanging listless in the cold blue sky. ("Challenging Disaster," p. 120-121.)

The Captain experienced a roller coaster ride of emotions in the seconds after the disaster. One minute on top of the world, the next on the bottom of the ocean. The large drifting, white Os hanging in the sky like markers, took him back to his billboard on Jeff Davis Highway, his mother, addiction and death. No doubt in a daze from the events of the last two hours, he yells "SWEET JESUS!" punches a nearby keyboard, reopens his window and throws his TV onto Bank Street ("Glass shattered, fractals rippled; knobs and nozzles skipped like rocks across a pond. Plastic ribs, circuitry and sad remnants splintered.").

Having replicated the last flight of the Challenger, he locks his office for the last time and walks to the Dixie Diner huddled against an ill-wind and takes a seat in his favorite booth. Rotisserie dogs spin in perpetual motion and the Lionel circles the room and emits small Os in a bizarre replay of the Challenger's last SOS.

The Captain would have looked at his watch, if he had one, to orient himself, for the seventh circle(s) is time. What about the sweep of the Hare-minute hand around the clock-face, and the Tortoise-hour hand? There is a measured duration in which the tropes, extensions, ellipses and compressions are recorded in "Challenging Disaster." It is a window stretching from 8:00 a.m. Tuesday morning of January 28, 1986, until noon; breakfast to lunch. From the moment the astronauts begin their ascent to the catwalk surrounding the shuttle until the 73 second disaster beginning at 11:38 a.m. that morning, only four hours have elapsed, but it feels like a lifetime. A little after 8 a.m. the Captain speaks to the waitress, Brea, serving him and singing "Rocket Man" to him:

"Got the time?" I asked.

"You got the money honey, I got the time," she said.

"Where's your watch? An impo-tent man like you needs a watch."

"Haven't worn jewelry since Vietnam."

"*Til touchdown brings me round again to find,*" she sang.

"No weddin' ring neither." She hoisted a Heinz ketchup bottle and sang into the mic,

"*I'm not the man they think I am at home.*"

"Who is?"

"*Rocket Ma-aaan.*" She bent forward in a crouch. "*I miss the earth so much I miss my wyyyiiife.*" She glanced at her Wonder Woman watch, "Zero hour, eight a.m." ("Challenging Disaster," p.p. 105-106.)

For the next four hours the Captain hops in and out of time over a period of 30 years. Speaking of Kurt Vonnegut—except for not visiting *Schlachthof Fünf* and the fire-bombing of Dresden—the Captain does as much time traveling in his four hours as Vonnegut does in *Slaughterhouse-Five, or, The Children's Crusade: A Duty-Dance with Death.* War and its hang overs. For Vonnegut, it was FUCKING World War II. For our Captain, FUCKING Vietnam.

Except for the television's announcement of shuttle delays during the morning, there is no time reference until the Challenger explodes, and as history has recorded, it did so because of the failure of the two redundant O-ring seals in a joint in the Space Shuttle's right solid rocket booster (SRB) frozen in a time period encompassing over-night and it did so at 11:39 a.m. EST (16:39 UTC).

The record-low temperatures of the launch reduced the elasticity of the rubber O-rings, reducing their ability to seal the joints. The broken seals caused a breach into the joint shortly after liftoff, which allowed pressurized gas from within the SRB to leak and burn through the wall to the adjacent external fuel tank. This led to the separation of the right-hand SRB's aft attachment, which caused it to crash into the external tank, which caused a structural failure of the external tank and an explosion. Following the explosion, the orbiter, which included the crew compartment, was broken up by aerodynamic forces.[59]

How does the Captain end this morning dive into these circles of disaster? Like he began it. Sitting at his favorite booth in the Dixie Diner while the Lionel train made its imaginary journey blowing its whistle for its imaginary travelers, and auguring the future with its perfect Os. But in this case, the descent seems to promise an ascent.

I removed the training schedule from my brief case. MUTA-6 three-day flyaway; Key West, scuba, scout swim, night infil techniques and shots at Papa Joe's until the crack of dawn. *Per aspera ad astra*. ("Challenging Disaster," p. 122.)

FINALLY! A disambiguation of this Latin phrase. It is used like it should be and the truth is that he most likely used Pall Malls as the device to introduce the phrase because his love of Robert Graves and his retelling of Virgil's *Aeneid* in *The Golden Fleece* (see Introduction, page 6) would have required him to use the phrase as Virgil (and Graves) did *"sic itur ad astra"* ("thus one journeys to the stars"). A phrase entirely befitting of the circle of the Challenger and its brave argonauts, but not so much fitted to the other circles of this story, unless deferrable to a pack of cancer sticks. For Thompson, and his Avatar, grief and regret are occurrences along the Ho Chi Minh Trail of life, and as in Vietnam, must be faced, survived and repressed. Key West. Night Infils. Shots till 6 a.m. at Papa Joe's. These are simply burdens that must be borne, and remembered. *PER ASPERA AD ASTRA!*

---

[55] Thompson references in "Black Hand," in one of his circles in that story ("I looked at Chen with that what-the-fuck look and gave over to muscle memory unsure of where I'd hit, Laos or Narnia.").

[56] Ray Bradbury, "The Rocket Man" is a short story in *The Illustrated Man,* Simon & Schuster Paperbacks: New York, 1981. p. 98.

[57] Kurt Vonnegut, *Welcome to the Monkey House*, New York: Delacorte Press, 1968, p. 4.

[58] Albert Einstein, "Weak people get revenge, strong people forgive, and intelligent people ignore".

[59] Rogers, William P.; Armstrong, Neil A.: Acheson, David C.; Covert, Eugene E.; Feynman, Richard P.; Hotz, Robert B.; Kutyna, Donald J.; Ride, Sallly K.; Rummel, Robert W.; Sutter, Joseph F.; Walker, Arthur B.C.; Wheelon, Albert D.; Yeager, Charles E., (June 6, 1986). "Report of the Presidential Commission on the Space Shuttle Challenger Accident" (PDF).

BLACK HAND

HUES *of* GREEN

"There is no such thing as a disembodied mind. The mind is implanted in the brain, and the brain is implanted in the body."

—Antonio Damasio, *Looking for Spinoza*

Anamnesis. You will now listen to my voice. My voice will help you and guide you from the open door of this UH-1D Huey, 1200 AGL, in a frigid wind that is not ordered by nature for military parachute jumping. Every time you hear my voice, with every word and every number, you will enter a still deeper layer—hallucinating, but receptive. I shall now count from one to ten. On the count of TEN, you will awaken from one bad dream and enter another. I say: ONE. And as you focus your attention entirely on my voice, you will jump with your MC1-1 parachute at 1200 feet above Fort Pickett airfield, one-hundred pounds of gear between your legs on a drop line. TWO. Your hands and your fingers, in black gloves, are getting colder and heavier. THREE. You feel a deep, hard, thump, thump, thump vibrate through the cold metal floor of your helicopter. FOUR. You are frozen with fear and curiosity as you float outside the chopper, peer into its cabin beneath a quiet blur of blades and see yourself sitting, with long legs out the door, rucksack balanced on shins, black gloves stuffed in your parachute harness, edged forward, touching the knife in your boot. FIVE. The beige ground of Southside Virginia has transformed to jungle green, the sky is now cobalt blue, the Annamese Mountains appear below, a vast expanse of triple canopy jungle, lush and forbidding. On SIX, I want you to go deeper. I say: SIX. You are again sitting in the open door of a UH-1D flying over Co Roc

Mountain. An immense sheer of landmark Laotian rock rises just beyond the Vietnam border as distinct and treacherous as the Matterhorn while you turn south and drop rapidly into the Ashau Valley on final approach. SEVEN. You sit beside Chen, Lau and Troung, your Nung counterparts, who are tightly wound and ready to spring. EIGHT. A baby-faced crew chief yells "GO!" but you hesitate and again, "GOOOO!" with a slash of his hand on your back and you jump, but there is no parachute and you are floating to the ground, oddly kneeling, already trying to send an encrypted message via the KY-38 handset with a gray-winged Cessna, 0-2 Skymaster circling above you like a hawk in updrafts and eddies. On every breath you take, you go deeper. NINE. You hear the ripple of small arms fire snapping through the leaves as Lau points with three fingers to enemy soldiers flanking you. You say *"Motherfucker!"* grab the handset and transmit in the open, *"Prairie Fire!"* A B-40 rocket explodes above you and you are running madly, and initiate a mad minute, each man firing a clip on full automatic at an unseen, closing enemy. On the mental count of TEN, you will be over Fort Pickett, looking up to follow your suspension lines to the skirt of your parachute. You are riding an arctic wind hard toward three concrete runways. Be there at TEN. I say: TEN.

It is no wonder Thompson opens "Black Hand" waiting to jump from a UH-1D Huey with these lines: "The cold brown earth blended with budding trees and spring wheat on this, the cruelest day of the year." It is another April and another challenging disaster, and what better way to preface it than with *The Waste Land?*

> *April is the cruelest month, breeding*
> *Lilacs out of the dead land, mixing*
> *Memory and desire, stirring*
> *Dull roots with spring rain.*[60]

Somewhere in the recent future, as "Challenging Disaster" concludes, the Captain is on a MUTA-6 (Multiple Unit Training Assembly) in Key West leaping from Mark-IV SOC boats into the crystal-clear waters of a shark-infested Caribbean, scuba diving for spiny lobster and doing shots at Papa Joe's until the crack of dawn. But as "Black Hand" opens, he is in the past on a MUTA-5 in Blackstone, Virginia, awaiting a parachute jump with his intrepid A Detachment and it is April, the cruelest day of the cruelest month. It appears to be Arctic training in a mission even more wretched than the Deerfield jump the previous April into the Valley of the DAMNED. But members of ODA 212 had suffered other cruel days on the DZ of Fort Pickett. A year before Thompson arrived to take over 212, both the Sergeant Major of 11th Group and the Sergeant Major Jump Master of Deerfield, Virginia, were severely injured on another windy day, one fracturing his back, the other snapping a femur and nearly bleeding to death. And it is a lousy day to jump equipment, a lousy day to be sitting in a frost-bitten UH-1D Huey, and a lousy day to be jumping into a Drop Zone (DZ) that was mostly concrete runways, and what wasn't concrete, was probably frozen harder than concrete. A frigid wind was blowing up to 20 knots across the DZ, and, Oh! Yes! The Captain says, "Tree landings were always in play on windy days." It is a different year, but another adrenalin-adventure fix. It augurs to be a bad day in Blackstone.

Toward the conclusion of "Black Hand," in Portsmouth Naval Hospital, the Captain is told that he has a concussion and a shattered wrist. "We need your anamnesis," the doctor-surgeon says to him. The Captain answers, "I don't remember?" (but he has remembered his sense of humor). The doctor explains he is not talking about amnesia: "Anamnesis is your medical history."

Anamnesis. VOILA! The Captain provides the key to this story about remembering. What is Anamnesis? It has several meanings, one of which, as the doctor said, is a personal medical history, but the real meaning of this word in "Black Hand" is a recalling to mind, or reminiscence. Anamnesis is often used as a narrative technique in fiction and poetry as well as in memoirs and autobiographies, perhaps most famously in Marcel Proust's *rappeler* brought on by the taste of a madeleine cake, or cookie, in *Swann's Way*, the first volume of *Remembrance of Things Past*, but it isn't Proust Thompson is grasping at in "Black Hand."

It is a combination of memory considerations—experiential, psychological and neurological—that Thompson renders in the scaffolding of this story and they are not accidental, random, or undirected. In France, a *madeleine de Proust* is a common expression referring to a smell, taste or sound which dredges up a long-lost memory. The truth of Proust's sensory-memory phenomena is that you never know where you may find it. The transformative power of one person's cookie is another person's gas/diesel mixture in helicopter fuel; a birdsong in *Combray*, can become the thump, thump, thump of a two-bladed semi-rigid, seesaw-bonded, all metal main rotor on an assault helicopter. These transformational experiences occur, as C.J. Jung records it in *Psychology and Western Religion*, because "It is not that something different is seen, but that one sees differently. It is as though the spatial act of seeing was changed by a new dimension."

Anamnesis. Take what we know about the Captain and his traumatic military experiences, and pair it with another traumatic injury in a military setting, and you should witness intense sensory and visual memories of war events which are often accompanied by extreme physiological and psychological distress, hallucination, feelings of emotional numbing, body loss, or more accurately body alienation, during which there is no physiological arousal. Sound like a bunch of medical psycho-babble? It's not. This "new dimension" may occur spontaneously, or can be triggered by a range of real and symbolic stimuli. You would guess that we are quoting from the intended definition of Anamnesis ("medical records") here, but on the mental count of ten, you will be over Fort Pickett, looking up to follow your suspension lines to the skirt of your parachute. You are riding an arctic wind hard toward three concrete runways. Be there at ten. I say: TEN.

The initial transport of Thompson's Captain is a hallucination:

> The visceral thwack of rotors, pitch and yaw, metallic judder, activated a kind of molten slag that shot up my spine. Ore from a smelting ladle poured into my brainpan and my sight whited out. I stared, frozen with fear and curiosity as I floated outside the chopper; peered into its cabin, disembodied and digitized, monochromatic, beneath a quiet blur of blades. I watched a jumper sitting with his long legs out the door, rucksack balanced on shins, as he stuffed black gloves into his parachute harness, edged forward and touched his boot knife. The jumpmaster struck his helmet and said "Gooo!" Swept away, he fell endlessly, back in time. ("Black Hand," p. 137.)

On the mental count of ten, you will find yourself in the year, 1969. I say: TEN. It is 1969, and the Captain is back in Vietnam, or to be more correct, over Laos, with seven other members of his Recon Team trying to dismount a helicopter in the middle of an enemy infested, triple canopy jungle with ordnance snapping and singing like an angry nest of wasps, and little chance for escape. The hallucination allows the Captain and his crew to vaguely, magically, reach the ground, whether by a parachute jump that started his monthly reservist fix, or a depot delivery by an earlier version of a UH 1-D Huey. The event the Captain now finds himself imagining turns out to be a *"Prairie Fire!"* What is a *Prairie Fire?* It is a GET ME THE FUCK OUT OF HERE occasion that is in SOG, allegedly, a contingency plan, but for the Captain and his men, a Catch-22.

> The heavy contact and my declaration meant that Covey [USAF grey-winged Cessna air support circling above Recon Teams to provide artillery calls, bomb runs, and escape plans, hence *Prairie Fire*] had to pull us out, now! Covey's voice filtered through the triple canopy jungle into my ear. "Break contact and

continue the mission." What the fuck? Unbeknownst to me, someone had added a codicil to what turned out to be my revocable trust. ("Black Hand," pp. 129-130.)

Trust meant that when the Captain said "We are encircled and threatened with annihilation," the deadly game of hide and seek was over. The support forces of SOG would unquestionably come and get their boys out. Once SOG found the enemy, or the enemy found SOG, they were finished with the mission, FINI. How do you break contact and continue a mission when B-40 rockets are exploding around you, claymores are cranking, toe-poppers are popping, and nothing but full-automatic fire is buzzing the length and breadth of hell's little acre? But Thompson explains that some fine-print in these warrior's sacrificial contract now hid a secret change. "But somehow the new number crunching, fast-tracked West Point leg commander, had altered our contract, added a codicil":

> *"The aforementioned agreement under paragraph 4 page 31 of a SOG, Emergency Extraction, hereafter known as "Prairie Fire" shall be subject of the sole discretion of commander, who may otherwise countermand said team leader, hereafter, "One Zero," and order him to "Break contact and continue the mission" regardless of intervening actions or consequences. The One Zero shall hold harmless the "commander" for any death, dismemberment or wounding suffered by any team member, to include but not limited to capture." ("Black Hand," p. 136.)*

Hence the Catch-22. If you are surrounded and call *"Prairie Fire,"* to escape annihilation, you most probably will be ordered to stay and be annihilated. This bureaucrat in camouflage, Lieutenant Colonel James Donohue, was later run out of the Army after an IG investigation found that he'd lied about certain valorous medals (Distinguished Service Cross, Distinguished Flying Cross, and others) that he'd written up and submitted for himself, by himself, that were the forerunner to the term, "Stolen Valor." And the specter of that "Warrior Contract" has been raised in "Black Hand" by what appeared to be a routine and safe Special Forces Reserve weekend jaunt in the park, but PTSD don't work that way, especially when it is abetted by a severe injury. Instead, the Captain floats the events of that "*Prairie Fire*" in Laos in and out of the routine MUTA-5 requirements of his A-Team's *practicum* in southern Virginia 13 years later (was that unlucky number purposive?), at first as a sensory hallucination brought on by Proust's biscuit, then as full-blown symptoms of accompanying neurological phenomena that threaten to tip him over the edge.

In the central part of this medical study, the Captain returns to consciousness as he inspects his suspension lines to the skirt of his parachute, pulls toggles, quick release straps and begins a wind-blown plummet into the concrete of runway One, or is it runway Two? Now a participatory dialogue takes place between the reality of his Reserve jump and the specter of his Laos Recon Team insert 13 years earlier. This dialogue outlines the interposition of traumatic memory with the new traumatic injury that awaits him on the tarmac. This is what the Anamnesis provides us with.

In the Laotian reconnaissance the Nung tribesman counterpart, Chen, has lost a hand in the ensuing conflagration, as others have lost body parts, or have died.[61] As the Captain "bounced along the runway; a manikin flung from a speeding pickup," and his arm slammed into "a concretized world," he heard the "sound of one hand smashing."

> I glanced down where my right hand should be, but something bent and bloated extended at a curious angle. A hideous lump of pretzel dough flopped along side, useless as Chen's severed hand. ("Black Hand," p. 132.)

Intermingled in the military ripostes tossed back and forth between the Captain and members of his team, or ground crew, conversation slides to actors in the Laotian reconnaissance then back to the drill at Fort Pickett, then back to Laos . . . . He is ensconced in commands to his former SOG team Sergeant Elder ("Maybe I should wait for Elder. I swatted blue gnats and ignored the church bells."), conversations with his Reserve Company medic, SFC Courtney (Pug), over the owner of his own maimed hand (he continually insists it belongs to his Nung Striker, Chen, but more of that symptomatology later) and other bystanders past and present. SFC Courtney answers his insistence on finding Sergeant Elder:

> "Newly assigned to the company? Pug asked. He wrapped the pusillanimous pile with chicken wire and left it resting on my stomach. "It must be Chen's," I said. Elder had tied off the stump and got the IV going as the team laid down a heavy base of fire. I reloaded a clip, spotted his hand and picked it up. It felt warm as a three-pound glove. The fingers curled into a fist and I dropped it. I cursed and stowed it in my ruck. Maybe they could sew it back on. ("Black Hand," p. 135.)

Even in the medical evacuation helicopter to Portsmouth Naval Hospital, a 30 minute flight away, the roar of the engines, the sweet smell of avgas and the thump of the rotors keep sending him back to Laos, to the Ashau Valley, to the "Prairie Fire." He dwells with this twilight incubus until he arrives at Portsmouth Naval.

> The roar of 20mm cannons deafened us; shredding all vegetation and life forms into mulch. Next came 250 pounders, explosions erupting like Vesuvius as the A-1Es worked the ridgeline and finally the *coup de grace*; napalm erupting into a fiery Armageddon. The smell of burnt hair and charred bone was choking. I coughed and opened my eyes. ("Black Hand," p. 137.)

On the count of ten, you may cough and open your eyes. I say TEN. The Captain has been delivered and rides on a gurney with rattling wheels between swooshing and swinging doors. The surgeon, a Major Powell, informs him he is at the Portsmouth Naval Hospital and that "You've got a concussion and a shattered wrist."

Anamnesis. What the surgeon doesn't tell the Captain, Thompson answers for himself in this book, and this story. From the separation of mind from body as he exits from the UH 1-D

Huey, to the detachment of body from mind (the loss of his right hand that, while still attached to him, doesn't belong to him), Thompson diagrams some of the medical maladies that have been more and more on the minds of neurologists and writers in the last 20 years, specifically, Oliver Sacks,[62] Antonio Damasio[63] and Bessel van der Kolk.[64] Their writings (and research) have been busily concerned with the mind/body experience in injury, disease and normalcy. That is, concerned with the human response to trauma and terms such as proprioception, scotoma, Anton's Syndrome, agnosia, primary consciousness, higher consciousness and alienation (both body and mind). And all of these terms inform "Black Hand," as surely as Special Forces Reserve, MACV-SOG, and the broken body of our protagonist.

When the Captain finally looks down at his mangled hand he sees "A hideous lump of pretzel dough flopped along side, useless as Chen's severed hand." This is not a random impression but one lifted directly from Oliver Sacks' *A Leg To Stand On* where Sacks describes falling-down-a-mountain accident caused by an encounter with a massive, white bull on a hike over-looking Hardanger Fjord in Norway. Sacks' leg, horribly mangled after the fall, is no longer his leg. In looking at it and touching it, "he finds a doughy pulp" where his left leg should have been and he disowns it and can no longer imagine, or recall, how to move it. *A Leg to Stand On* is a medical memoir recording Sacks' alienation from his own left leg in which he concerns himself with terms such as proprioception, scotoma, Anton's Syndrome, agnosia, primary consciousness, higher consciousness and alienation (both body and mind). To repeat, all of these terms inform "Black Hand," as surely as Special Forces Reserve, MACV-SOG, and the broken body of our protagonist.

The Captain, too, met his white bull on a concrete runway in Blackstone, but in direct contradiction of his solicitous concern for Chen's severed hand ("I cursed and stowed it in my ruck. Maybe they could sew it back on."), the Captain disowns his own, and would abandon it, if he could. Of course, this is in total agreement with Sacks who also denied his leg thrice. Thompson is addressing proprioception here, a sixth sense, for lack of a better term, by which the body possesses itself and knows and ceaselessly confirms itself, and what happens when it is gone. This is the most concerning of Sacks' preoccupations with his autobiographical, neurological study of his own travail with proprioception, scotoma, agnosia and alienation after he was left with the impression that he didn't have *A Leg To Stand On*. Sacks even delves into brain lesion, or injury, phenomena like Anton's Syndrome where a perfectly healthy limb, analogous to a perfectly injured limb, is discerned as "not me." In both these cases, says Sacks, a vital part of the organic foundation of reality seems to have gone missing. And so it goes for Thompson's Captain in "Black Hand." In his case, he is missing his hand, but joined with his Laotian hallucination, has found a victim for it.

- "I glanced down where my right hand should be, but something bent and bloated extended at a curious angle. A hideous lump of pretzel dough flopped along side, useless as Chen's severed hand."

- "Something near the end of his arm twisted backwards; spoiled hamburger, bloated and black. It had no doubt, fallen out of my busted rucksack."

- "He'd police up that busted hand and find its owner."

- "Gainfully employed as a detective between drills, I was confident Pug would find the owner of that hand."

- "I'm going to splint your hand." I looked down. "That's not mine. Must be Chen's," I flashed back.

- He wrapped the pusillanimous pile with chicken wire and left it resting on my stomach. "It must be Chen's," I said.

- "Maybe they'd tried to sew that hideous thing on my arm while I was out."

- "Where'd that come from?" I asked. They didn't seem to know what the hell was going on with the hand or with my flitting back and forth in time—and I couldn't tell them.

- "We'll stick your fingers in those clamps." "How many times I got to tell you? That's not mine."

- "That's one bad ass hand." "A mind of its own," I said, "Find the owner. He should be held responsible."

- The brazen Owl maintained his charade, kept the gnarly hand, wrist and forearm hanging nearby. I wanted nothing to do with it.

- "Just find Chen. They got to be working on him around here somewhere." ("Black Hand," pp. 132-142)

Thompson's study in "Black Hand" is a cinematic, detemporalized incoherence starting with an ethereal view from a helicopter, then a plunge into hallucination, then a loss of self, and then a delivery from hallucination. Where the initial transport of "Black Hand" is hallucination, the final transport is also hallucination. The Captain said, as he lay busted on a runway, "Lying there I tried to figure how I'd zipped through time, recursive, outside looking in or vice versa, or was this even my body?" Truer words were never spoke. "The smooth glow of halos, lux luminaries circled and elevated me as I floated in a white beam of light." "Confused, but convinced that time slid back and forth as easy as the zipper on my fly," the Captain comes to terms with time, his "missing hand" and Chen.

I looked at the hand and felt a sucking sensation, snatched backwards through a rushing wind. I struggled to focus, looked down fifty feet off the jungle floor in my Swiss Seat, D ring thread thru a handhold. Spinning, I gripped the nylon rope as the helicopter drug me through the thick tangle of vines ripping at me, limbs slapping my face. I caught my last fleeting glimpse of Chen propped against a tree, empty albumin bag, IV tube, holding his bloody stump, glassy-eyed and forever dead. ("Black Hand," p. 142)

As a finale, a doctor in the form of an Owl sums up what the H-E-double hockey sticks is wrong with him. "Dark round eyes magnified by his thick glasses; the owl blinked." Dr. Powell, aka Dr. Owl, decrypts the Captain's problem, with, or without his Anamnesis, as follows:

- Inspecting the Captain's mangled hand, prodding the swollen skin, black as a banana, he suddenly focused on metacarpal lumps on the Captain's ring and middle fingers. Realizing they were old injuries, rather than part and parcel of the new hand impact, he asks the Captain how he broke them. "Boxer?" And the Captain was. Dr. Owl says, "X-rays don't lie."

- Studying the new full-blown chest X-ray, he pointed to a white line that extended down the arm from the Captain's shoulder, then traced a thick, fibrous scar snaking from shoulder cap to elbow joint. "Tear of the mid-substance biceps *branchilii* muscle belly."

- Dr. Owl then shifted his gaze to the white phalanx of finger bones spread across the black X-ray. You've got a flexion fracture of the radius," he said. "We've got work to do." Pointing to the Captain's wrist, he said "All of this bone is gone." pointing to white specks that blotted out the otherwise black X-ray and squeezing the pasty dough where the wrist used to be, he said, "This is powdered bone."

- In preparing the hand for surgery, prepping steel rods, metallic clips, and Chinese handcuffs, Dr. Owl finds a new artifact. "Interesting," he said. He traced scars on the back of the hand. "Looks like they removed muscle for a flexor tendon repair?" The Captain answers, "That is one evil hand." Dr. Owl: "How'd that happen?" Captain: "How the hell should I know. Maybe the damn thing was holding a glass when it decided to punch somebody in the face." Dr. Owl: "That's one bad ass hand."

- As far as the Captain's anamnesis, Dr. Owl said, "Your body keeps the score." The Captain thinks that if what Dr. Owl said was true, that hand, his hand was his scoreboard. "'Talk to the hand,' Owl said. He extended his palm to my face. 'Universal language," Owl said, 'We're hard-wired for pain.'"

- "And the scoreboard?" the Captain asks. "People get the message when they've had enough pain," Owl said. "Men of your caliber have an inordinate capacity for self-denial. Some are just numb. You're a combination of both." ("Black Hand," pp. 138-143.)

What Dr. Owl is referring to, the Captain elucidated earlier after realizing his injury and pain: "An old trick enabled me to at once embrace and ignore pain. In this line of work discipline was essential and denial, *de rigueur*." In Dr. Owl's system review, he has discovered a history of musculoskeletal wounds the Captain has suffered over many years and, with his observation of the Captain's latest wound and behavior, he realizes that he is observing a man of highest caliber who has an "inordinate capacity for self-denial," one who has walked on the precipice far too many times, fell off, but pulled himself back up. He has survived but not, as Dr. Owl recognizes, intact. His body has kept the score and has been reminding him constantly now for a decade, or more, what that score is. When Sacks and van der Kolk use the term scotoma, they are speaking necessarily of the medical failure to recognize traits, or disabilities in the "self" that are obvious to others. At the highest abstraction level are intellectual scotomas, in which a person cannot perceive distortions in their worldview that are obvious to others. Sacks terms these scotomas, alienation. Thompson describes his missing hand as a spatial neglect in his body schema where the mind does not conceive of the hand as self, therefore his continuous attempts to give the hand to someone else, even a cadaverous one—in this case to the ghost of a soldier. What Thompson does, eerily, is consign his own hand in the space of a day in southwest Virginia to a Nung Stryker, brave and valiant, who thirteen years before was propped against a Nipa Palm with an empty albumin bag and IV tube, holding his bloody stump, glassy-eyed and forever dead.

After his time travel on this particular Reserve weekend, "back and forth as easy as the zipper on my fly," the Captain summates:

> Maybe I'd lugged the pain of Vietnam around all these years, heavy and useless as that KY-38 [the SOG rescue radio]. I'd ignored the messages, cryptic or chronic; dreams and night sweats from the underground. It was as if I'd ignored an insurgency, deep within. Everything about me, even my code of conduct, was broke. ("Black Hand," p. 143.)

In 2007 Oliver Sacks wrote a book addressing a wide array of psychological and physiological ailments and the connections to music and its effects on the brain (the book is entitled *Musicophilia: Tales of Music and the Brain).* He took the poet, W.H. Auden, who he had befriended as a young man, to one of his therapy sessions. Auden was amazed at what he saw and quoted to Sacks an aphorism of the German poet Novalis, something to the effect of "Every disease is a musical problem. Every cure is a musical solution." Sacks found that music could "center" his patients which also summarized his credo—to find and evoke "a living personal center, an 'I,' amid the debris of neurological devastation."[65]

In Maxine Hong Kingston's *The Fifth Book of* Peace, she records Larry Heinemann speaking at one of her writing workshops. He warns,

> "When you write the pain of war, you will relive it. You're going to live through the pain again. You do relive the war, the emotions, the smells. But this time, you have a method for handling it—writing. You can control it, put it down, pick it up. Writing is a craft of the hand."[66]

Thompson has his autobiographical Captain in "Black Hand" finally say, "But if I remembered the pain, used it sparingly, maybe that gnarly, black hand could pen a story that even I could understand." It is a reverberation of Heinemann, but a far more memorable one. And like Sacks' music to soothe the savage heart, Thompson finds his living personal center, an "I," amid the debris of his neurological devastation. To write, to return to the body, or, at the very least, to the hand in motion. On the count of TEN, you will return to your hand. I say TEN.

Anamnesis? No, first of all, a surge forward and, as the hand begins to race across the page, the feet stir, the body takes flight. ... And the eyes, the eyes especially, the eyes fix themselves on the horizon, a horizon searched for, then found, sliding far away, sinking close at hand . . . Nothing counts but the first glimmer, nothing but the light, nothing but the sun, persisting deep into the heart of the night. To write, or to run. To write in order to run. To run, and to remember. Forward, or back, what's the difference?[67]

---

[60] T.S. Eliot, *The Waste Land*, New York: Boni And Liveright, 1922.

[61] This is reminiscent of another Recon patrol member who triggered a booby trap in "Walking Point With Sergeant Rock." "An arm wedged high in a stand of bamboo, finger pointing like a washroom sign towards the crater." P. 59.

[62] Oliver Sacks, *A Leg To Stand On*, New York: Vintage Books, 1984.

[63] Antonio Damasio, *Descarte's Error: Emotions, Reason, and the Human Brain*, New York: Penguin Books, 1994.

[64] Bessel van der Kolk, *The Body Keeps the Score: Brain, Mind, and Body in the Healing of Trauma*, New York: Penguin Books, 2014.

[65] Daniel X. Freedman, "Where The Rest of Him Was," *The New York Times,* November 11, 1984, Section 7, P. 11.

[66] *The Fifth Book of Peace, Ibid,* p. 290.

[67] Assia Djebar, "Anamnesis in the Language of Writing, trnsl. Anne Donadey, with Christi Merrill, *Studies in 20th Century Literature,* University of Iowa: Vol. 23, Issue 1, 1999, p. 188.

YELLOW HORSE

"It's been ten years now since the troops came home, but until recently I had never once heard anyone admit to guilt or shame over not having gone to Vietnam—not in hundreds of conversations about the war. I find this strange; meager, I think, is the operative word."

— Christopher Buckley, "Viet Guilt"[68]

All of Thompson's short stories in *Colors of War & Peace* have been about the Vietnam War, tangentially, or directly, but "Yellow Horse" is about more than just his war. It is also about peace, and ironically, how it's never found. There are four emotional phenomena occurring after wars in the population that never served in the military, or did, but didn't serve in combat. ONE: Those who never served in the military later forge documents and war stories about valorous service. TWO: Those who protested, or avoided the war, but over time have come to regret their lack of military service. THREE: Those who served in the military and had valorous combat service, only to later forge stories about even more valorous service; and FOUR: Those who served, could have seen combat, but avoided it through administrative, or other tactics, and now regret that they never experienced combat. There is, also no doubt, a fifth category; those who served, protested, didn't serve, were heroes, were cowards, but didn't/don't give a SHIT.

It is the fourth category we are talking about here and included in this species, the apparently most honest of all of them, is a veneration now for all things military, a nostalgia for the thing that elbows were brushed with, then avoided, or given up on in youth. While these categories are generalizations, these behaviors have been documented after most wars and Thompson pivots the action, and inaction, of "Yellow Horse" around this one.

The gap between those who went to war and those who stayed behind was larger in the Vietnam War than in any other war in our history. Fifty-three million Americans came of age between the signing of the Gulf of Tonkin Resolution on August 7, 1964, and April 30, 1975, the day Saigon fell to the Communists. Of those fifty-three, eleven million served in the military; and of those eleven, fewer than three went to Indochina. That leaves forty-two million Americans who did not serve. Twenty-six million of these were women, who weren't called (though the 6,500 women who did serve were essential to the war effort). About sixteen million were men who were deferred, exempted, or disqualified or who evaded the draft. About 80 percent of the Vietnam generation did not participate in the dominant event of their time. ***About 6 percent of military-age males saw actual combat.***[69]

Corporal (CPL) Francis E. Kunkel, was assigned to F Company, 2nd Bn, 7th Cavalry Regiment, 1st Cavalry Division, as a rifleman when he was awarded the Bronze Star with Valor Device for his actions on February 15, 1951 near Konjiam-ni, Korea. He also received the Purple Heart for life-threatening wounds and was evacuated to Brook Army Medical Center, Ft. Sam Houston Texas, where he recovered for six months. The day before Kunkel helped turn back the tide of a Chinese assault on 2nd Battalion, a young rifle platoon leader named 1st Lieutenant Marinus Bruinooge in G Company, 2d Battalion, 7th Cavalry Regiment (Infantry), 1st Cavalry Division distinguished himself at Konjiam-ni by extraordinary heroism in action against the same enemy Kunkel would face the next day. With his platoon pinned down within 150 yards of its objective by intense automatic-weapons, small-arms, and mortar fire and suffering numerous casualties Bruinooge led his men forward, but was halted by a vicious barrage of fire from two machine-guns and an emplacement employing grenades.

Making a one-man assault at approximately 1800 hours, he advanced within twenty yards and was wounded, but gallantly forged on and, after lobbing a grenade into the position, closed with the enemy and killed its four occupants. Observing the nearest machine-gun was but twenty-five yards distant, he harassed the gunners with grenades and then, fearlessly rushing forward, fired his carbine full automatic into the foxhole until he was mortally wounded. His intrepid actions retarded the onslaught, enabled evacuation of the wounded, and contributed significantly to the subsequent accomplishment of the mission. (Distinguished Service Cross: General Orders No. 107, December 14, 1951)

What's the point of these interjections? Corporal Francis E. Kunkel, now deceased, was my father-in-law (Ed to me). He probably didn't have to go to that Cold War in Korea. His father, a South Beach attorney in Miami, ended a Brigadier General in the Army Judge Advocate Corps, but Francis volunteered as a raw, privileged recruit and ended horribly wounded by combat and returned home, never to mention the war again. His cohort, Marinus, never knew it but others mentioned the war for him, posthumously. Thompson opens "Yellow Horse" this way:

In 1961, Pete Starr and Terry Moore enlisted in the army during their junior year of high school. Three years younger at the time and sick of school, I imagined the adventure was like running away to Buffalo Bill's Wild West circus. Pete and Terry joined on the buddy system, finished Advanced Training and were shipped to Korea; further assigned to 2nd Battalion, 7th Cavalry, 2/7, The Ghost Battalion. Almost wiped out during the Battle of Pusan Perimeter in 1950, it withstood relentless attacks by the North Korean Army; counterattacked and broke out. ("Yellow Horse," p. 147.)

But Starr's Ghost Battalion is the 2nd Bn, 7th Cavalry a decade later, a peace-keeping force at Camp Howze in Bongilchon, South

Korea, near the Demilitarized Zone (DMZ) dividing the North from the South. This much renown and decorated unit of my father-in-law was the service unit for these high school drop-out friends of the Captain between 1963-1965. The "Yellow Horse" of the title refers to the patch of the 1st Cavalry Division (a distinctive, large, yellow patch in the shape of a shield crossed from upper left to lower right by a black line and a black horse head silhouette in the upper right quadrant), first made famous by General George Armstrong Custer, commander of the 7th Cavalry at the battle of the Little Big Horn, or as the Indian Chieftains named it, the Battle of Greasy Grass. The Captain thinks about this battle in the gulley washes, deserts and plains of southeast Montana being a precursor to a similar battle 90 years later in another plain of elephant grass, white pines and palms—LZ X-Ray. Like Custer, in this battle the 1st Bn, 7th Cavalry was surrounded and vastly outnumbered by other Indians, the North Vietnamese Army.

The battle of LZ X-Ray in the Ia Drang Valley with the 1st Bn, 7th Cavalry opposing, was the first major battle of the Vietnam War. It went down November 14-16, 1965, and the story was made famous in the 1992 publication of Lt. General Hal Moore's (the Light Colonel Battalion Commander on the ground at LZ X-Ray that November) *We Were Soldier Once . . . And Young*, and even more so when Paramount Pictures released its 120 million dollar, box-office smash by the same name in 2002 starring Mel Gibson, Madeleine Stowe, Greg Kinnear, Sam Elliot, Keri Russell, *et all of em*.

Little known, or never known by Pete Starr, his unit of service in Korea in 1962-1964, 2nd Battalion, 7th Cavalry, 1st Cavalry Division, was the unit Marinus Bruinooge died for on Valentines Day, 1951, and with whom my father-in-law suffered a lead-poisoning, post-love celebration. Nor did he probably know, regardless of the movie exalting the 1st Bn, 7th Cavalry, that his old unit was involved in the same battle the next day, November 17, 1965, and between the two, the 2nd Bn, 7th Cavalry had it by far the worst. It was the same battle the 1st Bn, 7th Cavalry had fought the previous two days, but it was about four kilometers further north as the crow flies, and while suffering the largest killed in action numbers recorded in the Vietnam War, the name, "LZ ALBANY," provided an after-action report that did not receive exaltation, nor go down in infamy. If you read the history of LZ Albany, you can see that Pete Starr would have had no chance. 155 troopers were killed on that 17th day of November, and 124 wounded. It was the single bloodiest day in the Vietnam War, ever. One can only suppose that 1st Bn, 7th Cavalry's comparably more modest (but huge, by any standard) statistics of 79 killed and 126 wounded were easier to turn into great victory than the decimation of almost two entire companies of the 2nd Bn, 7th Cavalry.

The young Pete Starr was offered two doors in Fort Benning; reenlistment, the 2nd Bn, 7th Cavalry, LZ Albany and the War or, his walking papers, an honorable discharge, and Peace. He chose the latter. "Yellow Horse," is a journal entry for Peace, which, in Thompson's hands, can become a very problematic kind of thing (for when you seek peace, you always have to deal with the "Fucking War"). While Starr was awaiting reenlistment, or discharge in 1965, Lt. Colonel Hal Moore was preparing to take the retooled 1st Battalion, in accompaniment with the 2nd Battalion of the 7th Cavalry, 1st Cavalry Division, under the command of Lt. Colonel Robert McDade, to Vietnam. The reflagging took place July 1965, two months before Pete Starr had the opportunity to reenlist, but instead was reassigned to his civilian replacement center in Petersburg, Virginia.

> In early July [1965], the Pentagon announced that the 11th Air Assault (Test) Dvision would be renamed the 1st Cavalry Division (Airmobile) and that it would take over the colors of that historic division that had distinguished itself in combat in the Korean War and in the Pacific theater in World War II—not to mention horse-cavalry skirmishes with bandits along the Mexican border in Texas and New Mexico in the early 1920s.[70]

The voice of our now retired, post-another apocalypse Captain, upon a November day dark and dreary, seven days before Veteran's Day, and eleven before the anniversary of LZ X-Ray, reads from a book that tells about the lies old men tell youth when they send them off to war.

After the French lost the Battle of Dien Bien Phu, 1954, and were kicked out of Vietnam, President Eisenhower explained why the U.S. should take up the mantle. "You have this row of dominoes set up, knock over the first one and what will happen to the last one is the certainty it will go over very quickly." Called the domino theory, Presidents Kennedy and Johnson parroted the line. ("Yellow Horse," p. 148.)

Markers tell us that we are past the Second Persian Gulf War, or the "Iraq II War," for the great warriors, G. Dubya Bush, Ricky "The Bruiser" Cheney, Donnie Rumplestiltskin, Karl "The Christian" Rove, Condoleezza RiceErroneous, and Paul D. Wolfowizard are invoked as current examples of the old examples.

Of all the U.S. Army's miscalculations, MacArthur's arrogant decision to send troops to the Yalu surpassed even Custer, that is until Iraq: Bush—Cheney & the WMD Gang. Deserters and draft dodgers, no matter what their political aspirations, shouldn't be allowed to send boys to war.

As he reads and continues to mull the war he fought in 30 years ago, a war that will not leave him alone, the Captain says,

> *As I flipped the pages faster,*
> *Harkened back to Nam's disaster,*
> *The air grew denser, perfumed from an unseen censer,*
> *Came a rapping on my door.*
> *I expected the shadow in the window*
> *To skirt through the breezeway like before."*[71]

This is a veiled invocation of Edgar Allan Poe's "The Raven." Why? Poe's poem, famous for all kinds of reasons and much imitated, is probably a symbol of the most mournful, never-ending remembrance in literature, albeit a remembrance of love lost, but the Raven can show up on your chamber door because of a mournful, never-ending remembrance of war, and this shadow of death can stay with us as we grow old, and bunkered. But the shadow also stays with those who have no need to be mournful in such never-ending remembrance, as you will see in the speech of Pete Starr in the latter half of "Yellow Horse."

I cracked open the three-inch thick oak door of what people on Reed Street call The Bunker. The walls, poured in 1946, were concrete and rebar. Summer nights they radiated like a brick oven—winter, cold as a coffin. The two-bedroom blockhouse had a small, reinforced fallout shelter, where I stashed the washer-dryer and the LuRP rations. Its Spanish facade was block and plaster. The flat tar roof, parapet with rolling arches and fighting wall resembled the Alamo and conformed to siege mentality. The block was along the front porch channelled avenues of approach but restricted fields of fire. From the living room I surveilled a T-intersection through four slim gun port windows. ("Yellow Horse," p. 149.)

It is Pete Starr rap, rap, rapping at his bunker door. A blast from the distant past, and the WHY of the visitation is the determination of Thompson's recitation in "Yellow Horse." Given the brief history of Starr's military service in the introduction, a concise capsule of the visit is rendered late in the story, but better to out with it now, than nevermore. Much of "Yellow Horse" is taken up with tracing Starr's exit from Fort Benning and the Army in 1965. From his drunken odyssey back to Virginia with fifths of Jack Daniels and cases of beer "iced down, cooler wedged behind the bucket seat of my red GTO convertible" playing a new game of poker, wherein the discharged throws clothing out the suicide window of his speeding

GTO, after a couple of beers, or shots, an item of his uniform or equipment from his B-4 bag, until he arrives naked in a snow storm at the family home.

Recounted at times by Pete himself, this mythopoetic journey of discharge poker continues the 617 miles, or nine hours, from Columbus, Georgia to Chesterfield, VA. He tells the Captain that "A good NCO always has a contingency plan." The Captain replies, "Drunk or super drunk." And so Pete arrived home, safe, maybe not so sound, to stand "bone ass naked except for dog tags and pistol belt around [his] waist" on the doorstep where his British father, in full British Home Guard uniform with corporal stripes, greets and salutes him. Starr's major impression, as he recalls this data years later, was pride at his father's recognition of him, and "That my father was wearing corporal stripes gave me immense satisfaction and arousal, since I'd risen to the rank of buck sergeant."

When Pete brings his pain and guilt to the chamber door of the Captain, his confessional is exactly about the thing with which we introduced "Yellow Horse." Wasn't it good enough to serve well and honorably in the Army, especially in Korea at the gateway of one of those tumbling domino countries, helping the U.S. of A. "maintain the equilibrium of the Dingdong by containing the ever-encroaching Doodah?" NO! NO! IT WAS NOT ENOUGH! It's never enough! There is always a sense of loss, and feelings that you could have done more, so much more.

This is the view of Pete 40 years later, drunk once again, this time in the antechamber of the Captain's bunker:

"I got out in September, just before the Cav deployed in '65'" Pete's jaw locked and he swallowed hard. He removed his black cap with Pathfinder pin and Air Assault Badge centered above a 1st Cavalry patch; black horse head silhouette on yellow background divided by a black diagonal line. He slowly traced its outline with his finger. "The horse we never rode, the line we never crossed and the yellow speaks for itself," chided Pete. ("Yellow Horse," pp. 152-153.)

He is repeating a much maligning, but false, phrase made about the 1st Cavalry Division after the Korean War, but he is speaking of himself and the Raven that has sat upon his shoulder since 1965. What Pete describes/confesses to the Captain is a transference syndrome where one's feelings of regret, inferiority, and even shame, can only be exonerated by a reinterpretation of the cause of that inferiority. In this case, it is Pete's election of discharge from a unit that, time has taught him, survived in battle glory (or was it gory?) after he left. And here is Pete's "Come-to-Jesus moment."

> "I was gung-ho when I came back from Korea, graduated Pathfinder and Air Assault School," Pete said. "The battalion trained hard. Just before the unit deployed, First Sergeant Lukevitch handed me some papers and said, 'Your time's up unless you take a burst of four.' I had to reenlist for four more years to get the experience of a lifetime and Uncle Sam would gladly throw in $100 a month for combat pay." ("Yellow Horse," pp. 153-154.)

Let me list the groundwork for Pete's transference syndrome as he mulls, sometimes with rhyming couplets and Poe's Raven on his shoulder, the explanation he has laid out 40 years hence:

- "It took a few minutes to figure my chances of returning from Vietnam. I figured it was more like the police action in Korea, but halfway around the world in a malaria infested, booby trapped, sniper-ridden jungle. All that appealed to my sense of adventure and camaraderie with the men of first platoon; 'A' Company, brothers in arms."

- "I played war games in Korea where the Ghost Battalion was wiped out because General MacArthur got caught with his pants down," Pete said. "I wasn't some new recruit. I'd spent four years in this man's army. I knew what happened in Korea and it was bloody fucking awful."

- "I can't explain it," Pete said, "but as I looked over those reenlistment papers the hair stood up on the back of my neck. I thought of home, school and doing what I wanted for a change; G.I. Bill, commercial art, 9-5 and never busting hump again."

- "First Sarge said 'Sign here and grab your gear,' which I figured was a life sentence, and I said, 'Thank you no, I gotta go.' I chose to muster out honorably from this man's army. Seven come eleven. I rolled the dice."

- "Pete chuckled. What memory or feeling had provoked him to hunt me down? He had served two years in an occupation army, came home and trained for war with the 1st Cavalry just in time to say *sayonara*. Fate, if you believe, dealt him a straight flush and in an odd reversal I drew a pair of deuces, won his slot in the Green Machine. But now he regretted cashing in his chips, choosing life over death."

- "Pete missed the next biggest foreign policy fiasco after Cuba in our country's brief but bloody history. He missed LZ-X-Ray [more precisely, LZ Albany] in all its savagery and death by fire, enemy and friendly. And now, I suspected, having lived the mundane life of a commercial artist, three failed marriages, corporate collapse, bankruptcy, no retirement and a passel of kids spread out over three states, he longed for the opportunity to die young, while immortal—be forever named on the beautiful black, granite, Vietnam Wall. Dominos tipped end to end."

- "Memories of the army, LZ X-Ray, dead buddies, father, judge, three failed marriages, job loss, bankruptcy, beer and more beer, must've overwhelmed him. It would take ten years on a couch and case of Prozac to figure this out and I wasn't prepared for either."

- "That salute was the best thing I ever got from my old man." Pete sat, lost in thought. Clothes and cans littered the room [of the Captain's confessional antechamber]. "I missed my chance, he said. "I'll never know." ("Yellow Horse," pp. 152-162)

"I missed my chance. I'll never know." Like the painful laments of Christopher Buckley, James Fallows and Bob Greene, Pete comes to the Captain, knowing him since they were kids— admiring the Captain's father ("The Colonel" to Pete), admiring the Captain's service in Special Forces, in Vietnam, the much-decorated hero returned home—to seek some kind of reassurance, some kind of closure.[72] There is an odd array of Poe's couplets in the center of "Yellow Horse," first coming from the mouth of Pete:

> *"Are you hurting, or deserting?" said the figure at my door.*
> *Sir, or Madam, it was drizzling, your forgiveness I implore.*
> *I am drunk and nothing more. Then she pointed,*
> *Self-anointed, at the cans that spread galore.*
> *"What of those?" She vaguely whispered, "All dead soldiers on the floor.*
> *Empty beer cans nothing more. ("Yellow Horse," p. 158.)*

The Captain responds, *"Quoth the Raven, Nevermore."* And with a desire to forget and an urge to remember, finishes Pete's rhyming couplets:

> *Pete seemed as lost and implausible as a talking raven,*
> *Sockless feet upon the floor, Crushed tin soldiers spread before.*
> *It was obvious, him so heedless, what his drinking had in store.*
> *With each beer he drank so quickly, downed a case, maybe more.*
> *Then me thought his soul was rendered, stripped of pretense*
> *And surrendered, metamorphose nothing more.*
>
> *He reverted and converted into something you'd abhor,*
> *EL-ZE-X-Ray all his buddies,*
> *Napalmed on the jungle floor,*
> *Crispy critters tangled, twisted, helicoptered out—no more.*
> *This, his vision and derision, Like a movie seen before.*
> *We were young, but nevermore. ("Yellow Horse," p. 159.)*

And that is the crux. The Captain sees that Pete has taken on the mantle of the unit(s) that was never his and in the war that was never his, and now lives vicariously through them. He certifies this surrogate life with justifications.

"Thing of it is, when I was in the army," Pete said, "I hated all that spit and polish, formations, inspections, drill and ceremony, close-order drill, bivouac, long marches to the rifle range, chow, everything about it," he said. "I couldn't wait to get out."

But now?

"But now," Pete said, "I'm Commander of a VFW Post and Commandant of the Color Guard. We present the flag on Veteran's Day at the War Memorial; honor guards, bury the dead. I present the flag to grieving widows, take comfort in the crisp pleat of a Class A uniform, spit-shined boots, marching, saber rattling, flags furling, twenty-one gun salute, fly-overs. They fill me up." he took a deep breath. "God help me, I love it."

As heavy snow begins to fall again in southern Virginia, a cleansing symbol in so much of literature, Pete says, "Funny how memory flips around." He had come to the Captain for a kind of "better late than never absolution," but the Captain doesn't have a lot of sympathy with that plan since he, himself, is seeking closure from his own unrelenting memories of war, and not an imagined one.

- "I missed my chance," he said. "I'll never know." "*Wake the fuck up!*" I yelled in his ear. "The Green Fucking Machine! You ever smell a crispy critter? It ain't melted marshmallows! You lit your own fucking way! This romantic bullshit about dying with your buddies on LZ X-Ray is *nuts*! Where the *fuck* you think *they'd rather be?*"

- Sure the first Cavalry at LZ X-Ray survived by sheer grit, the grace of God, and "most important, TAC Air. Imagine what Custer could have done with napalm."

- His house is a redoubt called The Bunker; it is Alamo-like.

- "I see the Colonel on Veteran's Day," Pete said. "I'm Color Guard Commander for the VFW. We post colors, do funerals and such." "Fuck the VFW," I said. Didn't treat us kindly after Vietnam. Said we lost the war. Not the five Presidents, Congress and the Joint Chiefs."

- "Isn't that a little harsh?" Pete asks. The Captain answers, "What'd they know about counter insurgency: terrorism, unconventional warfare, pacification, burn the village to save it, or the Ho Chi Minh Road? We all had our turn in the barrel."

- "Patton's Third Army had a Forward Edge of Battle Area, a frontline with good guys on one side and bad guys on the other. The ground you stood on in Vietnam was our FEBA. Mama san, baby san, they'd just as soon frag your ass as look at you. The corruption, spies and VC sympathizers spread from top to bottom. No flag waving freedom fighters along the roads urging you on to Paris."

- "Which anyone that's been in a firefight will tell you is bullshit. It's fight or flight, neurons firing and biochemistry; cortisol and adrenaline, heroin surging through your veins or freezing in place. "Freezing up" to the uninformed, equates to being yellow, cowardly. Most everyone freezes the first time shit hits the fan. It's nothing to be ashamed of—I'm not."

- "As for the rest, how you'd perform under fire? It's all speculation. Nobody knows until that first round cracks over your head. It's got little to do with yellow and everything with red."

- "Pete really had no real idea that the flip side of Korean cold was Vietnam hot. Jungle rot, delta swamp, malaria, triple canopy, vines, bamboo, leeches, two steppers, dehydration, infection, was just as much the enemy. The country was carnivorous. It took a bite out of your ass every day."

- "You can wash out the smell of pissed pants after a firefight but the stain of not showing up would have been too much for me to bear."

- After Pete had snapped to attention, drunk and naked again, saluted the Captain and said, "On behalf of the United States Army and a grateful nation, please accept this beer as a symbol of our appreciation for your honorable and faithful service." the Captain thinks, "Maybe this was as close to a welcome home as any Vietnam vet would ever get. 'On behalf of grateful nation', turns out to be the gratitude of one citizen soldier. Not some synthetic, 'thank you for your service' platitude—but one deep look in the eye; *one* resolute salute, from the Home Guard."

- "Memories of the army, LZ X-Ray, dead buddies, father, judge, three failed marriages, job loss, bankruptcy, beer and more beer, must've overwhelmed him. It would take ten years on a couch and case of Prozac to figure this out and I wasn't prepared for either." ("Yellow Horse," pp. 148-167.)

While the Captain has entertained politely his old friend's lament, his own memories and a volatile anger with them, always bubble close to the surface, especially where Pete's lament has turned into laments (see p. 158.):

> "*Sit!*" "*Wake the fuck up!*" I yelled in his ear. "The Green Fucking Machine! You lit your own fucking way! This romantic bullshit about dying with your buddies on LZ-X-Ray is *nuts!* Where the *fuck* you think *they'd rather be?*" ("Yellow Horse," pp. 164-165)

The Captain finally asks Pete, "You come here for absolution?" Pete asks "You a priest?" That question ended any priestly feelings the Captain may have been entertaining for Pete.

> "This has got nothing to do with me!" Bam! He'd flipped it around. I felt jujitsued by this crazy son-of-a-bitch. "Where the fuck would I rather be? I got nothin' for you." Something burned, whisky hot, in my throat. It was my old friend rage, bubbling. I cocked my right arm. I wanted to smash something, smash his nose for coming here and stirring shit up. A streetlamp spotlighted the last beer on the floor. ("Yellow Horse," p. 166)

But Pete's act of standing to attention, snapping a salute and offering the last of Old Milwaukee's finest to the Captain on behalf of the Army and a grateful nation, cools his anger. He knows that the drunken, confused man before him is only a man for all that and has offered him, perhaps, the most sincere recognition for his valiant service in the Army and Vietnam he has received in years of accepting synthetic platitudes of gratitude since his return.

What Thompson has done in "Yellow Horse" appears to be a radical swerve ("LEFT FLANK, MARCH!") away from the previous six stories of Colors of War & Peace. In this daily journal the emphasis seems to rest on the story of a contemporary military man who never went to Vietnam, the war which this book has documented with painstaking clarity—whether it's Vietnam, Laos, Iraq, Afghanistan, Ukraine, inner space, or outer space. But there is the thematic answer. "Inner Space." Vietnam is always in the "inner space" of Thompson's characters, even when they dwell in the category introduced at the beginning of this explicative chapter, the category inferred in the epigraph taken from Christopher Buckley's essay on "Viet Guilt." Category Four. Buckley said, "It's been ten years now since the troops came home, but until recently I had never once heard anyone admit to guilt or shame over not having gone to Vietnam—not in hundreds of conversations about the war." Thompson uses the same sentiment to evince this very emotion, "Guilt," from one who stayed home but now, 30 years later in a kind of agony, regrets his failure to sacrifice himself on the pyre of Vietnam.

Thompson used as epigraph to "Yellow Horse," a quote from Michael Herr's book *Dispatches*, which has come down as a kind of gnomic paraphrase of the Vietnam War:

> Not that you don't hear some overripe bullshit about it: Hearts and Minds, Peoples of the Republic, tumbling dominoes, maintaining the equilibrium of the Dingdong by containing the ever-encroaching Doodah; you could also hear the other, some

young soldier in all bloody innocence saying, "All that's just a load man. We're here to kill gooks. Period."

Thompson raised the "Domino Theory" early in "Yellow Horse," as he hears Pete rap, rap, rapping on his door. And now, as he ponders that "Fate, if you believe, dealt [Pete] a straight flush and in an odd reversal I drew a pair of deuces . . . ," the Captain tries to reconfigure the fallacy of that theory based on a 1930's moral precept, "If you let your daughter come home late from a date without punishment, the next time she may come home pregnant." Certainly, the theory was a product of the racist and misogynist era in which it was raised. He says:

> The domino theory has one axiom: Dominos in line continue falling until the last one falls. Uncle Sam sent me to Vietnam to prove it. But of course I'd disproved that theory many times in my youth after erecting zigzag patterns of dominos, odd shaped like Asian countries on a map. If one domino was slightly off line and didn't knock over the next one, then the rest were left standing. Any kid who played dominos had proof. ("Yellow Horse," p. 161.)

While there appears to have been a LEFT FLANK, MARCH! in "Yellow Horse," the rank and file of *Colors of War & Peace* have trooped on, unerringly, in a straight line. Thompson provides a bookend with "Yellow Horse," to his opening story, "Blue Tattoo." In "Blue Tattoo," he starts the beginning of his autobiographical enlisted man, who "broke free of his family and civil lashings as sirens with the voices of WW II marauders and sepulchral oracles beckoned him with the Ballad of the Green Beret, as haunting an ear-worm tune as anything Ulysses had ever heard."

> The blinking strobes mocked me; my choice to volunteer for OCS, forego Jump School and the Special Forces training for which I'd enlisted. If boarded out, there would be no Green Beret, Merrill's Marauder's, OSS jumping behind enemy lines. My rebellious nature craved the ideal of self-sufficient insurgency

while teetering precariously on this rigid plank of perfectionism. Airborne icons imbued from youth, at once lifted aspirations and loomed as a harbinger of failure. ("Blue Tattoo," p. 12.)

And his newly minted 2nd Lieutenant does walk the rigid plank, from Ft. Benning in "Blue Tattoo," to a Bunker on Reed Street in "Yellow Horse," where he has been forced to look back on a career that once was a harbinger of success. In the last paragraph of "Yellow Horse," the Captain parodies Pete Starr's confessional pride at his father's recognition of him, to wit, "That my father was wearing corporal stripes gave me immense satisfaction and arousal, since I'd risen to the rank of buck sergeant." Thompson closes "Yellow Horse," with the Captain's sardonic recall of this as they exit the door from his Bunker and Starr snaps a final salute on him.

I stood on the porch, snowflakes swirling and snapped a crisp U.S. Army knife-edged salute to Pete Starr. The thought that he'd risen in rank to buck sergeant gave me immense satisfaction and arousal, since I'd climbed the ladder all the way to captain. (Yellow Horse," p. 168.)

Never, in the procedural of "Yellow Horse," has there been a moment of one-upmanship, or a pissing contest, between the Captain and his friend, enlisted man and non-combatant, but the Captain finally lets himself go, a reward for the ordeal(s) he has been through.

---

[68] Christoper Buckley, "Viet Guilt," *Esquire*, 1 September 1983.

[69] *Ibid.*, Christopher Buckley.

[70] Harold G. Moore (Ret.) and Joseph L. Galloway, *We Were Soldiers Once . . . And Young*, Random House: New York, 1992, p. 15.

[71] Edgar Allan Poe, "The Raven," 1845. "Once upon a midnight dreary, while I pondered, weak and weary,/Over many a quaint and curious volume of forgotten lore—/ While I nodded, nearly napping, suddenly there came a tapping,/As of some one gently rapping, rapping at my chamber door./'"Tis some visitor," I muttered, "tapping at my chamber door—/Only this and nothing more."

[72] Christopher Buckley, "Viet Guilt," *Esquire*, 1 September 1983. James Fallows, "What Did You Do in the Class War, Daddy?" *The Washington Monthly*, Oct. 1975, pp. 5-19. Bob Greene, *Homecoming: When The Soldiers Returned from Vietnam*, Chicago: G.P. Putnam's Sons, 1989.

HELLO MY LITTLE FEAR OF WAR!

"What could I say to you that would be of value,
except that perhaps you seek too much,
that as a result of your seeking you cannot find."

— Hermann Hesse, *Siddhartha*

L eaving the content of the first seven stories in *Colors of War & Peace* is like trading in a Ferrari SF90 Stradale, or Porsche 911 GT2 RS, for a 1990 Lexus LS400. You move from galvanic to arcadian, from adrenalin to sedation, although the shadow of Vietnam is always lurking. In "Hello My Little Fear of War!", Thompson is providing a purely autobiographical entry on his venture into Buddhism, begun with his introduction to OMEGA in 1991. There are two tracks to this venture; "Hello!" and Maxine Hong Kingston's journal entries in her *The Fifth Book of Peace*. While they are both more journalism than creative writing they present decidedly different images and interpretations of the same events.

Village des Pruniers (Plum Village). 30 kilometers due east from the Bay of Biscay to Bordeaux, then 40 kilometers due east of Bordeaux, but the 5th Precept forbids the consumption of Petrus Pomerol. Is that an irony? Yes, and "Hello!" is a gathering of ironies. It is ironic that we should travel from beer drinking in Southern Virginia, to Bordeaux, the finest wine *terroir* in the world. It is ironic that we do not go ahead in time, but go back. It is ironic that Thompson's search for the Precepts of Buddhism to deliver him from the round-a-bout of phenomenal existence with its inherent suffering in the hopes for a reconciliation in "Hello!", ends ten years later with a Catholic Sacrament in "Yellow Horse" where confession leads someone else to reconciliation. It is ironic that the representative spirit of religious asceticism, a monk, a mendicant, a bonze, a monastic, the very epitome of humility and self-effacement, should be a man educated at the best universities in the world, a writer, a poet, a politician, an orator, and a self-promoter who sits, *cathedra,* as royalty does. Is it *la génération perdue* (the lost generation), or *la génération retrouvée* (the found generation)? It is ironic that France, the country that wayward veterans visit, each to come to terms with their Vietnams, is itself the original conspectus for Colonials in Indochina. And, finally, even the title, "Hello, My Little Fear of War!", is an irony. But as always in Thompson's hands, by design.

As related in the Introduction, in 1991 Thompson, picked up a magazine printed by the OMEGA Institute in up-state New York that advertised a Buddhist retreat for veterans after making a farewell dinner for the writer, Sloan Wilson and his wife.

> Goodbyes were exchanged. "Just keep writing," said Sloan. "You'll get there." It was by now after 10 pm when he found a copy of a magazine, *OMEGA*, stacked with mail near the front door. He'd never heard of the place or its holistic studies and programs. The magazine chronicled spring retreats and workshops at the Omega Institute, in Rhinebeck, NY. There, advertised on the first page was a week long "Retreat for Vietnam Veterans sponsored by Thích Nhất Hạnh and the Community of Mindful Living." The Vietnamese monk had invited veterans and their families for peace making; meditation, hugging, dancing, dialogue, bounded by the Buddhist rubric. Thompson was intrigued and inspired but the retreat started the next day? In a mindless effort he threw clothes into a travel case, gassed up the car and drove north on I-95. After the all-night drive, and 428 miles, coupled with an inadvertent turn across the Verrazano Bridge, he arrived at the forested camp site. (from D.M. Thompson's unpublished memoir, *Marble Mountain Redux*)

This was the beginning of Thompson's encounter with Buddhism and his search for a meaning to his life 20 years after Vietnam, four years after Special Forces Reserves, his career change, and his imploded marriage. He says in "Hello!" that a few days after he'd settled into the Veterans' retreat he had accepted an invitation and joined a group of attendees in an "impetuous pilgrimage in order to pay homage to Teilhard de Chardin." A brilliant geologist, philosopher, writer and defrocked Jesuit priest, de Chardin's gravesite was famously on the grounds of the Culinary Institute of America, Rhinebeck, NY, and was an intellectual and spiritual intersection with the renown Buddhist teacher at Omega. Two names he'd never heard uttered in his life before that week promised to be large influences on the rest of his life. Now, in search of *Big Mind,* a Zen tradition, he hoped Thich Nhất Hạnh would confirm Teilhard's imagination and inspiration.

> The Frenchman's teleological theory of man was based on the inevitable evolution of all thought and being converging at the *Omega Point.* All matter, he theorized, had an inherent compulsion to arrange itself into more and more complex groupings that exhibited higher and higher levels of consciousness. Atoms, cells, animal, man, galaxies, the universe, strove collectively to order themselves towards higher states of consciousness, and ultimately coalesce at the *Omega Point.* ("Hello My Little Fear of War!", p. 182.)

The very opposite view of this, of course, is "Entropy"; a "thermodynamic quantity representing the unavailability of a system's thermal energy for conversion into mechanical work, often interpreted as the degree of disorder or randomness in the system." In a story concerned with Precepts and Sacraments, the Second Law of Thermodynamics would seem to take precedent. It says that atoms, cells, animal, man, galaxies, the universe, strive collectively to order themselves towards lower states of consciousness, and ultimately coalesce at another *Omega Point,* a total disorganization. In more literary terms, it means, that existence tends toward a "lack of order or predictability, a gradual decline into death." Thompson poses this irony as a kind of overriding rubric to "Hello!". He says:

Was that why I'd been drawn to the Veteran's Retreat at Omega, where all these characters merged? Since there are no coincidences, it must have been synchronicity. Here I sat, speeding through space/time with a coalition of willing radicals; mentally, physically and spiritually bound for our next way station. Perhaps generation *trouvee*, bound by time and circumstance of war, hurtled towards the promise of higher consciousness. Maybe Plum Village was the intersection? ("Hello!", pp. 182-183.)

Maybe, but as will be revealed, maybe not. But this puts the cart before the horse.

Along with three other Vietnam veterans, Maxine Hong Kingston invited me to visit Thich Nhat Hanh, *Village de Pruniers*, in Southern France, 1994. Affectionately known as Thay, the Buddhist priest and Nobel Peace Prize nominee wrote books and poetry. ("Hello!", p. 171.)

Hong Kinston wrote in length of Thich Nhất Hạnh, Buddhism, the veterans' writing group, and OMEGA, in her *The Fifth Book of Peace*, published in 2004. She concluded the tale in "Earth" with her choosing four writing veterans to accompany her to the retreat at *Village de Pruniers* and her view and interpretation of that month-long retreat.

The BBC called me. They wanted to make a documentary about writers and teachers journeying across national boundaries: *Stories My Country Told Me*. Desmond Tutu would travel from Capetown to Johannesburg, Eric Hobsbawm through sections of the former Yugoslavia, Eqbal Ahmad between Pakistan and India. And I would visit my ancestral village in China. But I've been to my villages already. I suggested, how about taking me and a group of American Viet Nam veterans to Thich Nhat Hanh's community, Plum Village? We will find a great story in Plum Village. The producer said, "Plum Village is where your heart is. We'll film where your heart is." *La querencia*. The [BBC] budget would allow for me, Earll [Maxine's husband], and four veterans. I chose two from the East Coast, Dan Moen

Thompson and Jerry Crawford, and two from the West, Ted Sexauer and Jimmy Janko.[73]

Thompson recounts this conversation in "Hello!" when Maxine calls him to ask, "Can you go with me to Plum Village for autumn retreat?"

> "France?" he asked.
> "A month of Noble Silence, sitting and walking meditation, dharma talks, strict vegetarian diet, and no spirits."
> *"A Clean Well Lighted Place,"* I said.
> "It could be intoxicating." ("Hello!", p. 173.)

What Thompson does not speak of in "Hello!" is his return to Vietnam months before Plum Village, just as Maxine recounted he would in conversation at their first meeting at OMEGA, and she wrote of it at length.

> Dan then tells about a monk, or monks, shadows, he fired upon. "He or they disappeared behind the big bell. I don't know if I hit him. I ran around to the other side of the bell, but nobody was there. Maybe another monk took him away. I'm going back to Marble Mountain to find out what really happened. I just phoned my daughter and told her I'm going to Vietnam again. I want to visit my old haunts inland, and see Da Nang again, and memorize Marble Mountain for my book, Marble Mountain. I want to know for certain. They couldn't have had rifles. They were monks. (*The Fifth Book of Peace*, p. 305.)

On his return three years later, and nine months before his trip to Plum Village, he traveled to *Ngũ Hành Sơn* (Marble Mountain; one of five marble and limestone) just south of Da Nang to see again this holy mountain. He remembered the hidden entrances, serpentine tunnels, hallowed chambers with statues, incense tinged grottos, ancient pagodas, and Buddhist sanctuaries within its geography. He planned the trip meticulously with Minn, a close family friend, for two years. Minn lived in Anaheim, California, and had repeatedly asked Dan to make the trip. Thompson's family had sponsored

Minn's family to come to the United States after the fall of Saigon, 19 years earlier. Unbeknownst to Thompson, on a last minute impulse, Minn decided to take not only his immediate family back to Saigon/Ho Chi Minh City for the first time but also his wife's parents. Minn, first generation rags to riches entrepreneur, had done exceedingly well in the new cell-phone business.

Coincidentally, Thompson met with Maxine Hong Kingston and Earll, for lunch in Alameda to discuss the fall gathering of the Veterans Writing Group at OMEGA. He cautiously presented her the first draft of Marble Mountain, the novel which he'd been writing under her tutelage, and from what he'd learned from earlier teachers. He departed for Vietnam hoping that he'd learn even more from Maxine's edit.

When he left Anaheim, Alameda and San Francisco for Vietnam, Thompson had planned to use Minn as his guide in Ho Chi Minh City and then, together, head up country to Da Nang and further north to Hue, Dong Ha, Khe Sanh and Mai Loc, near the demilitarized zone (17th Parallel). Critical to Thompson's planning was Minn's ability to speak fluent Vietnamese. He felt secure in the knowledge that he would have someone he could trust when he traveled north. It was paramount that he learn as much as possible about Marble Mountain, its spiritual sanctuaries and the enemy who'd launched an attack on his basecamp, 23 August, 1968. Most important, he needed an intercessor who would enable him to perform a ceremony for the men who had been killed during that attack, missions in Laos and on the mountain itself. FOB #4, was a Top Secret, SOG, basecamp located next to Marble Mountain. It was from there that recon teams, RT's and HF's (Hatchet Forces, or Reaction Companies) had been stationed and then sent north to Mobile Launch Sites and inserted in cross-border operations into Laos. But Minn, now taking care of the logistics of family in Saigon, would no longer be that intercessor.

Having seen the south of Vietnam, a region as alien to him as Naples is to a Milanese, Thompson, alone, rode the resurrected Reunification Express train 935 kilometers from Ho Chi Minh City to Da Nang and began his Buddhist ministrations. Along the way he encountered a significant number of helpers to aid in his pilgrimage, namely his translator and chauffeur, Ha, a Buddhist poet, who taught meditation and the Tao, Madame Bui Tai and Monk Nguyen, who was instrumental in helping him conduct a memorial service. Madame Tai rang a bell and taught him incantations, practices he would encounter on his journey to the holy mount.

> I repeat after her *"Um Ma Ni pat Me Hum."* Again. *"Um Ma Ni pat Me Hum."* She says that she cannot explain what the words mean. I will learn their meaning in due time. I am to use it whenever I feel anxious or threatened. It will calm and protect me. I remember the Nungs chanting these sounds just before a firefight. Then plop, a gold Buddha, attached to chains around their necks would be thrown into their mouths. Two months later as I am reading Jack Kerouac's *Dharma Bums*, I'm excited to come across the same phrase, grouped differently but recognizable. *"Om Mani Pahdme Hum."* According to a character in the book, Japhy, it means "Amen the Thunderbolt in the Dark Void." (from *In Search of My Rune*, Thompson's Journal of his return to Vietnam, 1994, p. 49.)

Thompson's return to Vietnam to immerse himself in this theater was new to his practice and had as its main goal the creation of a "Calling of the Dead" ceremony on Marble Mountain. He saw in this ceremony a reunion and resolution with men killed in action on and around Marble Mountain in 1968. To that end he began arranging, with the help of Ha and Madame Tai, his next steps.

> After exchanging pleasantries Ha explains why we had come. The monk listens mindfully. He showed surprise when the ceremony is mentioned. He asked about the men and how and where they had died. I relayed through Ha the circumstances. He nods in sincere deference. He has never performed the ritual,

"Calling of the Dead." It will be his first time. He will do it. He tells us to come back tomorrow. The ceremony will take approximately two-and-a-half hours. The first part of the ceremony will be the calling, or securing the attention of Buddha. The second portion of the ritual was designed to summon the dead men by name. The third part is the feast prepared for the Hungry Ghosts. I had gone to the Vietnam Wall in Washington, D.C. to take rubbings for the names. (*In Search of My Rune*, Thompson's Journal of his return to Vietnam, 1994, p. 50.)

After the climb to the Pagoda on the morrow, Monk Nguyen hands Thompson two sheets of paper with the 31 names he had given Nguyen earlier. These had been transferred to a large sheet held by a wooden frame. He hands Thompson the list to read with instructions that he will motion during each ceremony when to read them, and when to bow.

I ask him to be patient when I read. It may take a while. He nods in understanding. Compassion emanates from the Monk. I am reminded of a mantra, "I am a Mountain, I am strong." I will learn his alliance with this holy ground. "I am the moon in a sky of utmost emptiness." I suddenly realize why I took so many pictures of the moon on the roof of the Top Hotel. The moon in the sky of utmost emptiness, part of the mantra. The monk calls for his two initiates to help begin the ceremony. We walk slowly to the large pagoda. (*In Search of My Rune*, 1994, p. 51.)

While Thompson kneels on the cold, marble pagoda floor, Nguyen begins a slow chant to call Buddha: "*Nam Mo Bon Su Thich Ca Mau Ni Phat Nam . . .*" Chanting, clacking of a gourd, chiming of a bell and aroma of incense. The delicate aroma encircles Thompson; three loud clacks on the gourd, chimes of the bell. Silence.

"Silence. I walk stiffly to the altar. I bow three sets of threes. My right knee feels swollen. There can be no relief. I return awkwardly to my station. Again the chanting, clacking, ringing, incense."

He is kneeling on the hard marble floor 12,500 miles from his home in Virginia, images of the 31 men he knew who died in and around this mountain, in the distant mountains of Ashau, in Laos and North Vietnam come back to him.

A deep sadness fills me. Gone are these men. I remember how they died, violently—25 years ago. I feel pangs of anguish as I kneel on this stone floor, this mountain of grief. How powerful these men are to call me, over this great distance of space and time. Over time. All is mind. Three loud clacks on the gourd, chimes of the bell. Silence. Silence. I open my eyes. Monk Nguyen hands me the names of the men to read. My throat catches as I begin to read. (*In Search of My Rune*, 1994, p. 51.)

TALMAGE H. ALPIN JR. - WILLIAM H. BRIC III - TADEUSC M. KEPCZYK - DONAL R. KERNS - JAMES T. KICKLITER - CHARLES R. NORRIS - RICHARD E. PEGRAM JR. - PAUL D. POTTER - ROLF J. RICKMERS - ANTHONY J. SANTANA

"My voice grows stronger as I read louder the names, pausing after each. A single bell notes, bares witness to their lives, then fades. I allow the bell's tone to extend itself into the otherwise perfect stillness."

GILBERT A. SECOR - ROBERT J. UYESAKA - HOWARD S. VAMI - HAROLD R. VOORHEIS - ALBERT M. WALTER - DONALD W. WELCH - STANLEY . SIETING - RAYMOND C. STACKS - NORMAN PAYNE - PETER H. MCMURRAY - Gilb

"Later, Ha told me of the tears tracing smoothly down my shaven face. I was not aware of them. I felt solid yet diffuse, the delicate aroma of incense encircled me, three clacks on the gourd, chimes of the bell. Silence."

**GARY L. MATSON - DONALD E. ROSS
- WILLIAM T. BROWN - GUNTER H. WALD
- MONROE SHUE - RONALD E. RAY
- RANDOLPH B. SUBER - STEPHEN J. CHANEY.Gilb**

The "Calling to Buddha" completes with the last intonation of the thirty-one names. And all the other missing and dead . . . . Monk Nguyen takes from Thompson the list of names and rolls it. He places it in a large brass vase. His helper lights the paper. Flame and smoke consume it. The ceremony moves to an antechamber where three tables are set with flowers, bowls, steaming rice and vegetables. The hungry ghosts have been called. Monk Nguyen begins to chant and his initiates strike hard the gourd and bell.

The chanting is now high pitched and with a faster cadence. There is a special intensity about the proceedings. I begin to hum the chants, heavy Omms, allowing the air to rise from deep within my belly, resonance filling my chest, sound flowing through my vocal cords. My voice grows in loud supplication for those that have so long not fed. Silence. Bowing. Chanting. Striking. Silence. (*In Search of My Rune*, 1994, pp. 50-52.)

Thompson reads again, in the feasting room, the 31 names of his comrades thereby completing, with Monk Nguyen's execution, a *puja* for the dead. They were each summoned by name and Thompson, full of the mystery of their reappearance, will escort them in his heart back to their homeland, along with the ashes of their cremated names, and formulated plans of how to present them at The Wall.

By the time Thompson returned from Vietnam, he had packed a years's worth of learning and experience into a month-long furlough. He would be called to take these new experiences to Plum Village eight months later.

Plum Village. After arrival, Maxine and her veterans are invited by Thich Nhất Hạnh to drink tea, listen to talk and, traditionally, ask a single question of the Zen Master.

It was tucked nicely into dark recesses of a tree line, blending like a VC bunker. Ted Sexauer, an old airborne trooper, walked point as we traversed the tall grass. He goose-stepped with a cane ahead of me. We walked from the veteran's hootch, a small billet with open bay, eight beds and a bathroom. Ever vigilant, I surveyed the narrow path and tall weeds. We shared an aversion, chiseled in bone, about walking trails in open fields. How to practice living in the present moment, wonderful moment, when a voice said, *never walk a trail?* Even after hours of sitting and walking meditation, some things triggered caution. ("Hello!", pp. 171-172.)

But as "Hello!" describes, serenity is hard to come by for these Vietnam veterans, even though willing allies and converts. Thompson uses the phrase, *"A Clean Well Lighted Place,"* in response to Maxine's invitation to Plum Village. This is a reference to Ernest Hemingway's short story by that name (Hemingway is bandied around when the group first hits Paris; the Left Bank, the lost generation, *A Moveable Feast*, Montparnasse, and dinner at a favorite haunt of Hemingway's). It sounds like a simple and polite reference for the description of Plum Village, but *"A Clean Well Lighted Place"* is a complex allusion to life, and the meaning and purpose of the Buddhist Retreat at *Village des Pruniers*.

In his short story, Hemingway is asking the question, "What is the meaning of life?" Talk about existentialism and the "Lost Generation !" Hemingway is writing this in 1932, just before existential thought in fiction becomes mainstream; before Sartre, Camus, Malraux, Beckett, Hesse, *et al*, began to publish (although Shakespeare predates all of them by 300 years). Yet he is writing it from the point of view of that lost generation (of which he identified himself as one) and revealing all the prevalent themes; the universe is indifferent to human beings, life has no purpose, and we must look to our own actions to create meaning, if it is possible to create meaning at all. The crux of "A Clean Well Lighted Place" is that the old man in the cafe, who has attempted suicide the week before, spends his time every evening drinking at the cafe/bar until it closes, or he closes it in his "despair." There are only two other players in the cast of characters, a young waiter who wants to get home to his young wife, and an old waiter who seems to understand the old man's plight. The old waiter muses that now that he is aging, he is also one who would prefer to stay late in the cafe, and mentions that people of that sort need to find "a clean well-lighted place" in which to spend their time. He says, "Each night I am reluctant to close up because there may be some one who needs the cafe." The young waiter, uncaring, says "Hombre, there are bodegas open all night long."

> "You do not understand. This is a clean and pleasant cafe. It is well lighted. The light is very good and also, now, there are shadows of the leaves."

The young waiter leaves the scene, and after "Good night," the older waiter begins a monologue with himself saying it is the light of course, but it is necessary that the place be clean and pleasant. What did he fear? It was not fear or dread. "It was a nothing that he knew too well. It was all a nothing and a man was nothing too." "Nada [nothing]" replaces words in the Lord's Prayer, and the first line in the Hail Mary prayer, a mantra, if you will.

> It was only that and light was all it needed and a certain cleanness and order. Some lived in it and never felt it but he knew it all was nada y pues nada y nada y pues nada [then nothing]. Our nada who art in nada, nada be thy name thy kingdom nada thy will be nada in nada as it is in nada. Give us this nada our daily nada and nada us our nada as we nada our nadas and nada us not into nada but deliver us from nada; pues nada. Hail nothing full of nothing, nothing is with thee.[74]

As stated, this story is no accidental allusion by Thompson but illustrates, as his earlier stories already have, despair and a search for a place "with light" and a "certain cleanness and order." When the lost generation comes up in Paris, Thompson can identify with Gertrude Stein's coinage (Hemingway; he used it, along with *Ecclesiastics,* as an epigraph to *The Sun Also Rises*). Thompson says, "Perhaps after three generations, two wars and a police action, a new generation of veterans, writers and poets would coalesce in those same old haunts or discover new ones." But he raises a little known aspect of *la génération perdue*, the flip side, *la génération retrouvée*:

> "What about the Found Generation," I said. But that story, sixteen hundred Chinese youth migrating to Paris after WW I, had already been written. Irony, or coincidence, take your pick. What had been the difference between Lost and Found, East and West, during the Roaring Twenties? Driven by apathy and detachment, Westerners lost all hope and faith in society, while Easterners were driven by optimism and purpose. ("Hello!", p. 174.)

A unique take on another history, and one I'd never heard before. Thompson summarizes all that by saying "One thing for sure, Vietnam vets had been tossed into the lost and found. This was my opportunity to answer lingering questions about Buddhism and mindfulness." And with that he catalogues the "lost" and "found" generation of veterans who were the chosen few from the Omega group.

The first and foremost, Thompson:

> I'd come to the same conclusion after years in Special Forces Reserves. Deep down I believed if I trained men to survive the next war, it would serve as a do-over. But then I'd been addicted to risk and rush, daring do; jumping from planes, boats, taking trains; hopscotching the globe. It took years of magical thinking to reconfigure my war. In the end I lost. ("Hello!", p. 176.)

There is Ted Sexauer, a gifted poet and former Airborne Infantry medic who now walked with a cane because of too many jumps, too many bumps, and who said, "I went to Vietnam to have something to write about."

Ted loved word play, coined the term "Dharma Nazi" for all the strident, born again Buddhists—Juggendbund in former lives. We'd experienced many of the same things, OCS, Airborne School, Special Forces Q School, and Vietnam. I'd graduated from OCS and been assigned to SOG, Studies and Observation Group. He was originally assigned to the 1st Civil Affairs/3rd Special Forces Group, Fort Bragg after he graduated from a nine-month Serbo Croat School in Pasadena. ("Hello!", p. 176.)

There is Jimmy Janko, who was also an Infantry line medic with the 27th Wolfhounds, 25th Infantry Division, a unit of great meaning to Thompson because it was the same unit his father served with in Hawaii on the day of the Pearl Harbor attack, and Dad to him was a bigger hero than any James Jones character in *From Here To Eternity*. Jimmy, wounded in action, was a published author who chose, after Vietnam, to work for 13 years as a night watchman at Alcatraz, a form of solitary confinement and deep introspection, you could say thirteen years hard time without a conviction. Thompson describes him as "more ascetic than troglodyte."

Jimmy was small in stature, wild-eyed, but mild mannered with spike hair. His eyes darted around a room like a humming bird; hovering never landing. His quick wit and disarming smile camouflaged wounds. He had tended the wounded during Renegade Woods, April 2-6, LTC George Armstrong Custer III, commanding. Surrounded by Indians, he ran out of morphine syrettes, gauze and IV's during the bloody battle. The stacked bodies kept him alive. He kept his scalp, but his spirit was wounded. ("Hello!", pp. 179-180.)

And finally, there is Jerry Crawford, a former Army Ranger (but by description, a LuRP).

Bald on top, his hair was pulled back into a samurai bun with wire-rimmed glasses. He wore black leather, rode a Hog in search of windmills. He was haunted by the ghost of a woman guerrilla he'd killed—after she'd killed his buddy. ("Hello!", p. 180.)

Add to this mix, Maxine, Earll, the entire BBC film crew, several Vietnamese of Hanh's acolytes, and more. Maxine describes the entourage:

> The next day, on the sunny train platform at Libourne, where we got off the fast train from Paris, we met pilgrims on their way to Plum Village, a monk from Japan and Patrick LaCoste, an Irishman/Frenchman. We're like Dead Heads, converging by plane, train, car, and van upon Jerry Garcia and the Grateful Dead. The little train came, and our group—the vets, the BBC—crowded into the last car, filled the seats and aisle with our stuff, sat on the equipment, and stood looking out the back window. (*The Fifth Book of Peace*, p. 369.)

The Vietnam veterans, I would estimate, did not feel like they were converging on a Grateful Dead concert. Rather, they were always poised for the Vietnam that lurks in the shadows. Thompson describes again, but this time from a more distant past, 1994, his move into a newly rehabbed home, which memory tells us, is the revetment he was living in a decade in the future, 2004, in "Yellow Horse." He described the WW II construction again, but for the first time:

> Commodities were still rationed and lumber was in short supply but cement, rocks, sand and rebar were plentiful. His idea? Cast the entire house in reinforced concrete. Summer, the walls and rebar absorbed the blazing Virginia sun. During sweat soaked nights the walls radiated like a kiln. Come winter, the concrete walls absorbed the cold. The cement slab and wood floors wore on the bones. Living in the bunker was like camping in a quarry. Concrete stairs led down to a fortified basement that could withstand any attack, foreign or domestic. ("Hello!", pp. 173-174.)

Vietnam is ever present. Hanh's chalet appearing "in the dark recesses of a tree line like a VC bunker"; aversion to walking too close together on trails, or even on a trail; the biographies of Thompson's,

Sexauer's, Janko's and Crawford's traumatic war experiences; the image of colonial France, which dragged the U.S. into Vietnam, is conjured by mounting the train at Libourne, an older, smaller model in the French railroad system "similar to those in Vietnam," which had been built to enforce the occupation, "sociologically and financially, of French Indo China." But gunshots on the meditation trail in the morning somewhere in the lower hamlet of Plum Village that upset Jerry Crawford's peace train; and, finally, a "little fear" of war. And that leads us to the point of Thompson's irony—Buddhism, mindfulness and war.

Thompson says,

> "But there had been a tear in the cosmic fabric that morning. The sangha had risen early for sitting meditation in the main hall and afterward each walked alone through the countryside. Wisps of fog purled above rolling fields of bent stalks and gnarly vines. Jerry Crawford heard gunshots that morning. ("Hello!", p. 184.)

Maxine describes the incident this way:

> Jerry talked. "I am confused now, I'm confused here, because I was walking on the—on the walk this morning, and I'm thinking very calmly, and then the shooting started. And it frightened me. And I have trouble breaking through that fear. I have trouble being calm when I have chaos going round in my head all the time. Perhaps this is not a question, it's simply to let you know that I'm, I'm trying very had to be mindful but it doesn't—it, it doesn't always work for me." (*The Fifth Book of Peace*, pp. 384-385.)

Thompson thinks, "Flashback. It was evident from his anguished look that Jerry heard shots and it kicked up a vivid memory." Hanh, hearing this, laughs and tells Crawford, "Don't try too hard to be mindful." One of Hanh's acolytes, Sister Chang Khong, allegedly got what Jerry meant and said "Oh, I understand."

> "I see his point, he said he heard the shooting of the hunter and because of that is revive the fear of the war in the past.

And so if you—you can say: 'Hello, my little fear of the war, my experience again, you go back, we are in a safe area. Here's Plum Village. Is not Vietnam in war. Here is Thay; here is Maxine, here's all your friends, and we are practicing mindfulness.'" ("Hello!", pp. 184-185.)

Two things happened here, and both angered Thompson deeply. First, Hanh had given several dharma talks on the need to suffer (Living Christ, Living Buddha), and then treats Jerry's reaction as if it is the behavior of an over-zealous child. In support of this, Maxine recounts in *The Fifth Book of Peace* that she heard that "Thich Nhat Hanh told the veterans to use the sound of helicopters as if it were the Mindfulness Bell." The sound of a UH 1-D to a Vietnam veteran is a "Mindfulness Bell?" AAAAIIIIIIEEEEEEEEEEEE ! Thompson:

> So you need to suffer in order to learn from your suffering— but we may suffer uselessly. The enigmatic shell game drove me to distraction. If his talks were designed so the pea was never under the husk, then all this running commentary, big answers to big questions was similar to *Midrash*; never definitively answered. ("Hello!", p. 185.)

And second, Sister Chang's misunderstanding of Jerry Crawford's little war. HELLO! It ain't NO LITTLE FEAR!

> My face flushed hot when she said, 'my little fear of war.' Thay had just lectured on suffering the wounds of war in a dharma talk. Didn't she understand that safety and trauma were incompatible? ("Hello!", p. 185.)

But Sister Chang had just heard the same clueless lecture Thompson had. The point was that Jerry had a flashback. "He didn't have control over his reaction, no matter how many breaths he took, how slow he walked, or how hard he did or didn't try to control it." Reaction, after immersion at OK corral, is an autonomic one made by the body to protect itself.

Jerry had been in firefights. His body was wired differently. His reptilian brain and limbic system detected danger a nanosecond before it registered in his conscious brain. His body knew he was in mortal danger and it responded. It pumped adrenaline and other hormones throughout his body. The visceral sensations from queasiness to panic in his chest were designed to get him moving in a firefight. Fight or flight, before the rational brain had a chance to take a breath and say, 'Hello, my little fear.' ("Hello!", p. 186.)

Thompson concluded that Hanh "threw all of that in reverse." And Buddhism had missed the point. And the point of Plum Village, ultimately, was for each veteran to ask the Master one meaningful question and get a meaningful answer: "By tradition each member of the group would ask the Zen master one question. Fortunately, due to my singular focus, one was all I had." The BBC signaled the one minute warning.

> I caught Thay's eye. It was my one and only chance.
> "Will Buddhism and Christianity merge into one" I asked.
> "Let's have a cup of tea," Thay said. His soft rebuke said, *Enough*. The BBC wrapped and Sister Chang chauffeured him back to the hermitage. ("Hello!", p. 187.)

It is said that Buddhism is existentialism with a method. When Thompson invoked "A Clean, Well-Lighted Place," he adapted method to existentialism. After having his picture taken posing with his head planted on a headless statue of Buddha near the Bao Tam Cham museum in Da Nang, 1994, Thompson wrote:

> It is a feeling similar to the one on Marble Mountain. I cannot puzzle together what I am looking for, what I need. I am at the beginning again and I haven't got it. What ever the questions or answers that I am supposed to have garnered are still vague and unanswered. (*In Search of My Rune*, 1994)

Nine months later, he closes "Hello!" with an unanswered question:

A disillusioned Dharma Bum stepped onto a cold, clean, moonlit deck. I shuddered; wondered if I'd missed the yabyum ritual. I'd journeyed all this way to rummage through the lost and found box and it was empty. I had no answers, no understanding and it was time for tea. ("Hello!", p. 187.)

We need only to look ahead of Thompson, and backward in *Colors of War & Peace*, to know from "Yellow Horse" that Thompson is no longer a Dharma Bum, but a priest who hears confession and offers no absolution. How can we know this? Remember what Thompson said earlier in discussing Teilhard de Chardin?

"Atoms, cells, animal, man, galaxies, the universe, strove collectively to order themselves towards higher states of consciousness, and ultimately coalesce at the *Omega Point.*

That's not how he puts it at the conclusion of "Hello!"

White moon filled empty sky. Transfixed by the shimmering reflection in double-paned windows, my face, hands, and threadbare jeans quivered like atoms under a microscope. ("Hello!", p. 187.)

The atoms under Thompson's microscope are quivering, not coalescing. "Hello My Little Fear of War!" will always conjure for me a clean well-lighted place and an eternal refrain from Hemingway's *Nada Prayer*,

> *"Our nada who art in nada,*
> *nada be thy name thy kingdom nada*
> *thy will be nada in nada as it is in nada . . . .*

---

[73] *The Fifth Book of Peace, Ibid.,* p. 359.

[74] Ernest Hemingway, "A Clean Well-Lighted Place," in *Winner Take Nothing,* New York: Charles Scribner's Sons, 1933, pp. 22-24.

ANNEX 1

DEPARTMENT OF THE ARMY
COMPANY A. 2D SPECIAL FORCES BN. 11TH SPECIAL FORCES GP (ABN)
MICHELLI USAR CENTER, 1305 SHERWOOD AVENUE
RICHMOND, VIRGINIA 23220

20 Mar 79

SUBJECT: LOI for MUTA-5 on 6-8 Apr 79

TO: All Unit Personnel

1. In accordance with the unit training schedule and previously issued operations order, drill for April is a MUTA-5 on the weekend of 6-8 Apr 79 staging from Michelli USAR Center in Richmond, VA, with operational area in the Deerfield Valley, VA. All personnel, except ODA-215, are directed to report at 1800 hours, Friday, 6 Apr, at Michelli USAR Center for initial formation, ration issue, parachute issue, safety briefing, and initiation of airborne operation in accordance with previously issued airborne operations order. ODA-215 will report as directed by Commander, ODA-215 to Fort Meade, MD, not later than 2000 hours, Friday, 6 Apr. Company S-4 is directed to insure that rations, 60 main parachutes and 60 reserve parachutes, rifles, radios, compasses, blank adapters, and blank ammunition are all available for issue not later than 1815 hours, Friday, 6 Apr. Company S-2 will insure that additional maps and additional updated target information are distributed to detachments not later than 1830 hours, Friday, 6 Apr. Final mission briefing will be given to detachment commanders by Commander, Co A prior to troop assembly and at 1700 hours, Friday, 6 Apr. This MUTA-5 will terminate not later than 1700 hours, Sunday, 8 Apr.

2. As planned in isolation phase, this drill will involve a night parachute infiltration at EDWARD DZ, Deerfield, VA, utilizing three C-7A aircraft. The operation is time critical, and it is therefore essential that all personnel report as required above and that key personnel report as early as possible but in no event later than 1700 hours.

3. Company communications section will establish CP at Deerfield, VA, vicinity EDWARD DZ and will maintain continuous radio contact with committed detachments by AN/PRC-77 radio, frequency 55.55. Communications section will additionally provide two AN/PRC-77 radios to the DZ party and will maintain alternate communications with ODA-213 utilizing AN/PRC-74B radio and establishing contact at times and in the manner previously specified during isolation phase. Finally, communications section will insure that commercial landline communications are established between EDWARD DZ and Byrd Municipal Airfield prior to 1900 hours, Friday, 6 Apr.

4. Rations will be C-rations and LRRPs. Uniform will be camouflage fatigues, bush hat, and black boots. Individual equipment will be as follows:

-2-

LBE (web gear)   Survival knife
Rucksack   Compass
Rifle   Flashlight
Blank adapter   H-harness
4 magazines of blank ammunition   Lowering line
                                        Jump helmet

5. The operation planned for April is an excellent training opportunity
for our unit, and each individual assigned is urged to maximize his
his own personal effectiveness in performing the mission. In that
manner, we will further build confidence in each other and in our
ability to meet any requirement.

6. The two-week mission in Europe for ODA-213 and the mission in England
soon thereafter are both still on track, and additional information
and instructions have been received in connection with both. Personnel
selected for the England mission will be notified at the conclusion of
the April drill. At present, basic AT for the unit is scheduled for the
period 7-21 Jul 79 at Fort Devens, MA, and will include a ten-day graded
FTX for ODA-212 with proposed operational area in the White Mountains.

7. Drill for May will be a MUTA-4 at Fort A.P. Hill, VA, on 5-6 May 79
and will involve makeup M-16 qualification firing, combat pistol range
firing for all personnel, PT test makeup, swimming test, and other activities
related to AT preparation.

8. CPT Daniel M. Thompson, USAR, has joined the company as Commander,
ODA-212. CPT Thompson is from Petersburg, VA, and is a veteran of the
5th SFGA. He has commanded a long-range reconnaissance company in combat.
CPT Thompson will be a definite asset to the unit and to ODA-212.

Quentin Crommelin, Jr.

QUENTIN CROMMELIN, JR.
MAJ, Armor, USAR
Commanding

ABOUT THE AUTHOR

* * *

The author was born in Würzburg, Germany to a British mother serving in the WAAF and an American father serving in the 82nd Airborne Division (they met in Leicester, England during World War II). The author had distinguished service in the U.S. Army in Combat in Vietnam having served in the First Infantry Division, the 82nd Airborne Division, the 509th Airborne Infantry Regiment (the 8th Infantry Division's airborne arm in Europe), and U.S. Army Special Forces. He graduated Summa Cum Laude from Old Dominion University, worked in Virginia government and retired to Florida where he now lives and writes.

(Photo of the author preparing for a parachute jump in the Phantom Airborne Brigade)